A TEENAGE HERO. THE FATE OF A UNIVERSE. EVERY SECOND COUNTS.

DISTORTION

a god among us

TEAGUE RUDACILLE

Year of the Book
135 Glen Avenue
Glen Rock, PA 17327

ISBN 13: 978-1-949150-01-8
ISBN 10: 1-949150-01-1

Cover design: Jay Aheer

DEDICATION

To those who are still searching
for their inner hero.

ACKNOWLEDGMENTS

Before anyone else, I'd like to thank the Good Lord above. Without a doubt, all of my talent and hard work is a gift straight from Him, and it would be foolish to claim any of it as my own. All praise to Him who sees, knows, and rules all.

Secondly, I owe an immense amount of gratitude to Demi Stevens, my incredibly talented and patient editor. She provided incredible amounts of insight in shaping *Distortion* and sanding off its many, many rough edges. Without her help, this tale wouldn't be the same as it is today.

Thirdly, I would like to thank my mother, Laura Rudacille. She gave me the first nudge to start writing, and hasn't stopped encouraging since. From *Smythers the Cat* to the very first edition of this story, she's been there. Even though it's been a rocky road, she's played a valuable part in the development of this story. Thank you, Mom.

Finally, thank you to my friends and family, who have showed me what real people should look, act and feel like, and thus bringing life to this story. I thank all of you for contributing reality to *Distortion*: *a god among us.*

ONE

Has it really been this long? Four whole months... four months since that fateful day when I faced destiny. Four months since my life was changed forever, and I was put into a world of grueling struggle and endless responsibility. In all respects, it was just another day. No flying banners, no glorious fanfare, nothing to warn me I would meet the end of life as I knew it...

Health Class.

The crisp light of morning twisted through the small classroom windows, marking another *wonderful* morning at school. Students from seniors to freshmen, each lazy in the usual morning daze, populated pristine rows of desks. The sharp crack of gum filled the air, along with the dull roar of chatter.

I sauntered between the desks, backpack dangling on one shoulder. *Glad today's my last day... this year.*

My muscle-toned body, clad in jeans and a crimson cotton T-shirt, found its way into my own small, uncomfortable school desk. With a flip of dirty blond bangs, I sifted in my backpack and wrapped my hand around a box of gum strips.

A familiar face turned and smiled. "Hey, Travis."

"Morning, Chad." I unwrapped a piece and popped it into my mouth. "You're chipper, as usual."

Chad gave a hearty laugh and his signature white-toothed grin. "Best way to be." He ran a finger

1

through his gel-tamed mane and grimaced. "Hair could use some work, though."

I sighed. "Check your estrogen levels."

"Says the one who can't leave a stack of dishes unwashed," Chad sneered. "Might as well be a housewife."

"Tell me that when *you've* lived alone with your dad for seventeen years." Folder edges buzzed against the zippers of my backpack. "You ready for this end of the year presentation?"

"Wait a minute..." The whites of Chad's eyes popped into view. "That's today?"

I flipped open my tangerine folder and held up a fan of notecards. "Dang straight."

"Man..." Chad's forehead went into his palms. "Why'd I stay up so late?"

Classic. I thumbed through the rest of the folder and handed him a few blank index cards. "Here. I'll go before you. Fill these out, talk in circles, and you'll be fine."

Chad nodded and clutched them in his grasp. "I owe you."

"I'll add it to your tab." I stood and moved to the front of the room.

My stomach lurched as I made eye contact with each of the blank stares from other students. Twenty pairs of eyes became more like a thousand and my knees became about as stable as eggs balanced on toothpicks.

Easy, Travis... I pushed my gum to the corner of my mouth. *Last time you ever have to say a word in this class.*

A radiant, albeit beyond falsified, smile appeared on my face. "Hey, everybody. As most of you know by now, I'm Travis Shepard." I glanced down at my cards.

"If I had to pick one word to describe my health class experience... mandatory." My shoes thumped against the floor as my subconscious sent me strolling. "Let's not pretend like we didn't have to take it." I caught a glimpse of a disdainful glare from the teacher. "Okay, things I learned this year in health class... I learned that Joey just can't stomach the idea of touching a CPR dummy."

Dull chuckles came from around the room.

"Not like there was much more to learn."

More laughter.

"And finally..." I shrugged. "If I could have one wish granted, it'd be to have not done a presentation on the last day of school." I turned and headed back to my desk.

Respectful applause rose and fell.

"You'd have to be an idiot to blow it." I plunked down in my seat. "It's not like you're giving the State of the Union."

Chad smiled and stood. "Guess it's my turn, then."

"H-hello," another voice murmured. "My name is..."

"Or maybe not." Chad slumped back down in his seat.

I nodded and gave my attention to the speaker.

"Strange..." Chad raised his eyebrows, "...to hear her actually talk."

"When I lost my mother to cancer, I lost everything..."

My body was paralyzed. In an instant, my stomach became heavier than an anvil and my heart grew numb.

Chad tapped my shoulder. "Whoa... just like—"

I brushed him off. "Quiet."

She was calm, perfectly composed. Tall, slender, beautiful, the kind of girl a high school idiot my age would dream about. There was a certain grace in her moves, a pliability only cultivated through firm hardships in life. She twisted her shoulder-length hair around her fingers as she spoke, the caramel stream waving as it came down. Her deep emerald eyes, however... pierced my soul.

She took a deep breath. "After our long study on cancer and how it can be prevented, I feel like I might be able to help people, one day. Maybe I can help prevent that kind of loss for others. If I had one wish, that's what I'd ask for."

I applauded. *It's a rough goal, but... worth it.*

"My turn." Chad zipped out of his desk and whirled up front. "Alright, I'm Chad Davis."

I rested my chin on my palm and awaited the bell to end class.

***

A couple classes later, Chad and I traversed the hallways together, side by side.

I adjusted the straps on my backpack. "Halfway done."

Chad pulled his phone from his pocket and swiped around. "One period left until we get to *eat*."

"I'm ready." My eyes snapped to a secluded corner just beyond the clamor of the moving student body. "What the—"

It was the girl from health class, with a bulky guy on each side and a look of absolute terror on her face. They each leaned in and loomed as vultures over an abandoned carcass.

I turned. "I gotta go check something."

A few steps closer, eavesdropping became easy.

"Come on, cough it up. I'm short on lunch money, and I know you've got some."

She shrank down. "No."

"Come on... you remember what happened last time we went through this."

"Let's go." Chad caught me by the shoulder. "Look at how huge those guys are. You're a pretty strong guy, but it's best not to get involved. We have no idea what kind of people they are."

I took a deep breath. "Yeah, you're probably right."

"Just call your *mommy* and ask her to give you some more." One of the guys took a step closer, his chest a mere inch from her face. "Oh, wait... I guess you can't." Both of them exploded into hysterics.

The girl sniffed and fell back against the wall, tears streaming down her face. Her head went onto her knees, cedar locks hanging over like a waterfall.

My muscles tensed up.

Chad took a step back. "Oh, boy."

Deep within my soul, a tiny spark flickered. All sense of self-preservation faded in an instant. I swung off my backpack and shoved it into Chad's chest. "Sorry."

5

"Travis." Chad threw up his arms. "It's the last day of school."

I gave him a smoldering glance over my shoulder. "Go get the school resource officer."

Long, resounding breaths rose and fell in my chest. *Two guys... uphill, but not impossible.*

"Come on, sweetie." One of the guys knelt down beside the girl. "Hand it over. You don't want me to get angry, do you?" He slid his toxic hand over her shoulder.

Her eyes grew wide. "Don't touch me..."

"Don't you worry about me, sweetie. Give me the money."

"Hey, numbskull." I stopped, and broadened my body. "She said not to touch her."

"Well, what do we have here?" he sneered and straightened up. "A hero, huh?"

The air grew thick with the stench of absolute dissension. "Leave. Now."

His partner left his position against the wall, and both stood side by side, squared off.

One on the left looks a bit heavy... one on the right's got a nice looking ankle brace. I drew a deep breath. *Three, two, one.*

The tall one cracked a smile. "And what if I—"

I darted to the side and made a sharp kick to the ankle. He turned and wheeled up for a heavy-handed punch.

I ducked under. *Easy.* I turned my attention with a backward step. *Where's his friend?*

My senses dulled on hard impact. *Head butt... that's where.* I staggered backward. *Keep moving, Travis.*

I caught the fist of my attacker and slammed my back into his chest. Sweat built as I heaved his body over me and onto the floor.

See ya, meathead. I spun and locked burning gazes with the other, who pulled himself to his feet. "Had enough?"

"You joking?" He faked a cocky laugh and lumbered toward me. "You don't have a chance."

Again I awaited the first move. He planted his foot and twisted his body into a quick jab.

An audible crack split the air, and he buckled over with a wail.

"Leave this girl alone." I got down on my knee and looked into his quivering eyes. "Got it?"

"Mr. Shepard." A deep, firm voice arose from behind. "I'll have to ask you to come with me."

"Fine."

***

The school resource officer groaned, "Kid, if I didn't know your dad, you'd be in for it... this really has to stop."

I tapped my fingers along the edge of the swivel chair across from his desk, each fingertip stroking the smooth black leather with a fine flit.

He buried his face in his thick hands. "Travis, you really have to learn to fight your own battles. You can't save everyone." He made eye contact. "You know that, right?"

"Yeah, I know." I rubbed my sore forehead. "Ticks me off, though... the way people are now."

"Travis, they don't make 'em like you anymore," he chuckled. "Bud, I see you in here just about twice every year. The only reason you haven't been suspended is because... well, you're a good guy." He took a drink of his black coffee. "It's the last day, and I've got those other two troublemakers waiting to be dealt with. I'll let you go home with no detention today... on *one condition*."

I raised my eyebrows. "What?"

He pointed at me with a stern expression. "Don't beat anybody up next year. If I catch you in my office as a Senior, I *will* have you expelled."

"I'll do my best." I stood and headed for the door. "Have a nice summer."

I stepped outside to find empty hallways, and Chad leaning against the wall.

"We're late to class," he said and handed me my bag. "Satisfied?"

I gave a short grunt. "You say that like it's a hobby."

"Bull." Chad gave me a light thump on the chest. "If you don't get something out of it, why do you do it?"

I smiled and started walking. "We've been over this before."

"Yeah, and every time you give me the same stupid answer. *Runs in the family, runs in the family.* I'm sorry, but I don't quite get how that works. My dad would have my neck if he found out I got in *a* fight, let alone twice a year."

"I'm hot blooded... just one of my curses." I scratched the back of my head. "What're you doing after school?"

"Working. Why?"

"Never mind, then." I shrugged. "I'm headed out to the woods tonight, since Dad's working late."

"Well, you have fun with that."

"Yeah... thanks for your help." I turned and headed down a fork in the hallway. "Bye."

Maybe we'll get a nice stretch of quiet now.

A soft voice emerged from behind. "Hey... um, Travis?"

My attention was ensnared. "What?" I stopped and turned.

Her eyes locked into mine. For a brief second which felt like an eternity, something in my mind just clicked. My heart raced, and my breaths grew long to compensate.

Is she going to say something?

"I..." She glanced off to the side and twirled her hair around her finger. "I just wanted to say thank you." She smiled. "I don't think I'll be hearing much more from those two."

"Don't mention it." I tapped the side of my leg as the gears in my brain turned. *Think, think...* "Kate, right?"

"Yep," she nodded. "That's me."

"Yeah, well..." I glanced around, looking for some kind of way out. "How are you doing?"

"How am I?" She gave a hesitant laugh. "Been better. Where are you headed?"

"You want someone to walk with?"

"Well..." she looked down to the floor, "...yeah. I'd rather not go alone."

"Okay, I'll come with you. I'm not too motivated to go to class, anyway."

Our footsteps echoed through the halls as we turned a corner.

"How long have you been living here? I think I'd have noticed if you were here longer than a year."

"My dad and I moved here last month." Kate ran a finger along her bottom lip. "You?"

"Born and raised." I looked at the posters on the walls. "Out in the hills, where all the farms are."

A pause of silence spread.

Kate bit the corner of her lip, glancing away.

Indecisive. I took the initiative. "What's on your mind?"

"Travis..." she hesitated. "Could I ask you something?"

"Shoot."

She tightened her posture and closed her eyes. "Why go out of your way to help me?"

"Simple," I sighed. "You needed help, and I happened to show up."

"Sounds awfully heroic." She loosened up and let out a giggle. "A rare quality, nowadays."

"Thanks... but I'm no hero." I leaned against the hallway wall beside her classroom door. "Looks like this is goodbye."

"Well..." Kate reached into her pocket and pulled out a palm-sized notepad. She scribbled with a hot pink gel pen and ripped out a page. "It doesn't have to be. Catch me sometime over the summer... okay?"

My awful poker face slipped. "Alright, then..." I accepted the gift. "See you around, I guess."

"Cool." She gripped the doorknob, but stopped. "I know it's a bit redundant, but... thanks again."

The door closing behind her bounced through the hallways, beating again and again in my ears.

I pocketed the paper and looked down each end of the hall, meeting welcome silence in both directions. *I should go to class... but that's not happening.*

I slinked down and had a seat on the chilled tile floor.

Glad to see her happy for once.

I studied my open palm with a long, steady breath.

More than worth the bruises, if you ask me.

TWO

The warm wind coaxed my cheek as a woman would a long lost love, flipping the edge of my bangs along the way. I reclined on lush grass and swung my feet over the rocky surface of a cliff overhang. Songbirds crooned to one another from the branches, their wondrous melodies synchronized with the flowing water and low rustle of leaves. Here, in the utopian stillness, the soul could leave its earthly cares and dwell instead in bliss.

Beautiful. I took a deep breath and leaned onto the sturdy, overturned log behind me. *What more could a man want?*

Behind me was the groundwork of a forest hangout. In reality, it was a few aged logs around a stone fire pit, but it made me smile. The mere sight brought back fond memories of camping with Dad and exploring the woodland.

I closed my eyes.

Peace... finally.

The caress of nature eased me to sleep, the wind, birds and evening sun all fading into a tranquil silence.

A hot, steamy puff of air spread against my neck.

I stirred in my daze. *...What now?*

A second wave of heat.

The quick, rapid chuffs of sniffing blew through my ears. More and more hot air pressed against my face, until I finally took the hint.

I stretched and opened my eyes... then they went wide. *What the—*

Beside me was the stately figure of a wolf, his pale fur the color of winter snow. His eyes were crisp and icy. He lowered enough for me to catch the beginnings of an intricate pattern of black fur with elegant curved lines on his head. Going down his body, more lines divided his white coat with beautiful curvature. His size alone incited a fearful paralysis throughout my body.

I rubbed my eyes. *I've gotta be seeing things.*

A soft poke from his muzzle blew that out of the water.

Oh, no.

My heart tensed until I could feel it beating in my neck. My limbs grew weak and jittered upon the slightest twitch. Sweat began to build on my forehead.

I don't know how you're here, but I need to go... now. I grabbed the grass behind me and slid backward at a crawling pace.

The wolf perked up his ears and took a seat with a thump.

Easy... I stood, then backed away. *That's good, stay sitting.*

The wolf gave a long yawn, clearly dissatisfied with my pure terror.

I turned away and took off at a quick walk. *Let's hope he doesn't—*

I lifted my eyes to see the wolf, once again seated and peaceful, right in front of me. He leaned forward and touched my nose with his.

I checked behind me to the empty space where he had just been. "You're quick."

The wolf stood and stretched. With a silent, elegant pad, he glided to the edge of the campsite, where my handiwork met the growth of the forest. He turned and stared.

A wolf appears out of nowhere and... toys with me? I lifted my hand to my chin. *Something's up.*

"Hey." I pointed at him. "What do you want?"

He sat down and sighed, turning his gaze once more to the tangle ahead. In a few seconds, he made up his mind and disappeared behind the growth.

"Hold up," I started after him. "I'm coming, too."

The white wolf snaked through the wilderness as it grew more and more exotic. Under waves of radiance in the foliage, the plant life changed. Vines withdrew into the ground and trees, flowers bloomed to form bridges and pathways to other locations, and clusters of pulsing pollen drifted through the air.

I followed the wolf across a bridge of vines, and increased my pace. He padded along with a majestic stride.

We came to a small clearing free of overgrowth.

The wolf stopped at a puddle with a diameter about two feet across. He sat on his hind legs, occasionally looking back at me. I stared down the mystic pool to see a long drop, and sources of light in the middle of the deep blue. It was warmer than the air, but thicker than the water of local creeks. I tasted it.

Saltwater.

I stuck my hand into the puddle... and it pulsed with a sky blue glow. I pulled my arm back, and the water rippled. Long and steady surges gradually ceased upon my withdrawal.

That's not normal. I examined the liquid as it swelled with a dim radiance. *Not in any way.*

Like a deer as it went out into a meadow, I approached again with sluggish yet vigilant movement.

I put my hand in the puddle once more, and then my forearm, and then my shoulder. An invisible force ensnared my whole arm and twisted around it like a snake. I planted a foot on the grass and pulled... unable to break free.

A single violent pull yanked me into the unknown.

Immersed, I was dragged down into a dark abyss where light could no longer breach the water. Pressure built in my lungs, growing by the second. I closed my eyes, convinced I would drown in a daydream where I fell into a puddle and found an ocean.

By the time I hit the bottom, the need to breathe was overwhelming. Despite my efforts to endure, my mouth burst open and water flowed in.

I heaved a few times, the liquid spilling all the way through my lungs... and contrary to every piece of experience under my belt, I found myself alive and breathing.

Dense fluid squeezed in and out of my body, bringing awareness with each inflation.

Breathing water... I steadied my breaths. *Impossible.*

Before me was an underwater cave. Luminous corals the color of the sun eliminated all darkness. As I inspected the area, a school of strange-looking fish blazed by me. A streamlined bunch, their propeller-shaped tail fins allowed them to move like small torpedoes. The fish were aglow as well, changing skin tones to blend into the coral.

I glided through the submerged paradise and examined every object I came across. One particular reef was much larger than the others—as long as a bus. I reached out to touch it, and the layers of coral faded into the murk.

I moved to a place of cover as the entire reef arose from the ground as a gargantuan fish emerged from under it. It had plates of natural armor, and resembled a whale-sized grouper. The fish searched the area, and then burrowed exactly where it was before.

When the light of its disguise reappeared, I swam over the beast and continued forward. The caverns led me to an area of open water. Ahead, a flooded structure like an ancient temple rested in a spacious room at the end of the submerged tunnels. Barnacles and sea grasses grew along it.

The creature patrolled around the area like a vulture seeking a corpse. A shadow passed overhead. I was dwarfed under the dark silhouette of a massive shark. Thick layers of kelp provided cover from the aquatic titan. An unavoidable force drew me to the temple, pushing me into the twisting green.

Seconds slowed to hours as the beast passed within arm's reach. Its soulless eyes saw nothing of me as it drifted past... and I waited for my move.

I shot out from safety, immediately gaining the attention of my pursuer.

I pulled my body through the open temple doors, the shark slamming into the narrow arch behind. Bits of aged stone crumbled and plummeted through the dense waters as the enraged beast writhed, unable to break from the grasp of its prison.

Aging and water damage indicated the temple had been here longer than the rock binding it to the ocean floor. Strange markings carved into the walls glowed a magnificent indigo as I passed them. A mystic feel was present throughout. I swam through every opening to completely explore the building. My travels led me to a pair of sizable doors. I used all of my strength, but they held their position.

The marks on the door became more prominent, the dye used to define their pale inscriptions clouding into the water. A sharp singe burned into my hands. I pried the door open, and felt my consciousness tear away. I drifted off as I was pulled through.

I awoke in a strange hallway, and coughed up a spout of water. Behind me, a set of doors were closed so tightly they seemed immovable. A good amount of oxygen must have been locked in, and luckily the water was held out.

Made of stone, the walkway was of the same material as the surrounding temple. Crystals grew from the walls to shed dim light on the hall. Images were etched into these walls as well, and told a tale of gods, beasts, villains, and heroes.

The sound of my soaked shoes hitting the floor grew clearer with each step. In time, I found the end of the hallway, another set of doors. I leaned against them and listened for whatever might be on the other side.

They swung open under my weight and revealed another vast cavern. I tumbled into a room overtaken by crystals, growing and splitting the architecture with a low, steady hum. In the center was a shrine of the finest sculpting and design. The statue towered over me. A knight whose armor radiated from within, filled with a layer of crystals. His hands balanced atop the hilt of his sword. His blade met a stone pedestal, and on the pedestal rested a book.

This book glowed with the light of a clear sky, an artifact out of ancient legend. I approached the pedestal, and touched the book. It had a brown leather cover. The pages were aged and torn, but I felt an unmistakable presence from within... the whisperings of fate. The air around this aged scripture overflowed with mystic authority. Uncontrollable anticipation blazed throughout my body as I cradled the tome in my hands. Moments later, the mysterious book snapped open.

"Destiny awaits, Travis." Whispers reverberated from every corner of the room, phantasmal echoes from the unknown. *"Follow the path of the Exalted."*

The book's pages became bits of golden light as they turned faster and faster. I was transported in a flash.

Around me was a wide, circular room, hollow in the center. The stars themselves gazed in from the open holes in the construction, pouring their essence into the blazing sphere at the heart of it all. The core—a massive, lavender globe of plasma—moaned as its pulsing radiance coursed through the floor tiles, walls, everything. On the outer ring of the massive area, there were numerous rows of bookshelves stacked with books beyond counting. Each was labeled in a strange language... the same one I'd found in the temple.

I stood slowly and began to explore. There were so many books in the library... too many for me. The windows were massive, each one giving a new view to the sea of stars.

"Super clean, super organized." I gingerly stroked the spine of a thick textbook. "Whoever lives here doesn't get out much."

"Actually, it's quite the opposite, young one."

My attention snapped to the center of the room, my heart barely staying in my chest.

A mysterious being formed from thin air. He wore a dark purple robe, carrying the essence of the night. His hood arched over a void, an absolute absence of his face. Beneath his cloak was a suit of onyx armor, articulate and ancient. A relic staff pulsated ripples of electricity in the being's right hand, the sparks racing up its shaft. The staff had a potent lavender glow in its etched patterns, running through every inch of the polished metal. At the head, it split into four parts, whirling in an unpredictable pattern above.

He dropped to my level, looking down on me. "Greetings, Travis. I've long awaited your arrival." He spoke in a dialect reinforced by eons of discipline.

Words ceased to come from my mouth, only a few indiscernible grunts. I turned around, desperately looking for another *Travis*.

"Me?"

"I am Mohandar, the teacher of the Exalted." The being bowed. "It's time you learned who and what you *really are*. Listen well, student. Your life is changing as we speak, and you will have questions as it does."

"I have questions *now*."

"When you're ready to learn about your heritage and your future, return to me." Mohandar raised his palm, and it began to swirl with violet light. "For now... you'll have to do a little seeing for yourself."

A burning pain seared into my chest, and the world around me spiraled out of control.

Can we just take a break for a hot second?

Sudden impact sent every bit of breath and focus out of my body.

I was surrounded by a dense forest unlike any I'd ever seen. This one was filled with bizarre trees whose trunks twisted and turned around one another and flowers of exceedingly vibrant color. The combined sounds of wildlife created a symphony of nature. Birds sang in the trees, part of a chorus of rustling leaves and gentle wind. A crater six feet deep encircled me, accompanied by fallen trees and bloody branches.

"You've gotta be kidding." I slowly looked at the dirt walls surrounding me. "Where in the world am I now?"

Silence.

"Doesn't matter, I guess." I loosened up and sank into the earth. "Wondering won't get me anywhere."

Mohandar's voice filled my mind. *"It's time you learned who and what you really are."*

"No time wasted." My body quivered at the thought. "Don't mess with the faceless dude."

I froze when my eyes met my hand, gleaming from within a metal shell.

For the love of— I twisted and turned, getting the full view of the situation. *Just stop, already!*

I was covered by a suit of plated armor, beaten and layered with dirt. The material was painted a dull shade of crimson, with bright platinum trim around the edges. The shoulder joints had prongs which arched up in line with my head, and the interior of my suit was lined with a tough black leather. Just on top of my chest rose a long white feather. I followed its color to my back... and discovered two snow white wings.

THREE

S unlight fell through the leaves above, accompanied by the soft chirping of birds. *Trees...* I paced through the wilderness with a slow and cautious step. *More trees...*

Twigs crackled under my leaden steps, and the occasional tree trunk swatted the flopping appendages on my back.

I stopped and shuddered under the unrelenting pressure of my wings. My knees buckled with a surge of infernal pain and my body weight tumbled onto the moist bark. *Why am I so weak?* My breaths grew short and I winced as I pushed back onto my feet. *I can barely hold my body up.*

Faint clicking rose in the bushes ahead.

I lifted my eyes. *Please be a hint.*

A spider the size of a motorcycle raised itself out of the foliage, with eight spherical eyes glaring at me. Covered in dirt and quivering, the fiend hissed and prepared to leap.

...Can't step on that one.

Tension increased, and my body kicked as blood pumped harder... it was a sensation never activated in me before—a complex brew of bloodlust, adrenaline, and inhuman strength. *No question about it, though. I have to get out of here.*

The hunger in the spider's gaze grew. With an ear-splitting screech, the predator sprang into the air and lashed with poisonous fangs.

I lunged into full sprint and missed the spider's bite by inches.

I moved through the foliage and hurdled toppled tree trunks, but it was no use. Its nimble legs jumped over any hindrance, closing in.

My knees buckled and I hurled to the ground with a grunt. My body flopped against the grass with all the grace of a rag doll.

The spider slowed and scuttled in my direction, almost teasing me with its prancing stride. It hunted just as much for the sport as for food. It screeched a horrible sound and pierced the harmony of the woods. In an instant, two more emerged from the dirt beside it.

Well, nowhere to go. I clawed the grass behind me and heaved my leaden torso in the other direction. *One thing left to do.*

The predators closed in and readied their venomous fangs. With a loud hiss they lunged forward, and any thoughts I had were blurred.

My right fist surged forward, and impacted the eyes of my attacker with a firm thud. Without thinking, an uppercut followed, toppling the squirming arachnid onto its back.

"Gotcha." I raised my fist in triumph. "Now, to deal with—"

All was still as I looked around the area with blank eyes.

The three spiders were sprawled out on the ground, legs in multiple directions. A gleam against their bodies caught my eye. I squinted, realizing the pattern was a dart carved out of shiny wood.

"Huh." I stretched my sore muscles. "Guess this place isn't so bad."

A soft rustle came from behind, followed by a jabbing pain in the side of my neck.

I went limp in seconds, with my vision fading away.

***

Light returned, the flame of a torch flickering on my heavy eyelids. Cloaked by leaves, twigs, and thorns which ran down the entire body, the torch's holder watched me from about two feet away. I understood how I'd missed it now—perfect camouflage. He'd blended in completely with the environment. The torch was transferred to another nature-clad being. A tan hand protruded from the cloak, painted with white oil in intricate patterns. The hand reached between the camouflaged garb worn by its master, and pulled out a rod lined with wooden spikes on the lower side. I shook in an attempt to escape, but came to a gruesome realization. I was bound to the tree behind me.

The figure in front of me leaned down until I could feel breath on my face. Taking a few sniffs, he twisted and turned as he studied me.

"Like what you smell?" I winked. "I do shower every day."

Unfathomable volume assaulted my ears under an endless train of exclamations, none of which could be deciphered... as well as a great deal of projectile saliva on my face.

"Alright, alright." I turned away, squinting. "Alright!"

My interrogator hopped off to a nearby tree trunk and gave it a whack with his club. After a few directives which went *straight* over my head, he returned and put his face back to mine.

"Look, I don't know what you want me to—"

That's all it took to start another episode of feverish yelling.

This is starting to fire me up. I took one deep breath and answered. "I... can't... understand you!"

No response.

I grunted, and narrowed my eyes. "Shut up!"

I cracked my forehead against his, and he stumbled back. He growled... and readied his club. In an instant, he lunged forward with animalistic speed and closed in, only to be stopped by a silent, square impact to the skull. With a little bit of squinting, I made out the form of an arrow black as coal. On it was the flickering fuse of what appeared to be... a gunpowder bomb?

My company inspected the sparkling fuse as it pushed its way to the arrow's payload.

I tightened up and braced. *Here we go.*

With a bright flash and an all-permeating boom, I was alone, covered in dirt... and tied in place.

A figure veiled in darkness dropped from the trees. The descent was flawless. The silhouette tumbled, revealing the agility-focused armor paired with an ashen cape. He rose, retrieving not one, but two bows from his back. Quick jets of air accompanied a pair of arrows above him. I watched as with incredible dexterity, he caught both in his bows.

Great, another executioner. I pulled against my constraints. "What's wrong with you people?"

With special prongs in his armor, he drew both bows.

"Hold still."

With synchronized impact, the tree behind me thumped... and my bindings fell away.

The silhouetted man glanced around. "We need to get out of here. More are coming."

I'll take any help I can get.

The crackle of snapping twigs arose in the distance, a ghastly warning of time slipping by. My unidentified ally took off into the woodland, and I followed.

"I have a camp set up a ways from here." His cape flowed as a ghost between the claws of tree branches and thorns. "Far enough to be out of their grasp. Just stick close and we'll be there in—"

A hearty shout erupted from the bushes, and the bowman was thrown to the ground. My eyes adjusted to the darkness and identified a sturdy wooden club, wielded by a shirtless, sweat-coated male. A bovine skull covered his face, giving him a sinister assurance as he raised his club upward for another strike.

The bowman rolled aside just in time to evade the crushing blow, and instead took a kick to the face. His cloak fluttered as he thudded to the crackling fangs of countless branches and thorns beneath his feet.

He's in trouble. I planted my feet and surged forward. *Here goes.*

I dropped my shoulder and heaved my mass into skull-head. The iron impact sent him over like a twig, and his club thudded to the ground.

"A little extra weight isn't too bad, I guess." I extended my hand. "Let's keep it up."

The archer took my hand and stood. "Thanks for the help." He once again continued through the growth.

Little by little, the sound of the tribe dwindled. We traversed the wild lands as ghosts, safe under the veil of night. Before long, we came to our destination, a cave. Abundant vines and fungus grew over the opening, a verdant curtain to the surprisingly homelike setup within.

I took a seat on a log resting in front of a fire sparked by my new friend. I watched as the silent archer went into a leaf-sewn tent, then emerged with two bowls. He filled them with a stew from the fire, and handed me one. The man removed his hood to reveal a lightly bearded face bearing the expression of the echoes of a long, deep past. Hair the color of the midnight sky fell just over his eyebrows, and came close to a scar which ran along his cheek. He had a light metal suit tightened around his body, made of dark materials which helped conceal him in the night. A dull gray cape laid overtop, tying into a scarf when it wasn't being used as a hood. His steel-born eyes made contact with mine as his hardened, masculine voice questioned, "So, how'd you get captured?"

"Spiders." I took off my helmet and set it beside me. "And not the kind you find in the garden."

"Burrower Spiders," the archer nodded. "They're nasty little fiends, for sure... but they teach a good lesson."

"What's that?"

"When you're in Reach..." the archer loaded arrows into his quiver, "...it's better to expect conflict than to be blindsided by it."

I raised an eyebrow, "Reach?"

"You're kidding." The archer shot me a look of disbelief. "You don't know where you are?"

I shook my head.

He fanned his arms out. "This is Reach. The whole land. How'd you get this far if you don't even know where you are?"

"It's a bit of a roller coaster." I leaned back. "I woke up in a crater this morning."

"Roller coaster?"

Dang it, Travis.

"Oh, uh... yeah." I stroked the grass. "Let me rephrase. It's a bit of a *long story.*"

"...Okay." The archer shrugged. "My name's Arvel, and I'm one of the best shots you'll find in Reach. Seeing you're also a skilled warrior, I think we can help each other out."

Skilled warrior? Is that a joke?

"What do you have in mind?"

Arvel looked up to the stars. "I came here for what rightfully belongs to me, an amulet stolen from my long dead mother. The tribal chieftain took it for himself. I've no intent of letting him keep it. I could use some company, and I'd be glad to help you figure out why you're here."

I reached my hand down to the small bag at my side, crafted from burlap and attached to the interlocking plates of my armor. My hand pinched an aged paper within the bag. "Sounds good to me." I pulled the sheet out, and read the looped ink scrawled across it.

Hello, Travis. Look up, if you will.

Weird. My eyebrows raised. "Hey, Arvel—"
"Yes, Travis?"
My eyes became golf balls and I recoiled backward, rapid stings of cold metal surging up my hands. "How did you—"
The forest had faded. Once again, I found myself among the stars, aboard the archaic library building adrift in the far reaches of the cosmic sea.
Mohandar, the wise, enigmatic soul from earlier, rested with crossed legs within an arm's reach. His cloak fluttered in an ethereal breeze behind him, and his staff stood upright at his side.
"Paradise... is it not?" He rose to his feet and extended his hand. "I suppose you're ready for some explanation."

FOUR

The enigmatic book from the temple hovered in front of me, emitting a joyful melody from a motley span of hums.

Alright... I extended my hand. *What's the deal?*

The ancient text recoiled just out of reach and twirled, as if taunting me.

Thing's got a mind of its own... I looked down, taking notice to my jeans, T-shirt, and the absence of wings on my back. *I'm back in my normal body.*

Mohandar paced around the walkways near the core of the Observatory, with his articulately crafted staff in hand. "I'll go slowly at first, just so you can take it all in." He waved his staff across the room, and manifested two chairs out of mystical gray smoke. "Please, have a seat."

I did as instructed and plunked down in the phantasmal seat, hit with a wall of overpowering anticipation. My heart pounded in my chest, my thoughts raced, and my fingers began to tap against the arm of the ghostly chair. *What's this guy have to say?*

Mohandar's robe whirled when he turned and took a seat across from me. He rested his staff against the chair arm and leaned back. "Let's begin."

Huh. First class I'm actually looking forward to.

Mohandar cleared his throat. "I'm sure you've already put the facts together, but the world you know is not as it seems. In fact, from here things will only get more and more bizarre. Do you have any curiosities as to why?"

"Yeah, I'm thinking." I leaned on my elbow. "Enlighten me."

Mohandar raised his hand to the ceiling, and the Observatory faded away into the stars, now a window into the cosmos surrounding the two of us.

A pair of planets formed in the absence, separated by a line of twisting light. On the left, Earth... covered in clouds and deep blue water. On the right, however... was a planet covered with vegetation.

"Behold, the *Sister Realms* of Earth and Reach. They may seem entirely different, but they're connected on an elementary level. Neither can survive without the other."

The color from the vision drained to monochrome.

"This leads to some complex methods of functionality. Seeing as you've now been to both Realms, take a guess at what they might be."

"Uh..." I straightened out the folds in my jeans. "The people of one have no idea the other exists?"

"True, but not what I'm looking for." The colors flushed back into the image. "These two work by *sharing* a flow of time."

My thoughts froze. "Huh?"

"If you think about it, the time since you first left my Observatory and now aren't far apart, are they?" Mohandar paused. "Think about it."

He's right... It's like I came back in the same instant I left!

"It seems this way because it's *true*." Earth started spinning, while Reach was grayed out and frozen. "If two Realms are sisters, only one can flow at any given time. If Earth is moving, Reach is frozen. However, when Reach wakes..." The green surface of Reach came forth, and the seas of Earth faded. "Earth will stand still."

"So, Earth's got a sister." I itched my nose. "Why pull me from my home and plop me in Reach, then?"

The book whirled between Mohandar and I, singing an indecipherable tune along the way.

"You've been called to something bigger than yourself... and you needed to see it before I could explain." Mohandar brushed the animated text away. "Your world, along with the world of Reach, is in grave danger. After being attacked where they're the weakest, they're moving on a path of certain destruction... In order to stop their downfall, we need an *Exalted*."

I shifted in my seat. "Exalted?"

Mohandar nodded. "An individual who not wholly, but partially, shares the blood and heritage of three legendary deities. However, this alone doesn't make one Exalted. It is the act of being chosen by a godly scripture which awakens the latent potential within."

I'm only human... not really anything special. Does this guy get that?

"You, Travis, have been chosen to unlock your true potential and live out your predestined purpose."

I looked around. "With all due respect, I'm not a superhero."

"I'm aware." He sighed. "I'd love to ease you into life as Exalted... but we don't have that kind of time." The stars once again became the Observatory. "Life will never be quite the same for you after today."

"Alright, I get it." I stood. "Anything else I need to know? I'd like to go home if possible."

Mohandar dissolved the two chairs with a wave of his staff. "Soon you will become an integral part of a life you've never known, but don't worry."

I wonder what he feels like, having an invisible head.

"There's no one more suited than you." He paced toward me, and rested a hand on my shoulder. "No matter how much you disagree, the book never chooses one who isn't destined to fulfill their role as Exalted. Yours is incredibly important, but we'll discuss it another day." He laughed. "As for getting you home, come right this way."

We came to an opening in the Observatory wall, leading to an extension of the floor which reached out into the stars. My lungs tingled as Mohandar and I breathed in the essence of the cosmos, accompanied by a wondrous view of space.

"Beautiful, isn't it? It's the last thing you need to know for today. Whenever you want to return home, approach the edge of this protrusion. This bridge is both the entrance and exit to my Observatory."

Try to be polite. I began the walk to the edge of the bridge. "Um... thanks, Mohandar."

"Come back in two days. You'll have learned some things on your own by then." Mohandar turned and headed back inside.

I tapped my foot. *And how am I supposed to do that?*

Mohandar laughed. "You'll figure it out."

The stars blurred into streaks and my body recoiled as I was rocketed from the Observatory with unspeakable force.

I gasped and straightened up. My heart pounded in my chest as sense returned. My legs quivered against the ground beneath me.

Lush grass coaxed the bottoms of my fingers, and gentle wind caressed face to security. Silence settled in, and with one deep breath, my nerves pulled back together.

I was still at my campsite.

Holy crap. I rubbed my hand against the log behind me. *No wolf, no temple, no Reach... I definitely need to get home.*

***

The sky had become a soft orange at my back as I made my way up the extensive driveway. Thick billows of cloud drifted through the sky as the air made a gradual transition from midday heat to the comfortable chill of a summer night.

The road home was a long slope of pure dirt and dust, with the house seated at the very top of the hill. Framed in the falling sun, I could make out its fading timber frame and well-shingled roof, as well as the wooden deck which extended down into the backyard. With every step, rest grew closer.

Weird dream... I glanced down at my dust-covered shoes. *Way too real.*

Dad's truck was parked in front of the house, a burly pickup with dull red and white paint job. Dirt from the driveway coated its fenders, adding contrast between the lower half and the sun-glazed topper. In crisp, well-printed letters was a license plate on the back.

BIGWADE. I chuckled.

I stepped around the truck and up the stairs to the front door. Upon opening it, I was slapped with a wall of aroma... all coming from a hot and ready crock pot.

Food... My mouth watered and my stomach rumbled. *Glorious.*

Dad awaited inside, with a big grin on his face as he chopped tomatoes, spinach and carrots into a salad. He was a tall guy, even without the extra inch or so added by his work boots. Thick muscles were prominent under his dull blue tank top, which bore the remnants of a long-worn graphic on its front. He turned and gave a big, hearty smile, deepening the laugh lines on his sun-tanned skin and making the hairs of his beard spring up.

"Hey, buddy." He motioned for me to come. "Why don't you give me a hand here?"

"Sure." I nodded and made my way to the sink.

"Uh..." Dad turned to his spread of vegetables and gave his receding hairline a light scratch. "You could peel these two onions here."

I flipped the hot water on and got some soap on my hands. "When did you get home?"

"A while ago." Dad glanced over at the clock. "Ten minutes, maybe."

"*Ten minutes?*" I raised my eyebrows. "That's how long it took you to start working?"

"No rest in my bones, Travis," Dad chuckled. "Don't even try to tell me you're not the exact same way, slugger."

"Slugger?" I flipped the sink back off. "Since when is that my nickname?"

"Well," Dad beamed with a smug grin, "since I got off the phone with Officer Davis."

I slouched a little and looked away, but he made his way over and leaned on the counter, waiting for an explanation.

"Sorry, Dad." I sighed and got to work on the onions. "The things people do set me off... and I don't necessarily play nice."

"It's fine, Travis." Dad patted my back. "Just try to reason with yourself before diving into battle."

"I'm working on it," I smirked. "Trying, anyway."

"You're a natural fighter." Dad lifted the lid of the crock pot. "Always have been, just like your dad." He rested his hand on the counter and looked me dead in the eyes. "Punch first, ask questions later, huh?"

I gave him a half-laugh. "Yeah."

"What's wrong?"

"It's nothing." I set the two peeled onions down. "I fell asleep in the woods today, and had a real whacked out dream. It's got me all screwed up."

Dad rubbed his beard and nodded. "About what?"

"It was too *real*." I felt around my pockets for a box of gum. "I woke up in the same place I fell asleep, and then got taken on this wild stroll with a white wolf. One thing led to another, and it was like I got pulled to another *world*. Scary is what it was."

"Huh." Dad took a deep breath. "It might not be normal for you personally, but... mystic dreaming has run in the family."

My eyes widened. "It has?"

"Yep." Dad nodded. "Your mother... she had all kinds of wild dreams in the few weeks before she left us. All pretty colorful. Nothing to worry about, though. Just the traditional vivid imagination you guys have."

"If you say so... thanks, Dad."

We worked together to finish, enjoy and clean up dinner, both beat by the end of the night and more than ready for the sleep which awaited us.

Or so I thought.

After I'd gotten ready for bed, I shut the door behind me, undressed, turned around... and there it was, floating in the middle of my room.

The book.

FIVE

The icy touch of morning wrapped around my body, along with an eerie silence. Sunlight crept its way through a curtain of dense foliage and glistened against my helm. A clatter arose when I shifted against the cold dirt, the tips of my widespread wings just flicking its surface.

Oh, no... I'm back in Reach?

I planted my ironclad fist against the ground and pressed, summoning a blitzkrieg on my muscles. With a brief struggle, I rose to my feet and stretched.

"Having trouble?" Arvel, the bowman, looked up from the smoldering remains of our campsite fire. "You sick or something?"

I paced around the cave walls, stumbling along the way. "Man, I wish."

"You told me you woke up in a crater, probably crashed." He sighed. "I'm not surprised your brain's fried. What's the last thing you remember before you got darted?"

"Like I said earlier," I lifted up my helm and tucked it under my arm, "I explored, and then ran like an idiot to get away from spiders."

"Yeah..." Arvel stood up. "I remember. Come on, then."

I lowered my helm to my hand. "Where are we headed?"

"The crater." Arvel stood and collected his bows. "How else are we going to have any idea what to do with you?"

We were off, and in due time, we stood at the edge of a break in the woods.

Pillars of sunlight crept through the forest canopy, giving a sanctified luminescence to the immense pit below. Mounds of earth rolled up in one big wave in line with a path of broken branches. In the center of the openness was a deficit of a man's height, riddled with feathers and broken twigs.

Arvel let out a long, high-pitched whistle. "I didn't expect *this* much."

"Yeah." I jumped into the crater and the grass became at eye level. "What exactly are we looking for?"

Arvel knelt to the ground and rubbed some dirt between his fingers. "Anything with the slightest hint of where you're from?"

We searched the area, combing every inch of dirt and grass.

"Arvel." My posture straightened and a wave of chills shot up my spine. "I've got something."

He popped out of the crater like a gopher. "What?"

"Up there, on the tree branch."

Above us was a small satchel suspended by a strap. It was too high to reach with my hand, but the tree would be easy to climb.

Arvel raised a hand to his forehead. "Jackpot. Good find, friend."

I made my way to the tree and placed my arms on a thick and sturdy branch. "Give me a second to climb up, and I'll get it."

A high-pitched whiz caught my ear. The thump of the bag when it hit the hard bark of a toppled log was the beacon of our success. "No need." Arvel put his bow away with a triumphant smile. "It's good target practice."

I crouched down. The key to the clues had been cut with an accurate slice from the edge of an arrowhead. I smirked at Arvel. "Nice shot."

Arvel pulled himself out of the crater. "Thanks." He froze and listened for a moment, and I did the same.

In the distance, the faintest of sounds surfaced— footsteps and a series of indecipherable whoops.

Arvel froze and I watched his eyes become those of a mouse in the presence of a hungry fox. "We need to go."

I followed him into the safety of the brush, and we kept moving.

***

Arvel lowered his hood in the glow of the fire and set the newfound bag in front of us. He knelt down, unbuckling its lock. "Let's see what we've got in here."

I took a seat with a thud, and emptied all the contents onto the dirt. "Answers. About time."

"Looks like a couple scrolls, about three *hundred* gold coins and some other stuff." He grabbed one of the parchment rolls. "A good start."

Nothing to be found on the gold. I pinched one of the coins in my hand, and rolled it in my palm. *If anything, it'll be in a scroll.*

"Here." Arvel tossed me one of the writings. "This should help you out."

The faded paper crackled as I unraveled it, a cloud of dust swirling around as I did.

In a rough sketch of ink was a geographic image labeled *Reach.* Scattered throughout the land were a series of landmarks, three of them circled.

"A map..." I studied it. *If only I knew where the heck I am.*

Arvel shifted to my side and pointed to the marked regions. "Looks like you had three places you wanted to go. The closest is the southern Jungle, but you've also got the tallest mountain in Reach labeled, as well as the Ruins of Sovengard. Who knows why you'd go there, but I'm sure it'll come to you."

"So, we know *where* I was going," I said, putting the map back in the bag, "but not why."

Arvel tossed me a second scroll with a hint of a laugh. "This might help."

On this scroll was a small list. I read it aloud: "Recover the three shards of Daedalus Tower's crystal. Recombine them to get back home."

"A man on a mission," Arvel said, leaning back. "I can respect that."

"Good finds, I guess." I picked up the final scroll, amidst the heap of items. *Last one... give me something.*

Grains of mysticism in the scroll tingled my sense of wonder as I eased a knot around the cylinder loose with a gentle tug.

Excitement ran wild in my mind as the scroll opened and revealed...

Well, isn't that just so incredibly helpful?

It was completely blank.

A tiny black dot moved on the parchment, a slow, sure crawl toward the center.

An ant. I pressed my thumb on the dot, and recoiled in amazement. *What the—*

The dot became a line. The line twisted and became a fan of ink-made tree roots, turning throughout the page. They all converged and formed the familiar English language.

If you're reading this, you're the Exalted who's inherited my body. You're probably confused. That's why I've left you this to help out. My name is Siris, and I'm the one who was previously in your current body. I'm the last of a race known as the Winged Knights (yes, very creatively named), but furthermore, I'm a warrior of Requiem, an airborne city which shares an energetic tie to the land of Reach (where you are). With you being Exalted... I need... a little favor. Please, finish the job I started, and go to the locations marked on that paper map. You'll figure out what you need to do.

P.S. There's a gift for you amidst the gold. Good luck, kid.

-Siris

The ink gradually seeped away until the paper was left blank once more.

I rolled up the scroll and tucked it away. "Now we're in business."

Six

A new day had dawned in my world, bringing a brand new struggle. At about noon, books laid flung about my bedroom. My desk chair was toppled over, papers and video games peppered the floor, and the ceiling fan struggled to whirl, its string coiled around its blades. My room had been hit by a virtual tornado, and I rested, exhausted and on my back amidst the chaos.

"You've torn apart my entire bedroom," I sighed, tossing a broken pencil at the cheerfully levitating scripture. "Satisfied?"

The book from the temple hummed some upbeat notes and floated all over the room, whirling about as it did so. Its soft golden glow pulsed slow and steady against surfaces untouched by its unstoppable curiosity.

Then it stopped in front of the bed.

"No." I sat up, lightning quick. "Leave it alone."

The book's aura grew brighter, and an extension of its light crept out toward the pages of my journal, the vault of my inner thoughts. Inch by inch, it drew closer until it was just a breath away, then stopped... and turned toward me.

Great. Acts like a five year old. I raised my finger toward it. "Don't..."

My journal fluttered as it was flung into the air and flown about the room. The Scripture stopped for another brief second, then shot out the bedroom door.

My blood boiled, and I clenched my jaw. "Get back here, you stupid antique!"

That's about all it took for the entire second floor of the house to become an earthquake site.

Storming downstairs, I managed to snag the Scripture by its cover. *Gotcha.* My eyes went wide when one foot glided off the wooden stairs to the first floor. My shoulder slammed against the wall and I fell, a toppling mess of limbs and pages.

My hips thudded onto the flat hardwood just before the front door. "See what you're doing?"

The infernal tome chimed and levitated up, still in my grasp.

"Do me a favor..." I tightened my grip. "Just drop it."

The journal hit the floor.

After all the trouble... I let go of the book and rolled onto my feet. "Thanks."

The book looped in the air around my living room, then took off toward a vintage clock at the top of a cabinet.

"No." I snagged it again. "If we're going to live together in this house, you have to learn you can't just go throwing everything wherever you want—"

The front door swung open.

Oh, boy. I swatted the book into the living room and out of sight. "Hey, Dad."

"Hey, Travis." Dad stomped in. "How's your day going?"

My body stiffened, and my eyes grew big. "Alright, I guess. What're you doing home so early?" I glanced over my shoulder. *What am I going to say when he sees the book?*

"I took a half day." Dad sat down and began to unlace his boots. "We're going fishing." He kicked off his boots and headed upstairs to change with his chest high and steps loud.

The book was gone, the only evidence of its presence being my sketchbook in the middle of the floor.

"Okay." I scratched the back of my head. *Where'd it go? I guess it doesn't matter, as long as it's not—*

"Travis, what the heck happened up here?"

My breathing stopped for a quick second. *Completely slipped my mind.* I ascended the stairs. Dad was staring at the absolute calamity of bed sheets, toppled furniture, and opened doors.

"Yeah..." I sighed and gave a fake smile. "I'll fix it."

"No sweat." Dad laughed and trudged through the hall toward his room. "We'll take care of it when we get home. Just get your stuff."

"Alright, give me a second." I went to my room and turned the brass knob on my closet door. *Good thing the guy's so mellow.*

My closet door groaned and swung open, and overbearing dust assaulted my nose. My fishing gear rested against the near corner, in my hands almost immediately.

Got my rod, got my bag... all checks out. My nose sent the tiniest pulse through my entire face. *Uh-oh...* the pulse evolved into an infernal jitter. *Here it comes.* I inhaled, squinted my eyes, braced, and...

Nothing.

Man, I really have to clear the dust out of here. I rubbed my nose and took a deep breath. *The dummy sneeze. Worst thing in the history of—*

A high-pitched chime blared from within the closet, and I was thrust back by sudden impact from scorching radiance.

The rod and bag tumbled out of my hands as I was thrown across the room and straight into my dresser, deodorant sticks thudding over me. My chest seared with pain as the burning ball of light forced against me, the dresser rattling away behind me.

Enough! My nostrils flared as I let out a violent puff of angry breath. *The foot's coming down.* I struggled to get my hand up to my chest under the gale force fighting against me, but with one heavy push, managed to get a grip on the book.

"Are you kidding me?" I stood, with the book wrestling against my grip. "Are you a sadist or something?" My eyes met the substantial length of bungee cords hanging at the top of my closet, and my gaze narrowed. *That'll do.* I clenched the bungee cords in my hand and bound the book to my closet shelf. "This should keep you out of trouble while I'm gone."

"What's all the racket?" Dad leaned into my doorway. "You trip or something?"

I stepped out of the closet and shut the door. "Yeah, I got my foot snagged on the door frame. Nothing big."

"Sure, but..." Dad lifted his hand to his beard and his eyebrows lowered. "What'd you do to your shirt?"

A sudden, chilling draft brushed against my torso, and my eyes got big.

In just those few seconds of burning contact, my shirt had transformed into more of a vest... losing its entire front left. The orange fabric was charred black on the edges, and fresh wisps of smoke cascaded off it.

Dad bit his lip, and his face twitched as every inch of his willpower came into use.

What'd I do to deserve this? I slapped my hand onto my forehead with a sigh. "Let's not talk about it."

"Sure thing, Travis," Dad laughed, and *hard*. I mean from the gut, and gasping for air. "I've had those kind of days. I can understand."

"Really?" I took off my shirt-vest and pitched it into the trash can. "You've had days like *this?*"

Dad stopped and cracked an ear-to-ear smile. "Nope."

I flung a new shirt over my shoulder, got my fishing gear, and followed him outside.

The truck bent on its suspension when I put my weight on it and pulled the door closed. I ran my hand along the old leather seat while I buckled the belt into place. The truck's engine rumbled upon the start and we were off.

I watched trees, cars and stop signs pass while we drove toward the spot where we would leave solid land and transfer to an aquatic paradise where every problem became nothing more than a ripple in the water.

The lake seemed to go on forever, a massive liquefied mirror containing a reversed image of the clouds and the trees along its bank. A few ducks paddled their way around the lake in a single-file line, and a kingfisher surveyed the waters with a watchful gaze.

Our boat bobbed in the calm water, bound to the dock by a tied rope. It was a small but sturdy vehicle with a single engine and three seats.

Boots thumped as we paced atop the wooden dock, accompanied by the occasional creak of a loose board. I handed our gear to Dad piece by piece, then stepped nimbly into our small boat to prevent it from rocking. Finally I untethered it from the dock.

I could use some time on the water.

A thunderous wake fanned out behind the propeller, distorting the view of the rock bed under the clear waters. I watched the kaleidoscope of color flow beneath us until they faded into the depths.

Dad steered the boat closer to the lake bank.

We slowed then came to a halt, with the sound of whizzing fishing line rising soon after.

I still don't get it. Me, Exalted? What's that stupid book or the world of Reach even have to do with me?

The two of us proceeded in our pursuit in total silence. After numerous cycles of cast and recall, I rested the lure in the water. "They're not hungry—" The rod immediately jerked forward in my hands.

With a sharp tug upward, I set the hook. I planted my feet on the boat and focused on the pull from the abyss. The rod crackled and the line whizzed while I brought in what felt like lead weight.

A vigorous splash at the water's surface heralded my victory. The eye of a foot-long bass made contact with mine while its body below flailed on the baited hook. I brought the wriggling body into the boat and slid my hand around it. I pushed its spiny fins down away from my palm. Copper scales glittered in the sunlight.

Alright, just to get a grip on things... the incident with the puddle wasn't a dream. Instead I picked up a mischievous book and an entirely new world to manage. On top of it all, this Mohandar guy's telling me it's only gonna get crazier. I popped out the lure before I dipped the fish into the water and gave it a push into the depths. *Why does he think I'm supposed to be some great and glorious individual?*

I wiped my hands against the sides of my pants. *News flash. I'm not.*

"So," Dad fixed his hook onto his rod and set the rod down in the boat. "Now that we're out here on the water, you want to tell me what you did to burn a belly hole in your shirt?"

Might as well tell him before the Scripture decides to start playing with him, too... I took a deep breath. "You're not going to believe me, but I'll tell you anyway."

Dad shifted in his seat and sat up, every bit of attention on me.

I hooked up my rod and laid it across my lap. "Remember that dream that had me all worked up?"

Dad nodded.

"You see, the thing is..." I tapped my fingers on the side of the boat. "None of it was a dream. At first, I thought it was... but now, I understand. That *dream* was another world, just as real as ours. If you don't believe me, I've got the book to prove it."

"You never mentioned a book before. Where is it?"

"After the Sacred Scripture tackled me across the room and burned off the front of my shirt, I left it tied to my closet with bungee cords..." My stomach lurched at the faintest glimmer in the sky, way off in the distance. "The thing probably escaped by now."

"But it's a book." Dad raised an eyebrow. "How could it have tackled you, let alone escape your closet?"

The glimmer grew bigger and brighter with every second, dead-set on the boat.

"That's it." I shrugged and pointed to the sky. "It's no ordinary—"

The living missile that was the book plummeted, barreling into my chest and nearly sending me into the water.

I gripped hard around the mischievous text, then lifted it for Dad to see as its aura slowly faded.

I smirked. "It's no ordinary book."

Dad nodded with big eyes, his face going pale before he toppled over in the back of the boat.

"Well..." I released the book, and it hovered beside me with grace. "Could've gone worse."

SEVEN

My eyes widened, a short breath pulling me back to the world of Reach.

Man, the shifts between worlds just come out of nowhere... what was I doing here last time?

A conglomerate of gold and silver coins jingled when I pulled them aside, an iridescent fire gleaming against them.

I remember now... Siris' gift.

Amidst the cascade of riches rested a cobalt gem the size of my palm. Cut with artisan precision to form a perfect triangle out of its dense, near opaque surface, it was overlaid with a glistening coating of ivory-like metal bent to divide the gem into perfect thirds. The finest etchings twisted and turned like miniature dragons across the numerous stretches of metal... it was a pure work of art.

Pretty sure that's the "gift" Siris wrote about. I glanced at the blank scroll, which moments ago bore the detailed message from the previous owner of this strange winged body. *What is it?*

I wrapped my hand around the gem and lifted it to my eyes. 'Smooth' didn't even begin to describe the pure bliss of this thing's surface.

Arvel dropped his scrolls and focused on the gem. "Check that thing out."

"Any idea what it is?"

"Not a clue," he said, leaning in to inspect the strange object. "It looks valuable, though."

A faint glimmer emerged deep within the dark blue shades. A sudden warmth crept onto my hand, spreading as it did so.

Must be too close to the fire. I moved my hand toward the cooler, darker portion of the cave.

The glow, as well as the heat, intensified more and more, until I dropped the crystal.

"Hey, come on." Arvel reached out to the steaming gem. "Don't just throw it on the—"

A high-pitched ring filled the cave, and everything went white.

Disarray assaulted my senses as I struggled to recover from a virtual supernova. I stood, and met the pure absence of my balance.

Whoa, there. I planted my feet and held still. "Arvel, I can't see. Can you tell me where the fire is?"

Silence.

Very funny. I clenched my jaw. "Arvel, I could use a hand, here."

A steady chill, as a ghostly snake, wrapped its way around my body... soon after, my armor became ice to the touch.

I took a deep breath. *Looks like I'm on my own.*

The white glare on my eyes dissipated, and my center of balance returned.

The cave, Arvel, and everything about Reach were gone. Instead, I found myself in an endless field, populated by blades of grass frozen to powder blue. The finest powder dusting of winter's icy cotton coated the field, as more and more of the tiny specks drifted from the sky to the soft ground.

"How about that." I removed my helm, and immediately felt the grasp of cold on my face. "Might as well see where I've been *whisked* off to now."

The grass crunched under my iron steps, and I shuddered as the ghostly touch of snowfall covered the tops of my wings.

On the far edge of sight was the smallest disturbance in the straight pattern of the field, a luminescent speck which appeared to rise above the barren surroundings.

Something's out there.

A faint chime—the sound of little bells—echoed through the field from the direction of the light.

I froze as the ringing bounced through my ears... my heart grew dense, and my stomach lurched.

What the— I fought to slow my escalating breathing. *I'm not afraid. Why is my body acting like it's on ice?*

The speck faded away, and the bells hushed.

Gone. I took a deep breath.

An eerie stillness overtook the field as a spectral voice passed by.

"Travis Shepard... the New Exalted One."

Deep. Imposing. Honorable. All would easily describe the astral baritone voice which made my spine quiver.

Behind me. I turned around, and got a close up look at my wing. *Glad I lived seventeen years and then just get wings one day...* I turned my shoulders, and the wing moved out of view.

Grass surged in a single united wave as a torrent of wind blasted through. Another chime—this one a massive tower bell—followed. Upon the sound, a gush forced my ironclad body backward, my heels dragging in the ground.

I planted a fist down and locked my body tight.

One more harrowing clang reverberated through every crevice of my being, and then the wind ceased.

The voice resurfaced. "Travis Shepard, the New Exalted One... are you deaf or just ignorant?"

Wise guy, huh? I shifted my weight onto my legs and stood. "Little bit of both."

I locked eyes with the source of the voice.

Just ahead was a translucent figure of bright white raging flames, twisting and turning to form the shape of a bulky suit of armor, unbelievable in complexity and design. The flames coiled themselves into prongs, divots and studs in every phantasmal plate, creating the unmistakable form of a human knight. Arms crossed in front of his body toward clasped hands at the hilt of a searing sword, rooted into the earth below.

"Who are you?" I folded my arms. "You look like some kind of fancy ghost."

"You're not wrong." The armored knight lowered his head toward the sword's pommel, and with an explosive burst of ember, wings of pure divine light fanned wide. "Do you know who I am now?"

Let me think. I rubbed my chin. *Do I know any winged knights made of fire?* "Nope."

"Look at yourself, fool." The spirit grunted and raised a hand to his chest. "I am knight—"

I sighed and interrupted, "—Siris of Requiem. So, what do you want?"

"I want to follow up on my note." He took a seat on the snowy grass. "Just to make sure you understand."

"Seemed pretty straightforward." I joined him on the chilling earth. "I'm Exalted, this is your body, you need my help."

"Well, I don't *personally* need your help." Siris shifted and stretched his blazing wings. "More like every living thing in this world and your own."

I nodded. "Give me the rundown."

"It's like this." Siris paused and gathered his words. "Your world and mine are Sister Realms... meaning if either dies so will the other. A *Channeling Crystal,* a wedge between the two, has been destroyed. With its broken pieces scattered about Reach, the tower can no longer support the barriers between the Realms... and they'll smash together if someone doesn't intervene."

"So..." I shrugged. "What's so bad about them merging?"

"*What's so bad?*" Siris' blazes intensified. "When Realms collide, they *completely implode.* The only way for you to keep my world and yours from going to absolute chaos is to collect and assemble the three broken pieces of the Channeling Crystal... all of which are conveniently marked on your map."

"Alright." I gave him a confident smile. "Then all I need to do is get a hold of 'em all, and everything will be fine?"

Siris sighed. "Every shard you find will turn back the damages of our worlds' crossover, and before you ask me what kind of damage... it's big, and you don't look like you're in any shape to fight it."

Jeez. This guy's no stranger to pessimism.

"With all of this in mind, I implore you to get moving. Get out of this forest as soon as possible and make a mad rush for the Lunar Jungle... because time's slipping faster than any of us would like."

I nodded. "Sure thing."

"On another note..." Siris lifted his blazing sword from the ground and rested it on his shoulder. "Are you familiar with the term *Rashaad*?"

Fastest subject change in history. "Never heard of it."

Siris' flames grew stronger. "Enough with the jokes. You and I are *both* hot-blooded. And me, quite literally."

"I'm not kidding." I raised a hand to him. "Take a breath or two. What's *Rashaad*?"

"Well, allow me to explain." He opened his hand, and his sword faded. "I'm not a fan of lectures, so I'll give it to you straight."

Hasn't been a minute since his last sermon.

"Before an Exalted awakens their true inner powers, they must fight a duel with the one who previously resided in their new body. Such a test is to find out who's more fit for the role." Siris shrugged. "In short, we have to fight... for *tradition*."

"Whatever." I stretched out my arms and loosened up. "So, what now? You want me to count to three, or—"

"No, no, no." Siris backed away. "We're not going to fight *now,* not after all this talk... raincheck?"

"*Raincheck*?" I chuckled. *A very knightly word choice... but what the heck?*

"Good, good..." Siris thrust his arm forward. "Well, off you go."

The ethereal bell clanged, and the valley warped.

***

"Hey."

My head snapped to the side under a fast whack on the cheek.

"Wake up."

Daylight caught my eyes. Ghostly wisps of smoke danced where the fire would be, as Arvel turned the ashes about with a stick.

Wait... I rolled, and with a stinging bend of the wings, realizing I'd toppled backward onto the ground. *How's the sun out?* I leaned forward and pulled my body up. "Arvel, you mind explaining to me how the sun's up?"

"Well, it's morning and..." he pitched the fire-poking stick and looked at me. "...the sun comes out at daytime." He pointed to the sapphire gem. "You passed out hard the second you touched that thing."

"I could've sworn we talked about it for a while." I stretched my arms out to the sides, and my wings fanned out behind me with a low fluttering sound. I turned my head and studied the massive, alien appendages. *Cut me a break, will you?*

"No." Arvel eyed up the gem, grimacing as he did. "After seeing what it did to you, I'm not even *touching* that thing."

My foot thudded against the bag, now packed up and resting against one of the logs. "Well... did we find *anything* useful?" I picked it up and slung it over my shoulder. "Anything?"

"Let me think..." Arvel rubbed his bristly chin before cracking a smug grin. "No, just your name, rank and occupation... *Knight Siris of Requiem.*"

Should I really let him call me that? I paced around the cave. *Ah, what harm could it do?*

"Alright." Arvel went into his tent and came out with his bows. "Listen, now that we know you're alright, you want to go climb some of the big trees in this forest?"

I laughed. "Like for fun?"

"No, unfortunately," he brushed an ant off his shoulder. "You remember why I'm here. I've got to take back what these savages stole from me, and we'll need a plan. The best view you can get of the village is from the trees."

"Fine with me." I put my helm on. "Let's go."

A short ways of travel, and we were there.

These trees were *huge,* and when I say huge, I mean ridiculous. I felt like a bug next to them, because they were thick as houses and seemed to have no end to their height. Even still, we somehow managed to get up in them.

"Better get comfortable, Siris." Arvel leaned back against the trunk of a tree, supported by its thick outreaching branches. "We'll be up here for a few hours at the least."

In a distant clearing below us was an encampment made by the Tribe, a series of huts surrounded by a wall of spiked wood. The structures' lack of stone or metal echoed the primitive state of a people integrated into the nature they relied on.

I struggled to get my wings in a position where they rested in a pleasant feeling among the tree branches. "Do we really need to be *this* high off the ground?"

Arvel chuckled and rested his hands behind his head. "It's all about quality, Siris. The best view for the best planning. I can see every building, but more importantly every person."

I felt the gentle breeze on my wings, a cool and steady flow of air between the bright green leaves. The wind coaxing the soft surface of my feathers was intoxicating.

Okay... I let out a long breath of pure satisfaction. *Maybe they're not so bad.*

The scent of bark and plant life filled my nose as I kept an eye on the establishment below. *Strange, the more I think about it. No time passes when I travel between worlds. It seems impossible, but...* A bright yellow hue caught my attention, and I turned to see a flower on the side of my tree. *What's this thing?* Orange patterns ran through each of the vivid petals which seemed to move in order to catch the breeze.

I reached out to touch the flower, and was met with an audible pop. It rocketed off the tree trunk and glided with grace to another. Roots flowed behind like tentacles, and wrapped around the next tree it decided to call home.

"It's called a Sky Blossom." Arvel tapped his boots against branches while he kept focused on the Tribe's village. "They can't fly, but they can climb trees and glide to other ones. You don't know a real challenge until you've tried to catch one."

I shifted and sat more upright. "Sounds like a blast."

"Yeah." Arvel nodded and gave a short laugh. "Gotta have fun somehow, right?"

I tracked the Sky Blossom when it transferred between trees once more. The abnormal wonder danced through the air and caught wind. It passed across my view of the Tribal village, and I grabbed Arvel's shoulder when my focus shifted away from the flower.

I pointed my finger down to the valley. "Look."

Within the walls of the village, a multitude of tribal people gathered. They stood still around their chieftain for a short time before they dispersed and began to exit into the forest.

Arvel grabbed a tree branch and pulled himself up. "I watched them for a few days before I found you. That's the hunting party, but they never leave at this time of day. What are they up to?"

A few more hours gave the answer.

"They're hosting a big ceremony at nightfall." Arvel turned to me in his tree. "We don't have any time to waste."

"You want to go *now?*" I said, standing on my branch. "Seems pretty stupid to just rush in."

"By the time we get down there, it'll be dark." Arvel paced to the trunk of the tree. "As for a plan, we'll improvise. Let's get this done, quick and clean."

I took a deep breath, and my muscles tensed up. *Great… just great.*

EIGHT

The house was silent, and gave off an air of emptiness as the evening wind fluttered in through open windows. The fading orange of the sun illuminated the slumbering face of my father, still out cold from the events on the water.

"Did you really have to make such a startling entrance?" I spun the Sacred Scripture, floating in the air between Dad and me. "I had to haul him to the truck and drive us home because of you... and he's heavy."

No response from the book.

I hope he's okay. I took a deep breath and watched Dad from a chair across the room. *Come on, Dad... Wake up.*

The book hummed and drifted to my father. With a hidden majesty, it circled around Dad and began to glow its bright aura once more.

"No." I raised my hand to it. "You've been nice and mellow so far. You hurt him, and I *promise* you and I are going to throw down."

Its glow manifested with tranquility rather than ferocity, spreading throughout the room and radiating on every surface. It extended in waves of aurora around Dad, with golden glimmers streaming from each band. The light coated his body for a short few seconds of divinity before the book stopped and returned to my side.

Dad wheezed once, and his eyes opened. "Holy sh—"

The scripture chimed and twirled in the air with joy.

"Sorry." I paced over and knelt down in front of him. "Last thing I thought you'd do on the water was pass out."

"It's fine." Dad cracked a smile. "Do me a favor. Go into the top drawer of my bedside table and get the black box with a blue ribbon on it. Bring it here."

I did as I was told and returned with the container.

Dust had accumulated on its polished and blackened wood composition, and the faintest scent of lavender stuck to its edges. The box was only about the size of both my hands, but something about it made my insides crawl, so I offered it to Dad.

"No," he pushed it back toward me. "It's for you."

"For me..." I glanced down at the box, and shivers went down my spine. "How?"

Dad laughed and straightened up, still a bit lethargic. "Just open it, Travis. I've wanted to know what's in this thing for eleven years."

I sat down beside him and pulled on the edge of the ribbon until it popped off, leaving only the box. The lid made a satisfying *whiff* when it came off, along with a tiny puff of dust.

I set the lid aside and was met with a small piece of paper on top of smooth indigo cloth. I pinched it between my fingers and held it up.

"It's in cursive." I looked to Dad. "Mom always wrote in cursive."

Travis,

Your destiny has already begun to reveal itself. This is a gift for you. Take it and go to the place where your father and I met... be strong, my little hero.

Love, Mom

I took the cloth in my hands, and Dad leaned over my shoulder.

"Here goes." Pulling the gift's wrapping aside, my eyes shot wide.

A triangular gem, cobalt and plated with pale alloy, pulsed upon contact with my hand... identical to the one given to me by Siris.

Dad picked up the keys to his truck. "Come on, bud. We're going for a ride."

***

The stars radiated in the cloudless night sky, ancient sentinels over the land below. Gentle moonlight glistened on the grass, giving it a dark purple glow in the night. The air itself was charged with a subtle electric feel. When combined with the chilling, but not harsh, nip in the air, it caused every hair on my body to stand tall. The only sound present was the low rumble of Dad's truck.

I cradled Mom's gift in my hand, and lifted the lid to get one more look at the gem.

Exactly the same... can't be a coincidence. I closed the box up. *But how did Mom get a hold of this?*

"Well, the note said to bring you where she and I met." The truck silenced, and the thud of Dad's door echoed in the night. "Here we are."

Ahead, in the glow of the full moon, was the silhouette of an old Japanese maple tree, a stout, but incredibly wide plant whose lavender leaves carried a mystic radiance in the moonlight.

"Go ahead." Dad paced to the front of the truck and leaned against the grill, causing the front of the raggedy old thing to dip down. "I'll stay back here. This is for you, not me."

The book hummed beside me and twirled in the air as its aura grew.

"You heard the man." I faced the book. "Let's go."

Immediately, the scripture blasted forward and raced toward the tree.

No rest... I leapt into stride and followed. *Typical.*

After a brief moment of running and some *very* heavy breathing, I reached the crest of the hill.

The book raced around the tree in circles, carving a pale signature in the night as its aura brushed against the brownish gray tree trunk.

Man, I'm out of shape. Long breaths relieved the pressure in my lungs as I looked the tree up and down. *This thing's huge. A fitting place to meet your love, I guess.* I drew closer and ran my hand along one of the many twisting outreaches in its trunk. *Hundred years old, at the least.*

I stepped around to the other side of the tree, and my knees collapsed from under me.

From this incredible overhang in the terrain, you could see untouched natural land as far as the eye could discern. Flowing creeks, tall mountains, ranges of forest... all were visible in the sanctified gleam of the full moon and the watch of the stars.

Mom... you said to come here. I set the black box down in front of the overlook and removed its lid. *Here I am.*

Upon contact with the skin of my palm, the gem's blue portions at the points of the triangle began to emit a soft, baby-blue glow, with tiny sparks of white racing through it. I bowed over the divine radiance and held it against my chest.

Oh, so it's a lantern.

Through a creeping wave, the glow expanded into my heart... soon the beating fuel of life in my chest brandished the very same luminescent quality. My veins followed, and then my entire bloodstream, until my skin was radiant, accompanied by a gently undulating blue aura in both my blood and the air around me.

My heart pulsed slow, crisply audible in my ears. Every inch of my body was alive with an unspoken joy as the flowing waters of life coursed through me.

I get it now. I looked down at my hands, and a smile crossed my face. *This is...* I lifted my gaze to the stars and stood up. "This is a part of me."

"Indeed it is."

Just off the cliff, the air bent into a vortex and began to pulse a soft purple aura, growing brighter and brighter until it was a serene white.

A fleeting silhouette shot out of the portal, with a fluttering cloak trailing not far behind.

The grass in front of me sifted upon the silhouette's arrival. "The son of Jennifer Shepard."

"You again, huh?" I leaned back on the twisting trunk of the tree and crossed my arms. "What do you know about my mom, Mohandar?"

"Quite a bit, actually." Mohandar planted his staff on the grass and stood upright. "More than you, though it pains me to say."

I squeezed my arms and took a few long breaths. "Do tell."

"For starters," Mohandar chuckled and had a seat just ahead of me. "Your mother was *not* human. Far from it, actually."

I rolled my fingers into fists. "You expect me to believe that? What kind of justification do you have for such a *stupid—*"

His fingers stretched, creating a reflective vortex much like a ghostly mirror. I found myself eye to eye with the narrow-eyed, jaw-clenched face of a ticked off teenager... whose whole body was filled with an electric blue light.

"Yeah, that makes sense..." I sighed and loosened my posture. "Sorry."

"No need." Mohandar allowed his creation to fade. "I understand you're hesitant, if not *completely* closed off, to revisiting your past. Even so, I need you to listen."

I nodded.

"Now is a time of great peril, Travis." Mohandar turned and faced the vast clearing ahead. "As we speak, life as we know it is drawing closer and closer to its abrupt end."

"So..." I took a seat beside him. "What do you want me to do?"

"I'm sure you know of your task to collect and assemble the pieces of the Channeling Crystal." Mohandar stroked the blades of grass beside him. "Your doing so is the sole thing standing between the chaotic end of both your world and Reach."

I rubbed my chin. "Is that it?"

"Of course not. Even if you were to recover the shards with an *immense* level of speed, damage to the Realms would be inevitable." Mohandar looked over at me. "Your task in Reach will be hard enough, but you'll have your work cut out for you here as well..." he said with a clenched fist, "...as the defender of your *world.*"

Seriously? My eyes popped wide. *Of the whole—*

"There's a phenomena which happens when the boundaries between Realms weaken... things get moved to Realms they shouldn't be in, often times very *powerful* things." He wrapped his arm around my shoulders and outstretched his open palm. "Imagine this entire valley is a city, full of people. Workers, merchants, wives, husbands, even children."

A brief span of silence took over as my blank gaze combed over the field.

"Now... imagine a single being with the strength and motive to reduce it to nothing but ash."

Not sure I like where this is going...

"Traditionally, an Exalted is trained for years, mastering the ways of their new life. Unfortunately, you don't have such a luxury. You'll have to fight off these terrifying foes... for if they manage to destroy Earth, Reach will also—"

"Hold on," I interrupted, then wiggled out of his grasp and paced away, the night falling eerily silent as I drew to a halt. "Listen. I may be all glowy like a strip of neon, but I've lived my life as human. Human. If you're dealing with the possible end of the world here, you're not looking for me." I looked at him over my shoulder. "You're looking for a superhero, and quite frankly, I'm nothing special."

I turned away and headed down the hill. *I'm just not what you—*

"Stop, Travis."

My legs froze mid-stride, in complete disobedience to my will. In an instant, they'd become like the pillars of a statue, both unwilling and unable to budge.

"You may not believe in yourself," Mohandar said powerfully, "but *I* do. So you're going to stay right here and hear what I have to say. Many can be *called* great... those who uphold the law, those who dive into the fire to save lives, even those who aspire for the greatest personal success. However, there's only a handful in every era who are *called*, driven for something far beyond themselves."

No. I shook my head. "You don't—"

"*They* are the ones who rise to the task at hand, and become something every man dreams of becoming."

I turned and slowly faced the flow of emotion coming from behind, growing more and more intense with every line. Little by little, the walls around my heart withered away like sands amidst the tide.

"Travis, these are the *heroes*. Every day, they awake and charge toward danger, wherever it may be. They delve into the dark alleys, the caves, the *hallway corners* of life and put themselves on the line for the *good* of those around them. Look around you, at our dying world. We need a hero... We need *you*."

My vision grew blurry under quickly moistening eyes, and my knees began to tremble. *What a case.*

"Travis, I'm calling you to stand every day, boldly charging to places where no man dares to tread, for the sake of everything you hold dear. I'm calling *you* to take hold of your destiny and become what you were forged to be. I'm calling you to be *Exalted!*"

Diamonds fell from my eyes. For an eternal second, the two of us waited in the moonlight... as the strands of fate awaited.

"Travis... this is your *one* chance."

What am I supposed to do? I wiped my eyes. *Heck of a speech, but I can't—*

"*Will you be the hero this world deserves?*"

I turned... and gave my answer.

***

The easy rattle of my ceiling fan overtook my room, filling it with sound when paired with Dad's snore.

Ugh... I thudded onto my side in bed, twirling the blankets around me like a fluffy cocoon. *Maybe this way.*

My mind drifted off into stillness behind my closed eyelids.

Yeah, this is better. I yawned. *A yawn. Yawns are good...*

My eyes shot open and I let out a long sigh. "Still awake."

I rolled onto my back and put my hands behind my neck.

Wonderful... I tossed my blankets aside. *Can't sleep. I've tried covers on, covers off, all the fan speeds... We went to bed around ten, and I'm still not asleep.* I sat up and looked over toward the hallway. *Dad's out pretty hard... Maybe I'll go outside and look at the stars for a bit.*

The Sacred Scripture wasn't on the shelf. *Where'd that stupid book go off to now?* I stood. *Time to go find it, I guess.* I threw some clothes on and crept outside to the back porch.

Made from a great deal of straight wooden planks—once a golden brown, but now faded to a duller gray—everything about the deck was wooden, including the benches around the outside and a single round table in the center. A triad of wind chimes hung on the porch from a tall central pole, each one letting out a soft jingle in the nighttime wind.

Sudden light caused me to squint.

The Sacred Scripture zipped around the porch, sure to collide with just about anything that could make noise. The whole place sounded like a gunfight from all the racket.

"Hey..." I rubbed my forehead. "Sacred Scripture."

The book froze in midair with an attentive focus.
Since when does it ever listen?

"Keep it down. Dad's asleep." I took a seat on one of the porch's wooden benches. "What're you doing out here?"

The scripture gave no answer... not like it could. Instead, a long silence took hold.

So, I'm supposed to keep the Triangle Stone— uh, Realm Stone, on me at all times... it's supposed to let me know when the Realms shift. Should be nice to have some warning for once.

In the distant sky, a transient streak burned for a passionate second as it tore past the stars around it. One moment it was there, the next, gone.

"Look at that." I turned and pointed. "A shooting star."

The Sacred Scripture turned and watched as an armada of additional stars followed, a rain of sanctified flames from the untouchable cosmos.

"A hero, huh?" I smiled as I watched my book track each streak across the sky. "Maybe finding you wasn't a freak accident after all."

The book turned with a hum.

"I'd have never made a really good worker, anyway..." I leaned back on my seat. "Watch out, bad guys. *Travis* is out to get you," I chuckled. "Like that'll scare anyone."

A growing heat rose in my pocket... burning from the Realm Stone.

One of the stars made a sharp turn and plummeted toward us with incomprehensible speed, a blazing jet of pure heat from the distant reaches of space.

My face caught the glare of the ever-hastening star, and my stomach lurched as I stood up.

"Oh, boy."

NINE

Arvel and I had arrived at the home of the tribe... and the night was still. I stared at the towering barricade of spikes barring us from our destination. The wall stood high and appeared to touch the stars, its dark silhouette looming.

I need to get to work with Mohandar and the shards... but this guy needs my help.

I watched as Arvel hoisted himself onto the grainy surface. "What are you doing?"

"You got a better idea?" Arvel paused. "It's not like we can just *knock*."

I grabbed on and followed. Soon I was within arm's reach of a pointed post marking the top... and not too long after, I had my hands on it.

The crack of breaking wood echoed through the night as all of my weight lurched backward.

Uh-oh, going down!

Balance thrown, my body tumbled, and I braced to prepare for...

Nothing.

Arvel's face was silhouetted by the moon as he held me with one arm. With a bit of effort, he managed to bring me back to safety. "Be careful, alright? Hurry up and grab something, or we'll both be on the ground."

Close call. I hoisted myself up, this time careful to grip two crevices instead of one. Within the barrier were numerous huts networked by pathways of beaten dirt. A massive ceremonial fire burned bright, as the shadows of shamans danced in the twilight, their amorphous silhouettes transforming into avatars of the wild. The steady pulse of tall drums echoed through the streets, along with the songs of the villagers.

Now to get in and out, quietly... like a game of capture the flag.

A tribal spearman gripped his weapon with both hands and came around a distant corner before he leaned against the side of a nearby hut. The white oil which created mystical patterns on his face and bare chest glistened in the flickering flame.

Arvel reached under his cloak. "They've got guards set, so be careful." A low swish came from him when he lowered his hands and pulled a sturdy rope tight against the post he stood on. He held out another to me. "Take your time on the way down. Your armor's not as quiet as mine."

I took the rope and fastened it to my post.

Arvel swung over and fixed his feet to the aged wood, facing it as he began a slow descent.

I dropped off the side, and felt the quick jolt of the rope as it pulled tight. My wings didn't help when their weight began to pull my center of balance. *You know, you could make yourselves useful.*

Arvel snapped and got my attention. "Easy, easy. Take your time."

When we got within a few feet, Arvel and I dropped to the ground.

I gave the rope a few tugs, and it remained sturdy. *We should probably take these down.*

Arvel peeked around the edges of the hut we were concealed behind. "Leave them." Arvel grabbed his bows from his sides. "We're leaving the same way we came."

He moved like a ghost between the buildings and dirt pathways, a mere whisper in the night. No matter how close or how far the enemy was, not one of them could pick up on his presence.

The chieftain's hut was a large single-floor home carved straight from the elements. The various rooms were dark and thick with humid air. Arvel and I sifted through cobwebs, bedrolls, and shelves filled with bows and tomahawks, searching for the one true prize... Arvel's long-lost amulet.

Arvel inspected every trunk and storage area he could find. "Make sure you check everything."

My hand delved into the mouth of a leather bag, thick and slightly moist. With a bit of groping in the darkness, my fingers wrapped around a dense sculpture with what appeared to be a thick, string-like band around it. "Think I've got something."

Pulling the mystery object from the shadows, it caught the faintest glimmer of the moonlight... and sparkled.

Arvel rushed over and cradled the ornate metalcraft in his hands. "That's it." He headed for the door. "We need to get out, *now*."

"Why?"

"You don't hear that?"

Voices conversed in an indecipherable language, barely audible above the ceremonial drums. A shadow passed over the doorway, a slow and solemn omen of what was soon to come.

"Things are about to get rough." Arvel reached into his cloak and pulled out a handful of dark and shining pellets. "Hope you're ready."

A sudden shout came from outside, followed by a frenzied, charging mob of spearmen.

Primal, unfamiliar battle instinct took over. My senses sharpened, elevating me to an indescribable level of focus and prowess. I grabbed the attacker's spear by the shaft, and pulled its wielder toward me. I followed with a sharp blow to the back with my elbow. *Poor weapon choice... only vertical attacks.*

Arvel executed a swift flurry of blows which landed his attacker on the ground, and hurled the pellets from his hand toward the door. In seconds, they burst and covered the entire room in thick smoke. "Let's go."

The chase began.

I checked behind us and saw a small group of tribal bowmen in pursuit. The sound of their bare feet as they struck the grass became my only focus as I ran beside Arvel.

I watched the ropes come closer, our way out of the village. "Almost there."

Arvel snagged his rope, with me right behind.

The bowmen pulled their strings back with readied arrows as we scaled the wall.

With a single firm hoist, Arvel brought me over the top. I gave him my hand, and he switched over to the outward side... but we'd held still for just a little too long.

The whiz of furious airborne darts filled my ears. Air brushed my head when they blew by... only to be followed by a low, surly grunt at my side.

Bloody sculpted wood jutted from an opening between Arvel's shoulder and chest. An airborne barracuda had succeeded in its hunt for blood.

Arvel lost his footing and fell.

I swung the rope over to the outer side and dove after him.

My weight caused me to fall faster though, and I succeeded in taking his hand and clutching the rope with my legs and free hand. Our forceful descent halted mere feet above the grass.

Arvel shuddered and breathed, though heavily. "Thanks."

"We're not safe yet."

The village gate groaned as it opened.

I took my new friend under my arm and helped him to safety amidst the seclusion of the forest. Within minutes, we were shielded by the protective veil of the mighty trees and dense leaves.

Arvel opened his hand and revealed the Eagle, crafted out of silver. Its intricate feathers and majestic wings sparkled in the moonlight, glimmering into the radiant chain wrapped around Arvel's fingers.

"Finally... peace." He made a feeble attempt to pat my shoulder plate before the loss of blood claimed his consciousness.

I looked up to the stars and trudged on. *Now what?*

TEN

A reverberating boom overtook my backyard, followed by a tidal wave of cosmic flame. Surges of stinging pain rushed through my entire body as the biting embers flowed over me.

Of all places for a shooting star to crash... can I just catch a break?

The assault finally relented, allowing the environment to shift from one extreme to another when inferno was swapped out for winter's chilling grasp.

Ouch. I wheezed and rolled onto my back, The Realm Stone's singe fading. *There goes the house.*

My eye blinked under the gentle touch of a snowflake, illuminated under the overpowering radiance of the full moon.

"Welcome, Travis."

I turned and was met with the searing gaze of a familiar, flaming spirit.

Siris lifted his astral wings and unfurled them outward, reflecting the lunar gleam in the horizon. His body of embers grew brighter by the second, until his entire form was a pure white.

He gripped the handle of the celestial blade on his back and pulled it free from its scabbard.

The air rippled around Siris' weapon, a talon forged of the very aspect of the sun. The snow on the grass melted in its mere presence, consistently pushed back by its flow of power.

"The fate of both our worlds rests on your shoulders." Siris lifted the sword straight toward me, my body immediately heating through. "The time has come for you to prove you've got what it takes."

"I just woke up," I took a step back and raised my fists. "Your timing could use some work, but if you insist..."

"Excellent!" Siris beat his ghostly wings and arced backwards the length of a school bus. "Straight to the point."

Alright, what am I up against? I took long, deep breaths and studied Siris. *Weapon, wings, flaming body... triple disadvantage.* I rolled my tongue in my mouth. *Not like it'll scare me off.*

"How are we going to do this?" Siris shrugged. "You want me to count to three?"

"That's my line." I let the breath out of my lungs. *Yeah... this was a bad idea.*

Siris rolled his shoulders and stretched his neck. "One."

My heart kicked in my chest, and a pulse of awareness spread through my brain.

"Two."

My muscles began to tingle under the fleeting rush of nerves. My lungs grew more aware of the chilling air as my mind became entirely focused. Even the low thump of my heartbeat banged in my ears, clear and defined. My body stopped quivering as an eerie silence fell between us.

Siris and I exchanged looks of complete focus, two unbendable wills in conflict.

I can do this... I narrowed my gaze. *Right?*

The valley shook under the sovereign ring of an invisible bell tower. Its reverberation shattered the peace.

Siris bent his knees, wings outstretched. "Three."

I lunged forward into full sprint. *So what if the odds are against me?*

Siris let out a furious cry and blasted forward in a gush of flame, his solid body slamming into mine along the way. I grunted under the force of the shooting star that was Siris, searing into my flesh and lurching my stomach under the sheer power.

I toppled backwards, and after a couple brutal impacts with the icy ground, was lucky enough to land upright. *Could've gone better...* My skin screamed as a fine vapor swirled from it, and a metallic aftertaste spread through my mouth. *Again!*

I rose just in time to meet Siris, with his sword in both hands. With a golf-like swing, he caught me in the torso, and my body rocketed upward.

Talk about strength. Darkened drops of war's ink plummeted to the snow. *He's on a whole other level.*

Siris' wings flashed past me, and a sudden warmth circled my lacerated torso. In a blinding second, the momentum reversed, and I found myself barreling to the ground in the clutches of a phantasmal eagle.

"Big mistake, buddy." I seized Siris' iron head, braving the immediate singe on my palms. "Try a little taste of *this*."

I threw all my body weight backward and rotated Siris underneath me, allowing him to absorb the violent impact into the frozen earth. His wings flopped to either side as both of us became surrounded by a shimmering mist of snow and broken grass.

"Good one, Travis." My leg was seized in the clamps of a bear trap in the form of Siris' hand. "However, if that's your best... you should concede now."

The valley began to spiral, and I soon met another crushing impact. I grunted as the brittle, icy grass scraped against my back until my body finally dragged to a halt. In just a few moments, I'd been transformed into a mess of rashes, cuts and burns.

"You see, that's the problem." I rolled over and planted my hands against the snow. "I don't know the word *quit*."

I lifted my body up once more, this time to meet a sharp pain in my chest. I hunched over and wheezed under the absolute agony in my lungs, and watched as a spattering drizzle of red stained the snow.

The breeze caught what remained of my shirt, a wrapping of tatters around my shoulders. The once white cloth had now become a crimson banner, a mark of unrestricted battle.

"Well, this sucks." I shuddered and managed to get out a broken laugh. "I liked that shirt." I reached up with one hand and grasped the torn neck of my ragged cape.

Siris lingered in the near distance... waiting.

"Why'd you stop?" With a clean rip, I sent the cloth into the wind. "I thought we were just getting started."

A right hook to my face connected with blinding speed, putting me back onto my hands and knees.

"What a waste of time." The searing tip of Siris' blade met my eyes. "Pathetic."

Come on... My shoulders cracked, and my torso thudded to the cold embrace below. *Get up, you've still got fight left.*

"I should've guessed." Siris sauntered past. "If you were truly Exalted, you would've known sooner... and probably kept your mother from death."

What did you say?

"You're weak." Siris stopped walking and turned, just enough to catch me in his peripheral vision. "Just like that frail excuse for a woman."

The snow crunched under his boots as he sauntered away.

"Get back here, you glorified torch." I pressed my hands into the ground, my arms cracking as I raised up once more. "*Nobody* disrespects my mother... I don't care who you are, or what authority you think you have." I stood and popped my shoulder against my body. "We're not done yet."

A familiar, distorted hum came from my side.

The Sacred Scripture faced me, steady and intent.

I'm in really bad shape. I gave Siris a cold stare. *All talk, I'm afraid to admit.*

"Siris—" My chest burned with gripping pain, rubberizing my legs. I gasped as the air left my lungs, and the pulse escalated in my neck.

What? I clutched my chest, and watched as a faint glow emerged from under my hand. *Can't breathe!*

My heart became an overpowering bluish white, feverishly beating a soft warmth through my body. I trembled, and my joints tightened as my chest was forced outward.

A violent explosion of crackling electricity surged throughout the vicinity, a gush of flailing claws of the storm. Lightning dropped from the sky and coursed through the ground around me, each lance touching down as an elemental dancer amidst the raging voltage. My hair was flung upward from torrential winds racing around my body, an unstoppable gale which returned breath to my lungs and balance to my body. An overpowering sense of strength filled my mind, unshakable amidst the chaos.

I was the king of the storm.

This feeling... I clenched my fists together, intensifying the miniature hurricane around me. *So familiar.*

The Sacred Scripture burst through and linked to me in a concentrated ray of blue energy, and with a rippling wave over its cover, took on the aspects of my new form. Its cover morphed into a crystalline blue, networked with an array of intricate platinum.

This is more like it. I held my body still. *Now... let's try it out.*

I took a step forward, and was met with a vicious blast of awareness through my entire body. The air transformed and became a deep cerulean as my blood vessels emanated a divine glow. In response my skin grew a pale white. Corkscrews of sky blue aurora twisted around me with unspoken grace, laden with tiny surges of sparks.

The bell tower clanged once more.

The lightning stopped, and the wind died down to a steady breeze to reveal my fiery gaze.

"You're right... it would appear we aren't finished." Siris laughed and drew his sword once more. "Your true power—"

"Shut up." I tightened my fists and watched my forearms inflate. "I'm done chatting."

I lunged forward, this time backed by awoken power. My body thrust forward with impossible speed, my arm drifting back as I did. I tightened my fist, and plowed Siris' face with the wrath of a tempest.

Siris' armor made a dull ring as his phantasmal body bounced off the ground. He stabilized himself in the air and leaned forward to charge.

My shoes sounded like a jackhammer as they struck the ground with incomprehensible speed. In less than a second, I met him once more, this time with a leaping knee to the torso. *How? He was wiping the floor with me a second ago.*

Siris rooted himself against the ground and pushed into me with his shoulder, just enough to knock off my balance. He followed with a swift horizontal cut against my ribs.

Amazing. I took a step back before sweeping a leg out from under him. *Didn't feel a thing. Maybe that's not as good as it sounds.*

Siris beat his wings and blasted away, just in time to evade the crushing blow of my fist. He executed a precise barrel roll and glided in from afar, gaining aerial momentum as he raised his burning blade.

I took a few thunderous steps forward and met him head on. Our bodies interlocked, and both of us let out deep grunts of exertion as we pushed against one another.

With a mutual shove, we each were sent backward for a mere instant before clashing once more, this time with a flurry of blows at relentless speed. A finishing elbow from Siris to the gut halted the action just long enough for him to get hold of my neck.

"Doesn't matter if you're as strong as I am now." Siris raised his wings. "You can't fly."

We were both rocketed toward the full moon, and I pried against his grasp.

A streak of blue caught the edge of my sight.

The Sacred Scripture whizzed as it rushed up beside me, a radiant missile which easily kept pace with Siris.

Again I was thrown toward the ground, this time with Siris' moonlit silhouette barreling down on top of me to deliver the killing blow.

The Sacred Scripture whirled around my side, then chimed.

Immediate focus rushed into me, and my eyes opened wider. I kicked my legs and flipped to land on my feet, with eyes to the stars.

The Sacred Scripture bent its radiant glow into mine, and harmonized with my very being.

"Here we go, Scripture." I braced myself, and tightened one fist behind my back. My forearm bulged as the energy around me coiled and formed a surging veil. Waves of heat surged from my powerful body as I held my breath and concentrated with everything I had.

My heart raced, my pulse still reverberating in my ears. With a raging roar, I twisted all of my body weight and forced my arm upward.

Siris plummeted to the earth, and his blade collided with my fist.

A deafening boom tore through the valley, followed by a supernova of light as racing electricity met furious inferno, becoming one at the center of a cataclysmic explosion.

The chaos subsided and I found myself on my knees, the mysterious power from within no longer present. I fell back and let out a long sigh in the tranquility of the valley.

A peaceful silence fell, leaving me alone with the moon and stars.

"A splendid duel." A fanning cloak cast a shadow on my face. "It's a shame there's no such thing as a dueling tradition among the Exalted. *Rashaad...* even sounds like a fake name."

Mohandar, the faceless sentinel from the first days of having my book, loomed over me silhouetted in the moonlight. His dark gray armor glistened in the soft glow, along with his staff.

I sighed. "I'm gonna pretend I didn't hear that."

"Come on, we're headed to the Observatory." Mohandar nudged me with his boot. "It's time to make an Exalted out of you."

I stood with a little help from my teacher, and for the first time since I met him... I got the sense that his faith in me wasn't misplaced.

Maybe there was a heroic fire somewhere within me, waiting for a bit of kindling.

ELEVEN

The shadow of my wings danced over Arvel's sleeping form. His arm was bound and wrapped in shabby, blood-stained patchwork. His breaths were light... barely moving the amulet on his chest up and down. *I tried my best... not like I know a thing about bandaging. I just hope he's alright.* I turned from the fire. *Where's the stick?* I groped about and seized the gnarled fire poker. *Let's see if I can get some more heat on Arvel.*

I flipped the burning wood around, feeling the flame grow stronger.

My eyes caught the rising globe of light creeping over the horizon.

Holy crap, the sun's out? I sighed, posture slowly drooping down. *I still haven't gone to bed...*

A sudden snort came from just beside me.

Awake! I jolted and straightened up.

Arvel moaned and rose with a mindless stare. In a few moments of emptiness, he gazed about the cave with the eyes of a sloth.

"You're alive." I set my fire stick down. "That's good."

Arvel ran his hand across his cloth binding and winced. "Could be worse. Bring me the bottle of amber-colored liquid in my tent, would you?"

I did as I was asked, and handed it to Arvel. "What is it?"

"Scotch." The cork topper popped when it came off.

"You *just* woke up. What do you need booze for?"

He raised the bottle to his lips and took a few gulps before he reached for his shoulder. "This."

With a more than audible rip, he exposed the inflamed, reddened sight below the bandage.

"Yeah," Arvel bit his lip and set the bottle aside, "definitely not healed yet. In my tent, there's a box full of—"

I started toward the tent. "This better not be more booze."

"It isn't." He raised his good arm. "It's a wooden box about the size of your palm."

I brushed aside the tent's curtain for a door and rummaged through Arvel's belongings until I came across a finely-cut little cube of oak, smooth to the touch.

Arvel's eyes lit up when I brought it out. "Yeah, that's it."

I handed it over and watched as he immediately divided the cube in half to reveal a pool of tiny beads inside, each one hot pink and glistening in the fire. He pinched one of the pea-sized orbs between his fingers and held it up to me.

"These things are *fantastic*." Arvel smiled. "Watch this."

I stared as he placed the sphere between his teeth and crunched down on it.

The moment the ball shattered, his pupils shrank and he took one big gasp. His torso dipped down over his bedding, and within a few seconds, his body had taken on the aspect of an earthquake.

My stomach churned at the sight.

"Hey." I put my hand on his back. "You look like you're hooked up to a jackhammer."

The inflamed flesh on his shoulder rippled, and with a few steady waves, the redness drained to his pale skin tone. Eventually, the shaking stopped, rendering Arvel flat on his back.

"Hurts like hot coals... but recovery's a painful business." He extended his arm and wrapped his fingers around his bottle. "That's why I needed *this*." He tipped it up once more. "Much better."

Well, that just happened. I paced around the fire. "You sure you're alright?"

"Sure am." Arvel grinned and held out the box. "You want one?"

I shook my head faster than I could process the question. "No way, man."

"I'm kidding." Arvel gave a light laugh and closed the lid. "Why don't we gather up our things and hit the road?"

I picked up my helm from the ground, but stopped when my brain finally caught up. "Where to?"

"...I don't remember." Arvel paused for a moment. "Open up the one scroll with the map on it."

The crunching of aged parchment arose. "Well, we've got options."

The map was scribbled together with no sense of craftsmanship... even still, it seemed to provide a decent idea about the lay of this land. A few locations of interest were marked on the map with prominent black dots, one to the west, one to the south, and one to the north.

"You'd think it'd be a little more detailed."

"Doesn't have to." Arvel pursed his lips and studied the drawing. "They're all well-known landmarks."

"Really?" My wings fanned wide, just brushing the walls around us.

"You've got the Lunar Jungle, The Stairway to the Stars, and the Ruins of Sovengard marked..." Arvel nodded. "The Lunar Jungle's only a two-day walk from here, so that's where we're headed first. You figure out a reason why we're going yet?"

"It's funny." I scratched my chin. "We need to go pull together three pieces of a giant crystal, or else this world's going to smash into another."

Arvel brushed his bed roll aside and went for his armor. "If that's what you call funny, I don't even want to know what you call serious."

Just like that, we were up and out... the scent of pine and oak growing weaker with every step.

I pulled the bushes aside, and was met by open air. Rolling hills, green plains, and streams came together to form a wonder of nature in the valley below. The breeze caught my wings and gave a gentle chilling push, caressing each feather as it passed.

Arvel chuckled. "Wind feels pretty good, huh?" He gazed across the open field. "We'll have to stop at a town overnight. *Stonebrook.* Nice place, nothing but a few farms and an inn."

"Anything you can tell me about the Jungle?"

"You bet." Arvel nodded. "Boy, The Lunar Jungle's an incredible sight. By day, it's calm and quiet, not to mention full of wildlife. When the night falls, though... that's when the fun starts."

"Your kind of fun or mine?" The wind on my wings felt like I was in a hammock relaxing on tropical islands.

Arvel began to descend the slope to the valley below. "We'll only know when we get there, won't we?" He clutched the glimmering amulet on his chest. "Thanks for helping me reclaim this, by the way."

"Don't mention it." I joined Arvel and began the trek to the village. "By the way..."

"What is it?"

"We're going to be stuck with one another for a bit." I rubbed my chin through the bottom of my helm. "What's your story?"

"My story?"

I nodded during the long pause right after.

"I thought we were over this." Arvel shot me a stare which made even my eyelids fall motionless, as if my soul had been grasped by the claws of a wraith. "I lived with my family for eight years, and then I lost everything."

"Alright, alright. Sorry."

"So you say." Arvel lightened his piercing gaze, but I could still sense the ice behind his eyes. "You don't see me trying to dig up your biography, do you?"

I angled myself away, with muscles tensed. "Fair, I guess... forget I asked."

"Hold on." Arvel was silent for a moment as he watched his boots tread through the grass. "Sorry... you're right."

"Arvel, you really don't—"

"You brought it up." He took a deep breath. "...After my village was attacked, my grandfather got me out quick, all the way out of Reach. I was just a little one then. Didn't think much when he left me in an inn alone for a few hours at a time... he always came back with food, so it seemed alright."

"That's rough." I looked away.

"That was the easy part." Arvel grimaced. "One day, he left me alone like usual, but then hours became days. I went out looking for the guy, and instead found him cold, and ripped open by a rusty knife just because he walked into the wrong alley." He paused. "The wretch who did it was quick to spring for me, too... but he instead met the loving embrace of an arrowhead in his eye. Being a little boy, I was petrified even as my masked, caped rescuer took me by the hand and led me far away, to her home in the mountains."

Wow... to think he's gotten this far.

"The woman was the absolute best with a bow, could hit a fly across her house with a quill... she took me in and showed me her ways. While wearing a suit of armor by her own design, one can use its edges to fire a longbow with one hand, and... with practice, one in the other as well. I took to her well, but the more time I spent with her, the more I noticed something." Arvel made eye contact. "She never spoke. Not ever. Not while teaching, nor eating... the woman would *hum*, even *write*, but of all the days I knew her... she never uttered a word." Arvel laughed. "That answer your question?"

I've got no room to complain about anything anymore. I nodded, slow. "Beyond answered."

"Alright, then." Arvel watched as a butterfly flittered past him. "Your turn. Where do you—"

I twisted my shoulder, and my wing jumped just the right way to smack Arvel square in his back. Immediately, he became acquainted with the ground, his fluttering cape behind him.

"*Whoa.*" I stopped walking, and used every bit of self-control I had not to laugh. "My bad."

"Firstly, ouch." Arvel pushed his body off the grass. "Secondly, for what reason?"

"I said I was sorry." I knelt down and helped him up. "I'm still trying to figure these things out."

The golden sun transformed to deep tangerine as it sank toward a distant layer of trees. Among them, a swirling column of stone stood high above the surrounding leaves, an ancient sentinel over the woodland and the vast field. Before long, we arrived... at the little village of Stonebrook.

The town wasn't much more than a few buildings placed around a pathway of rocks embedded in the earth. The numerous dents and cracks in the structures revealed generations of age, giving me the sense I moved in a marvelous painting of harmony and depiction of peaceful countryside living.

Arvel spotted the inn. "I'm going to pay for our rooms."

"Okay."

A smile crossed my face as I marveled in the glorious absence of technology, business, and modern-day idiocy.

I rubbed my chin and contemplated the metric crap ton of information laid on me in the past few days... *Between Mohandar and Siris' teachings, everything's headed for a total face plant if I don't do something about it. Arvel and I need to get moving, and fast.*

I headed into the rustic, welcoming building, and allowed the commotion in my restless mind to ease.

The silence of the outdoors was drowned out by the uproar of clinking glasses and voices inside the inn. Round tables were scattered throughout the room, along with mingling travelers. Their joy was likely driven by the frothy drinks given to them by the beautiful bartender who wore a jade dress made of fine cloth with a darker green trim. She had a shine in her red, wavy hair matching the sparkle of her emerald eyes. Arvel went to the bar and pulled up a stool beside the counter. He ordered a flask of ale, and was met with a kind smile from the tavern maid, who scrubbed out another glass.

Never been in a bar before... I took a seat at one of the tables. *Haven't had any reason to.*

"Well, you're clearly from out of town." My shoulder plate dinged when a finger tapped against it. "You here for the climb?"

I turned. "Excuse me?"

A woman with chocolate brown hair and pale white skin took the seat beside me. She propped a slender arm up to rest her chin and twirled her locks between her fingers. She wore an earth-tone dress and worn leather boots. "You know, the climb?"

"I'm sorry," I raised an eyebrow. "What?"

"It's pretty much the only reason people come through here." She relaxed back in her seat and sighed. "Everybody thinks the big tower's real special, and a rumor got fired up that if you get to the top, you can talk to some spirits, or whatever."

"Get *out*." I propped my elbow on the table. "Any truth behind it?"

"Couldn't tell you." She shrugged. "Everyone who's tried to climb the thing either fell off tryin' to get up, or fell off tryin' to get down."

"Sounds fun to me." I stood. *Anything's better than sitting here.*

Arvel was still at the bar, chatting away with the beauty behind it.

I patted his shoulder. "I'm going to take a look around."

"You be careful." Arvel gave me a serious glare. "Don't get lost, either."

"I'll do my best." I waved and left the tavern. *Now, to find the tower.*

A short way out of the village, behind the trees, stood the colossus of stone. It had been here for ages, given the layer of moss, vines and lichens among its grainy surface. It was massive, and had to be at least five stories high. Dark clouds parted around the masterpiece of sculpting as it went up.

I took a feel, and my hand slid right off.

It's gonna be a pain to climb. This isn't a tree in the forest back at home... this is video game level.

I ultimately decided to stop fighting myself and go, driven by the insatiable desire to discover what could be waiting at the top.

For what felt like hours, I scaled the spire... blending into its moon-cast silhouette I pulled myself onto the flattened peak, and sprawled out on my backside... resting for the first time since starting the ascent.

The sky of Reach was filled with stars, too many to comprehend. Among the cosmic sea was the gigantic moon, sharing its light of assurance with everything below.

"Made it." I caught my breath and stood. "Now, to see what—"

I found myself standing on a circular surface about four feet in diameter.

I slapped my forehead and sighed. "You've gotta be kidding."

Nothing.

Not a thing.

Not even a little welcome banner.

I paced over to the edge of the tower and looked down to the grass. "That's just going to be a *wonderful* trip back."

A hefty crack reverberated through the night, and the footing underneath me scattered. The world flipped upside down as I was suspended in a gush of air... headed straight for the ground.

Well, this can't possibly end well.

TWELVE

My lungs screeched for air as the flash wave of adrenaline subsided... and the Observatory was a welcome sight.

The triangular crystal in my pocket cooled. *Talk about timing.*

Mohandar set both of his hands on my shoulders, his metallic fingers chilling to the touch. "Easy, Travis... breathe. Rough transition, I presume."

I clutched my chest and gathered some composure. "Still getting used to flipping between worlds."

"Yes, it is a bumpy ride." He laughed and gave me some space. "At any moment, you could return to your wonderful place in midair!"

"Yeah." I tapped my foot. "I just have zero say in when I switch places, huh?"

"Indeed." Mohandar studied the palm of his hand. "The Realm Stone will warn you when the change comes, but you have no say when it happens. Though the duration of your stays change, they'll always be equal between both Sister Realms."

I rubbed my temples and took deep breaths. "So... if I'm here on Earth for a week, I'll be on Reach for a week?"

Mohandar nodded. "And then you'll have to be prepared in case the next shift lasts a day. Your soul can only move between your own body and Siris' once it's under the effects of frozen time."

"How fun." I groaned. *At least I've got the Realm Stone for a bit of warning.*

The Sacred Scripture blasted from my side and raced about, bringing my view to a marvel of architecture.

Mohandar's celestial home possessed a mesmerizing shimmer from all directions. The very construction of the place shattered my definition of possibility. Not an inch of the structure was connected, held together only by the gravitational pull of the flaming orb in the center.

Looks like something off the Sci-Fi channel. I returned from the no-man's land of my mind. "What's the deal with this place?"

"The deal?" Mohandar chuckled, and made his way across the room. "It's old."

"I get that," I said as the Sacred Scripture descended to my side, "but how does it even *work?* Why don't the individual pieces up and drift off?"

"Good question." He stopped at a wide space in the observatory floor and faced me. "If this place allows me to see and travel to every Realm, isn't such a matter trivial?" He tightened his grip on his staff, and it flared an innate violet glow. "Anything else on your mind?"

"Two things, actually." I popped a strip of gum into my mouth. "A while ago, you said I was picked to be Exalted by some kind of god?"

"The gods, yes." Mohandar brushed his cloak off his shoulder. "Looking for a bit of history, I see."

"The way you put it, it sounded like they're in charge of us." I fixed the sleeves of my shirt. "What kind of powers are there above the Exalted?"

"Well, the Prime Deities Alcyon, Cydea, and Grrogum are the authority you speak of..." Mohandar made his way over to his bookshelves and started searching. He froze about halfway down, snagging a resource from the rest. "Ah, here it is. *On Deities, Greater and Lesser.* I have a feeling you'll get it easier with a visual... this way, please."

He really does have a book for everything. I followed Mohandar to a table, where he set the book down and cracked it open.

"Greater and Lesser... there's different classes?" I asked.

"Yes. The Greater Deities include Alcyon, Cydea, and Grrogum, but there's far more Lesser Deities than you can count. These would include deities like Yaris, Lord of Domination..." Mohandar tapped his fingers against the table and stepped aside. "Quite a famous Lesser deity, but we're not here to discuss him." Mohandar pointed to the pages of his book. "Here's what you need to know."

I brushed the Sacred Scripture out of the way and looked over a well-printed graphic.

Aged ink stained the ancient page, creating a triangle on its grainy surface. Each point was marked with a circle flashing its own unique symbol. One was a winged sword... another a balancing scale... and the final an all-seeing eye.

"This is the symbol of your god, Alcyon." Mohandar guided my eyes to the symbol of the sword. "Typically, when you communicate with other Exalted, you'll introduce yourself as Travis, *Exalted under Alcyon.*"

I rolled the idea around. "Will I get in trouble with this Alcyon guy if I don't?"

The Sacred Scripture zipped into my face and yapped away.

"Not exactly." Mohandar gave my book a playful shove. "The gods, both Greater and Lesser, live separately from us. So long as the barriers holding the Realms apart stay intact, we won't have to worry about any kind of divine wrath."

The Sacred Scripture bumped me on the shoulder before floating off.

Mohandar closed the book and headed back to the shelves. "You said there was something else?"

"Yeah... what's going to happen to the Realms? You told me they'd fall apart, but—"

"Yes..." Mohandar opened his palm. "Hold still."

His hand was on my face in an instant, blotting out the world around me.

Swirling plasmids bent into conscious shapes in the blackness, forming an entire village composed of vibrant color. The streaks were completely flawless, from the towering mountains all the way down to insects flittering between buildings. Amidst the neon paradise, a streak of red overtook the skyline... expanding to become an oval-shaped disc with a deep black center.

"It begins with invasions." Mohandar's voice was calm. "When powerful individuals cross into realms where they don't belong."

In a surreal wave, the colors intensified and became crisply detailed.

The auras shifted into terrified faces of fleeting people, every one with a jaundiced skin tone. Man, woman and child alike ran in desperation to escape the grasp of a rampaging hydra whose endless heads snaked from the scarlet disc in the sky. Hellfire rained down as each maw spewed its searing fury.

I held my breath as I watched an entire family transform to ashes under the beast's scorn.

"This alone leads to countless deaths and incalculable levels of destruction," Mohandar sighed. "It gets even worse."

Worse? I tried to move, but my body was trapped within the illusion.

The massacre in front of me faded before morphing into another scene. Ahead was a futuristic metropolis built from polished white metal.

"As the forces holding the Realms apart cease to exist, they undoubtedly begin to merge. At first, it's physical."

Right in the center of traffic, the air rippled... like an intense heat wave. With a flash, a crystal the size of an apartment building shot up from the ground. The world itself surged airborne as thousands of crystalline fangs jutted upward, tearing out building foundations along the way.

"However," Mohandar's voice quieted. "None can prepare for what follows."

With a final blinding flash, everything came to a halt... horrified citizens, falling metal, and the burning sky became but mere parts in a lurid painting. Time itself had screeched to a halt, leaving behind petrified remnants of a world in ruin.

"The end of time." The pressure of Mohandar's hand left my face. "Once it's gone this far, it isn't long before both Realms are completely annihilated."

I'm up against the freaking apocalypse. What am I supposed to do to stop it?

"This is why you *must* reassemble the shards of the crystal in Reach. Follow Siris' map, and save the Realms from destruction." His footsteps shifted as I opened my eyes. "Today, we're going to start your training. You're not going to get off easy on this side, either."

He tapped his staff against the floor, and we were catapulted across the galaxy.

***

Rays of mid-morning sun trickled through the trees, and gave the emerald grass a wonderful glossing on the tips of their blades while the easy wind and trickling streams provided a calm background to the silence.

I looked around and found myself in my woodland campsite.

"What a nice place." Mohandar took a seat on one of the toppled logs and gazed over the rolling treetops ahead. "Wonderful craftsmanship, Travis. This will make a fine place to develop your skills."

"You teleported us *here?*" I paced, my face in my palm. "You couldn't pick anywhere else?"

"Why not here?" Mohandar turned around. "Calm, quiet, you can hear all the birds singing..."

"You're a bit of a fruit cake." I plunked down beside him and flung my arms across the grainy bark. "Alright, then. What're we doing?"

Mohandar laughed. "First of all, *you're* standing back up."

A sudden, excitable hum arose as a ghostly net snatched the back of my shirt and pulled me to my feet.

The Sacred Scripture danced around as it withdrew its grasp.

"Any tips for this thing?" I sighed and gave the book a stern look. "Honestly, it's more annoying than a cloud of mayflies."

"Unfortunately, Sacred Scriptures have their own minds... not a word of advice would help." Mohandar stretched out his shoulders. "Now, focus."

I straightened up.

"Our first task is to get you into your Power State... but on command." He rose from the log and faced me, his cloak flapping. "It's quite challenging at first, but it all comes down to one single step."

I nodded.

"You need to call upon the bond between yourself and the book, not physically, but in a partnership of souls. The stronger the connection, the easier it will be to slip into your true power."

Partnership of souls? I looked at the Sacred Scripture, and my heartbeat immediately accelerated. *So what, like feel the energy in the—*

My chest kicked outward, and my muscles inflated. "Oh, boy."

A gush of electrical energy exploded across the area, a neon scramble of racing little sparks.

The miniaturized storm subsided, leaving Mohandar in the presence of the pale, storm-born recreation of myself... only this time, with none of the rage, and none of the lightning on my undulating wisps of spirit.

Mohandar withdrew his forearm from his face. "It would appear you two get along quite well."

"Yeah," I sneered and glanced at the book. "Quite."

"Now, for the next step. Tell me how this form affected you during your battle."

"Well, I was already pretty mad, but it really stoked the fire." I ran my fingers along my skin. "It got more intense as we kept going."

"Do you see the connection?"

I scratched my chin, and thought hard for a nice stretch of time. "Nope."

Mohandar raised a finger. "Your Power State was wild and uncontrolled because you were. You're calm now, and your Power State mirrors this."

"So in other words," I recalled the immense strength of my past experience, "angrier is stronger?"

"Wrong entirely." Mohandar lowered his plated hand and allowed a spider to crawl on. "When you allow rage to take control, you become vulnerable, predictable, and most importantly, you stop thinking. However, if you deliberately control your mind and spirit as one..." Mohandar held out the palm of his hand, and a gentle, rose pink ember emerged from it. "You can do the impossible."

"Cool." My legs began to quiver. "Show me."

He released the ember, and allowed it to flicker away. "Hold out your hand, like so."

This is awesome. I extended my pale, open palm. "Okay."

"Now, we're going to take this easy, so you can develop strength of mind." Mohandar lowered and studied my pulsing energy. "Harmonize your mind and soul. Will them together to create…"

Anticipation drew the moment out for eternity.

"…A sphere."

I took a deep breath, and looked into Mohandar's void of a face from the corner of my eye. "A sphere."

He nodded. "Visualize it in your mind, and keep it in focus. Waver for a second and your creation will break."

"Alright." I focused, and all the sounds of the wilderness faded. Nothing existed except myself and my open palm.

Sphere. A ball. Like a big, floaty beach ball.

I channeled everything I had, and immediately, a growing weight bore down on my body.

A subtle flicker arose, then a spark, then… creation flowed.

"A cube?" My heart sank. The cube vanished in a shimmer of specks, and the strain on my body released.

Mohandar laughed and patted me on the shoulder before walking off. "You'll get it eventually. Once you make an orb, try to get creative. Play with your powers, if need be!" His voice deepened to a more serious tone. "Tomorrow's when your *real* training starts."

He blasted off into the stars, leaving me to my work.

"Okay." I cracked my knuckles. *Let's do this.*

Two hours passed.

I was toppled on the grass, limbs stretched in all directions. My chest heaved up and down as I panted, sweat streaming over my forehead with an unshakable ache as if I'd just blasted out a full-body workout.

"*Alright...*" I raised my hand to my eyes. "*Two hundred* times I've tried, and *two hundred* times I made a freaking cube instead of a sphere." I groaned and pulled myself up to a seated position. "I'm done."

The Sacred Scripture was in the bushes, humming as it played with a wilting, shriveled shell of what used to be a lively tiger lily, but get this. Whenever the book's divine essence touched the lily, the bloom sprang up again... all the color and perkiness restored. Likewise, the moment the Scripture let the blossom alone, its petals reverted to their state of death.

I watched for a while, until the book gave its task a rest.

"So, Scripture... any idea how I de-Power State?" I looked down at my hands. "If I can help it, I don't want to be glowy all the—"

With an audible click, everything about the Power State faded.

"Huh... thanks."

The Sacred Scripture hummed, and drew my focus once more.

I put my hands on my knees and pushed. "Let's go for a walk."

The book and I ranged through the peace of the forest until we came to its end, where the lake, fields and trees met. Out in the distance, I spotted our fishing boat lingering near the water's edge.

"Let's go check out the lake." I turned to the book. "I'm sure there'll be some fish you can—"

The book was gone, with no warning or trace.

"Ought to get a leash." I shook my head and kept on walking.

When I got to the docks, I was met with a welcome surprise.

Out on the edge of the aged, moist wood was the glistening figure of a beautiful girl, with her long legs swaying over the easy-moving water. She stroked her caramel hair between her fingers with grace, resembling a nymph of the fables in waterside serenity... such unspoken wonder made her a goddess in a lime green V-neck shirt and jean shorts.

I took a hesitant step onto the wooden planks. "Excuse me."

"Hmm?" She turned, and revealed a soft gaze which struck me petrified. Upon sight, her emerald eyes lit up and a smile curled across her face. "Hey there, Travis. Been a while, hasn't it?"

I stopped, and with an inaudible gasp, recollection struck me.

Last time I saw those cheerful green eyes, they were welled up with tears. The faint echoes of crying rang throughout my mind, along with the tiniest sense of... vulnerability.

Kate.

"Yeah, it's been a whole... *week.*" I feigned a smile back. *Between Reach and Earth, it feels longer... funny how things work out.*

"So, then." She swung her legs onto the deck and stood up, making sure to grab her shoes in her fingertips along the way. "What're you up to?"

I brushed a fold out of my sleeve. "Just coming to check on the boat, maybe clean it off a little. You?"

"Just enjoying nature..." Kate smiled and gazed over the water. "Well, go ahead. Nobody's stopping you."

"Thanks." I strolled toward the edge. *Wait a minute.*

"How's summer? Lame, fun, somewhere in between?" She plunked back down, this time facing the side as her bare feet eased back and forth.

Well, where's the tally? I fell in a puddle, met an ages-old spirit, got a new body, killed a few giant spiders and fought a ghost knight, so... The boat swayed on the water as I got in its small body. "Been pretty mellow so far. I got myself a new job that's kind of fun." I took a towel from under the driver's seat of the boat and polished off its console.

"A working guy, huh?" She leaned in with big eyes. "Punch any more bad guys lately?"

I returned from the labyrinth of my head. "Not lately, no. Sorry if it's a disappointment."

The boat gently sloshed in the water as each of us hesitated to speak.

I took a seat. "What are you doing here?"

"I told you, watching the lake." She raised an eyebrow. "...You don't have a head problem, do you?"

"No, I'm just not all that smart." I put the towel back. "I mean, what are you doing *in this area?*"

Kate giggled. "I live here. You really don't get out much, do you?"

"Well, it's not that I don't get out, I'm just either in the woods, or—" Without warning, a burning sting surfaced in the side of my cargo shorts. My eyes tightened up, and I shot my hand into my pocket.

Kate's hand went over her mouth. "Travis, are you okay?"

I pulled out the Realm Stone, the gift from Mom. Sure enough, the thing was all fired up, and ungodly hot to the touch. The mere second it hit the floor of the boat was enough for it to raise a fine steam.

The wind shifted, howling as a pack of ghostly hyenas. Clouds billowed up over the lake, creating an ominous blanket of darkness from which there was no escape. The guiding light of the sun was no more.

This isn't good. My senses focused amidst the chaos, my thoughts in full clarity. *That thing's never burned so bad before, usually it's just a little before I switch worlds... this is different.* I looked over to Kate. *She isn't safe here.*

"We need to go." I snatched the Realm stone and sprang onto the dock. "I don't know what this is, but my gut says it's bad."

She took off and headed for the grass. "Do you think it's a tornado?"

"Signs don't point that way." I followed, close beside her.

"What do you mean, signs don't—" In the transition to grass, she lost her balance and toppled right into me... sending us both to the ground.

I put my hand on her shoulder. "You okay?" At this point, I was hollering over the screaming winds.

Kate rubbed her ankle, but nodded. "Yeah."

The ground trembled beneath us...

"Travis." A dull red light cast across Kate. She froze with wide eyes. "Behind you."

I turned, and found myself staring into an endless chasm of scarlet sliced into the air, as if by an invisible blade. The pit radiated with an essence of calamity.

Two eyes appeared from within the laceration of reality... each one as big as myself.

A bellowing, distorted voice erupted from the crimson portal, the very sound making my skin crawl.

"Human... Fear me!"

The Sacred Scripture sailed in from afar, holding fast at my side... and like the striking of a flame, my Power State roared to life.

I scoffed. "No."

THIRTEEN

Reach returned, and with it, the absence of footing beneath me. I plummeted to my demise, layers of the stone tower whizzing by. *This is it.* My joints started to lock up. *I'm dead, right when everybody was starting to need me.*

A white blur flitted into my vision...

A feather.

The majestic fluff twisted and turned in the air, in utter defiance of gravity.

Kate.

Panic shut its fat mouth and made way for conscience.

Stop and think about Kate! If you quit now, she's as good as gone.

Clarity pulsed through my brain. Breaths became the rolling surf, and my body took action.

Never surrender.

The grass came within arm's length... and then, in a moment of brilliance, they unfurled.

My wings stretched high and wide, unleashing the breath of a tornado with a single mighty beat. A sudden dizziness overtook me as the momentum shifted entirely, throwing me toward the stars above.

With one more beat, the daze was gone and replaced by pure turbulence. Intense wind hit my face, immediately causing my eyes to water.

I'd become a living missile.

I can't believe it... I cracked a huge smile. *I'm flying!*

I let out an uncontrolled cackle as I lifted my right wing and initiated a long banking turn. The rush refused to die down, relentlessly conjuring up goosebumps, quivering, and most of all... laughter.

I burst through the clouds and came upon an entirely new world.

"Incredible." I snapped my wings open and halted. "Just incredible."

Cascading bands of the aurora borealis greeted me with grace. In the silence of the night, the flowing river of cosmic wonder became a dancer, waving and undulating across the entire sky. Greens, yellows, and pale whites all twisted and turned through one another, a mark of beauty far beyond what any man-made invention could give.

"To think this was up here all along." The rays reflected on the corners of my helm. "Unbelievable."

I'd have stayed and marveled forever, if not for a sudden pale blaze which came barreling toward me with incomprehensible speed.

"Look out!"

I thrust to the side, just barely evading the streak of pure heat. *That voice.* I followed its transient trail of smoke... and found myself right back at the peak of the tower. I descended and landed, taking a good look at the results... and believe me, it took a few seconds to get a grip on what I was looking at.

The tower's top had been beaten into a steaming crevice, charred black and adorned with fizzling embers the color of snow. In the center... the expressionless gaze of the phantom knight Siris. He'd been reduced to nothing but his astral helm, merely a foot tall and with none of the imposing armor.

His body clinked as he rolled to face me. "It seems we've crossed paths again."

I closed my teeth together and tried to fight off a chuckle, but to no avail. "*Jeez.* What happened to you?"

"You happened." Siris sighed in his severely altered form. "Thanks to your fit of rage, I now have accepted a more... *humble* appearance."

"I'd say I'm sorry, but..." I lost my composure and collapsed to the warm, rocky surface beneath me.

"Will you cease your foolishness?" Siris grunted. "This is no laughing matter."

I howled as I rolled about on my back. "You're a yammering tin can!"

"A tin can who'll fling you across the horizon." His blaze flared as he hopped over to my hysterical body, each bound accompanied with a tiny metallic *clink.* "Now, I have very important—"

"Alright, alright." I took a moment to pull myself together with one last sigh, my gut now screaming from its joyous torture. "What's up, metal head?"

Siris rolled his gaze to the side. "I'm terribly sorry, but could you pick me up?"

"Feeling lonely?" I sneered.

Siris bounced. "Pick me up so I can be at your eye level. Give me a shred of dignity, at least."

"Fine." I lifted him by the edges in his headpiece until he and I were staring each other eye to visor.

"I'm indeed terribly ashamed of what I said about your mother, Travis." Siris took a deep breath. "She was an incredibly enduring, honorable individual who deserves no such disrespect."

I narrowed my eyes. "Then why'd you say it?"

"I knew the only way to tease out your Power State was to unleash that nasty temper of yours." Siris trembled in his limited stature. "But anyway, I'm not here to apologize. I've come to make an offer."

I need to get back to Kate. I remained silent. *Frozen in time or not, she's not safe.*

"I'm sure you've figured out our little tradition was a sham," Siris sprang out of my grasp, "and seeing as you've *completely* defeated me, I'd like to offer you my assistance. A payment, of sorts."

I shifted up onto my knees. "What help can you offer? As far as I know, the life of an Exalted is dangerous... and I can punt you."

He's a jerk, and tried to kill me a little while ago... I eyed up his tiny stature. *But I do feel a little bad for him.*

"Alright," I shrugged. "You can tag with me as long as you don't pull anything weird. Don't go trying to take *my* head off."

"Oh, good golly!" Siris bounced. "You won't regret this, Travis. Now, let's get down from this tower."

We dropped to the base of the tower with an easy fan of my newly usable wings. "The tavern's a pretty decent walk from here. How do you want to get around?"

"I can manage on my own." Siris shook free of my grasp and plopped to the ground. "If need be, I'll roll to keep up."

"Answer me something." I joined Siris as he hopped his way along the beaten path toward town. "How are you in so many different places? First you're in the triangle stone, then in my backyard, and now here. What's up with that?"

"It's not a *triangle stone*. The gift I left you is a *Realm Stone*, and it picks up abnormalities in the balance of reality." Siris kept on hopping forward. "To answer your question, in order to intermingle with your world and my own, I do one simple thing... I *invade*."

I took a step back and tensed up. "You're an invader?"

"I guess you could say so." He turned. "Without evil intent, that is. Travis, while invasions have a very nasty undertone when talked about, not all of them have ill meaning. Does every apple have a worm in it?"

"Making a hurricane in seconds and tearing a hole in someone else's world is a bit of a big worm."

"I suppose you're right." Siris shuddered and kept on. "It's a shame how these crumbling worlds function... especially for you."

"Especially for me?"

"None of these people know they're petrified in their struggles, that for hours, sometimes days at a time, they're held in the very same moment... never meant to leave. This goes for every kind of instant... a kiss, a farewell, even a stabbing. At any given time, these poor individuals could be entirely frozen in whatever they see." He sighed. "Not one of them knows... but you, Travis, are cruelly aware."

"Don't be such a downer." I reached down and spun him by his crescent. "I've got somewhere I'd rather be, but you don't see me yammering about it. Doesn't matter if I'm *cruelly aware* or not. I can worry all I want, but it's not going to change the fact that I'm here with you, and we've got things to do."

Siris chuckled. "Perhaps I can learn a few things from you."

"From me?" I snorted. "No."

A horrible screech, like an entire kindergarten class raking their nails against a chalkboard, split the night.

"Oh, no." Siris halted. "Travis, we need to get to town *now*."

Out in the distant path, a fleeting blur of man-sized shadows crossed from one tree line to another, in a feverish sprint toward the village. After the tiniest break in the movement, the woodland rustled to life with the sound of the rolling surf. More and more of these scampering silhouettes converged upon the town, an invisible army under the darkened trees.

The ground beneath us shifted.

"Travis, pick me up!"

I snagged Siris by the crest of his helm and sprang backward, met with the menacing grin of an arachnid face bursting from the earth below. A shower of fine soil rained down on us as the screeches continued on all sides...

"This doesn't look good..." I looked around. "Not at all."

At every angle I was met by the quivering form of a beady-eyed, man-sized spider, their choppy breaths puffing with the volume of a horse. Each one's furry abdomen was coated with a dusting of soil, fresh out of their unseen lairs.

The faint sound of yelling came from the direction of the village, followed by the clang of a great bell.

One by one, each scourge hissed in a baleful chorus and readied their fangs, toxic saliva dripping from their mouths of avarice.

"Travis..." Siris shifted in my hand. "Put me on over your helm."

"Why don't we just fly off?"

"They're in the trees, you fool." Siris let out a long breath. "Slide me on, over your helm."

The spiders dipped their heads down and tensed their legs.

Sweat beaded up on my forehead, and my heartbeat began to pick up.

"Travis, *put me on your head.*"

I hesitated, just long enough for an advocate of death to rocket into the air toward me, its fangs of pestilence bared.

Siris' flaming aura arose. "Do it, now!"

FOURTEEN

Thunder crashed behind howling wind. Rain pounded down as I stood, surging with awoken power. My breaths grew intense as every muscle in my body bulged.

Kate was collapsed on the ground behind me, absolutely petrified.

An arm the size of a school bus thrust from the moaning portal.

No doubt about it. This is the start of it all.

"Fearless." Another titanic arm stretched into our world. "What are you?"

I refused to break my gaze, tightening my posture. "Exalted. You?"

Clawed fingers curled and pulled forth the torso of a colossus.

Look at the size. I should be shaking in my skin... Why am I so calm?

Eyes of scorn leered down from a black stone mask. The great beast's head fanned out to the sides revealing a net of horns, broken and gnawed from previous battles. Its body inflated with a mountain of scaly muscle, legless and home to four burly arms.

A loud ping ensnared my attention.

A sword, hooked inward like a scythe, protruded from the ground. The silver fang was fit to harvest trees with ease, just like its matching left-hand sister.

His voice rumbled, so powerful I could barely understand. "I am Ulanog... this world's new overlord."

I broadened my chest. "Not so long as I've got a say."

"Get in my way, and you'll be dead." The titan pulled his blade from the earth, and a stream of mud dripped from it.

Kate stood up on nervous legs. "Travis, look at him. You're tough, but are you serious?"

"What have we here?" Ulanog craned his scaly neck and extended a clawed finger. "How *delicious*."

All sense of reason blew from my mind, my entire being uniting under a single overwhelming purpose. My vision sharpened, my heart kicked in my chest, and my Power State snaked and encircled the swelling muscles of my forearm... then pulled the trigger.

With a jet-powered leap, I threw my body and delivered a fearsome uppercut to Ulanog's jaw. "You stay away from her!"

"Insolent slave." He dug his claws into the earth and threw his boulder of a torso toward me, flinging mud. "Die!"

I sprang to the side, just barely evading a brutal swipe of Ulanog's blade.

A scaly wall smashed into my side, flinging me airborne.

Ouch. The Sacred Scripture raced beside me. I thumped against the grass, but whirled back to my feet. *Gotta be quicker than that.*

"Little slave girl..." Ulanog dragged his way over to Kate. "Where's your protector now?"

Kate's eyes narrowed, and she rolled her weight to one side. "You know, you shouldn't turn your back on the enemy."

I lunged forward and seized Ulanog's stubby tail. Adrenaline overtook my brain, the aspect of rage now coursing through my bloodstream.

"No." Ulanog's eyes got big when my muscles swelled, and the great brute's body began to slide. "Impossible!"

"I know." I hurled my scaly foe onto his back, the earth trembling upon his impact. In a mere second, I sprang onto his chest and cracked my knuckles.

Thunder rolled as I laid into his exposed chest, my fists becoming a relentless jackhammer.

Ulanog bounced against the ground under my vicious assault. "Enough of this game."

Ulanog snatched me up with a single hand and heaved me away.

His muscles are too thick. I pulled my balance together and stuck the landing. *Blunt strikes won't work.*

"There's more in you." The giant crossed his blades in front of his chest. "Show me!"

What was it Mohandar was trying to teach me? I ducked a whistling horizontal swipe, and a few of my hairs flittered into the air. *Fighting angry is fighting poorly?*

Another iron claw bore down just in front of me.

He's right. I have to think... I sprang onto the car-sized fist of my enemy and sprinted up his arm. *I have to control my Power State intentionally.*

I pushed off of Ulanog's shoulder and twisted my hand to my face.

I have to take another approach, something to pierce those scales. I pulled my mind together and gathered my focus. *Give me a sword!*

My pupils pulled tight under a short-lived flash, and...

Just the thing I needed.

"A sphere?" I rolled my fist around the infernal ball. "Seriously, *now?*"

The structure of the orb shattered in my grasp, and unleashed a ravaging sensation in the nerves of my forearm as my pale skin grew brighter and brighter. Without warning, my curled fingers expanded.

The crackling radiance became a translucent longsword forged of my very spirit. Its blade hissed under the raindrops, converting them to wisps of steam upon contact.

The two of us stopped for a moment to take a short, spiteful glance at one another.

I smirked in the face of hate. "This is more like it."

Ulanog bellowed and lashed out with his hooks.

By raw instinct, I threw my sword out and caught the curved blade, my entire body rocking with the blow. I pushed the sword away and followed with a clean vertical slash up his chest.

Good hit. I nodded at the dark ooze dripping from the cut. *I just might—*

Sharp pain bit into my hip as the point of Ulanog's other hook shoved its way through my gut. I buckled as the blade pulled back out with a clean coating of my blood, casting me to a knee.

I deserved that. I wheezed up a fine mist of crimson. *I was getting cocky.*

My body went limp when another rend raced down my shoulder, a grim cocktail of reddened rain flowing out. Without a moment of mercy, Ulanog's open hand buried me in a fine-tailored hole.

The pale glow in my skin died out like a wax-drowned candle.

I shuddered and managed to press off the wet terrain, my left arm dragging against the moist dirt along the way. "Never... give... up." Each word sent a jab into my lungs, arousing a nasty fit of coughing.

"I don't know if you caught on, but your strength's already left you," Ulanog growled. "Why won't you just stay down?"

"That's what anyone else would do." I raised my arm, coated with the scarlet signature of battle. "You can kick me around and call me a worm all you want. Fine... I won't care in the slightest. But so long as you're a threat to my friends, I'll keep coming!"

I lunged forward and pounded my frail fist into the virtual brick wall ahead.

"Courage." Ulanog didn't even flinch. "An intoxicating wine for the fool." He curled his finger behind his thumb and flicked me over, as if I were a little ant.

Don't stop, Travis. I pushed with everything I had, but my lacerated core refused to rise. *You're not done until you're dead.*

"Not one foe has been able to withstand my strength as long as you." Ulanog lifted his blades. "You will die with your honor intact, Exalted—"

A frenzied cry erupted from behind, and my executioner turned around. With a pained yell, Ulanog's head snapped back.

Wedged in Ulanog's blazing eye was the fat end of a wooden paddle... at its handle, Kate viciously pressed it further in, ignoring the fleeting pyre. Her soaked locks hung over her as she drove with all her might, until she slipped and rolled off.

Kate, no!

"My eye!" Ulanog dropped both of his swords and stretched all four sets of claws wide. "I'll tear you apart!"

What the heck were you thinking?

Ulanog flailed his torso toward Kate in a deadly embrace.

A fleeting gush of air blew past.

In an instant, Kate was beside me, embraced in the safety of the Observer's arms.

Mohandar set Kate down on the grass and stood tall. "Are you alright?"

"Thank you," Kate nodded. "Whoever you are."

"Good. If I'd come a second later, you'd have been *killed*." His blowing cloak gave him the appearance of a real-life superhero as he pulled his staff from its holder on his back. "Travis, this will only take a moment."

Ulanog straightened up as Mohandar, with unbreakable composure, took firm steps toward him. The torrential wind, the pounding rain, the sheer size of his opponent, not a bit of it could even dent Mohandar's poise.

"You." Mohandar raised his hand. "Leave this world."

Ulanog bellowed a hearty laugh. "Never!"

"Poor decision." Mohandar spread his outstretched hand wide, and his staff flared a blinding purple as the forces around him bowed knee. The rain, the grass, the ground itself, all emitted a shimmering strand of violet and converged upon Mohandar. Together they wove into one, becoming the lance of life itself. The divine javelin blasted forward in a shower of sparkles, burrowing into the invader's chest and permeating flesh with its powerful glow.

Mohandar turned toward us as Ulanog exploded in a supernova, blinding me of anything in the world other than our silhouetted rescuer.

Well, that makes me feel useful... I turned my body for a better view. *To think he gave me all that trouble, and Mohandar just—*

When the blast cleared, hardly a sign remained of the invasion... no wind, no rain, no portal. Just the torn up lakeside and bloodstained grass.

The familiar rumble of Dad's truck came into earshot as Mohandar took a knee at my side.

"My, my," Mohandar laughed. "You're quite a mess."

"Mo—" I clutched my side with a shivering hand.

Mohandar wrapped his arm under my shoulders and lifted me. "Easy, Exalted One. Did you really think you could handle your very first invasion on your own? You've had *no* training and *no* experience. I'm shocked you lasted as long as you did."

Kate rested her hand on my knee.

"Travis!" The sound of the truck ceased, along with a quick thud. "Son, what happened to you? You look like you were through a meat grinder!"

"Don't worry, Wade." Mohandar lifted his gaze as Dad skidded down in his work jeans. "He'll live."

"What do you mean, *he'll live?*" Dad grabbed Mohandar by the sides and shook him, whipping me around in the process. "Look at him, he's got a broken arm, his entire front is ripped open, and—"

"He's Exalted." Mohandar returned his staff to the sheath on his back. "He's lost a lot of blood, and yes, he's in bad shape, but with proper care... he'll be fine."

The edges of my vision began to blacken, as the voices grew more and more muffled.

"Let's get him out of here." Mohandar lifted me in his arms. "The boy fought well, from start to finish."

I mustered what little focus I had left. "You were watching the whole time?"

Mohandar leaned over me, the fresh sunlight framing his lack of a face. "Yes."

How convenient.

FIFTEEN

A rush of bliss filled my lungs. Light cascaded through the window of a small bedroom, the rich scent of pine filling the air. *Feels good to be able to breathe...* I lifted my head. *Where am I?*

My armor stood on guard at the foot of the bed. Its shining plates remained still and upright, as if it were watching me.

Last thing I remember, I was about to get jumped on by a pack of spiders... I stretched as my wings expanded around my bare upper body. *A dream, maybe?*

"You're awake." With a grinding sound, the suit shifted and faced me. "Having memory issues, are we?"

I grabbed my forehead and sighed. "Unfortunately."

Siris, who just recently was a phantasmal piece of metal, now appeared to inhabit his physical helm. Taking it on as his new physical form, his spiritual glow flared from within. "This may be a bit confusing at first, but allow me to fill you in."

"Siris, I *just* woke up." I lifted the sheet of my hay-padded bed. "Can I at least put some clothes on first?"

Siris popped off and clinked against the wooden floor. "Go ahead, I won't peek."

"I don't even want to know how you got me undressed." I made my way over to the armor and grabbed it by the shoulder. "How do you put it on?"

"You've never—" Siris sighed. "Undo the clips around the waist. The upper and lower body will separate. From there it's straightforward."

I snapped open a line of tiny latches, and lifted the upper half overhead. "Thanks. As you were—"

"Legs first." Siris bounced up onto the bed. "Last night, you asked me what kind of help I could offer you. This morning answers your question."

"You give me amnesia. How helpful." I put the torso down and stepped into the plated leggings.

Siris bounced closer. "When you put me on your helm, surrounded by hungry burrower spiders, I merged into your armor. By transition, I also bound myself to you... slightly."

"What do you mean, slightly?"

"Until your bond with the Sacred Scripture grows stronger, you'll be deprived of your Power State here. By only partially connecting my spirit to yours, I can give you not only a window into my *vast* knowledge of the sword... I can entirely take over if things get ugly."

"Let me get this straight." I picked him up by the edges and shook him. "You up and *used* my body without even asking?"

"Relax!" Siris' metal heated up and singed my hand. "As long as your book isn't here, you're just another idiot flailing around a blade." He took a deep breath. "Consider stepping outside and taking a look around."

"Siris, wake up." The door to the room banged against the wall. "The people want to see their—"

Siris and I both turned to see Arvel, with a fading grin on his face.

"Hey," he let out a hesitant laugh, and shifted glances between the two of us. "Are you talking to your helmet?"

"Apparently."

"I am not an *it,* I'm a *he!*" Siris rushed at Arvel. "I am Knight Siris of Requiem, and I—"

"It talks, huh?" Arvel raised his hand and caught Siris by the crest as he yapped away.

I puffed my wings out from two vertical slits in the back of my armor. "Let's go outside."

"Sure." Arvel passed Siris to me. "Like I said, the town wants to see you."

As we made our way out through the tavern, early risers didn't hesitate to smile and whisper as we passed through the door. With a loud creak and an assault of sunlight, reality became clear.

"Siris." My eyes got big. "What happened here?"

The street had become a morgue of arachnids. About twenty of them were sprawled out maimed, carved, and stabbed through... utterly massacred. Villagers moved about, stained with blood up to their elbows from dragging the fallen beasts to the butcher.

"They attacked in the dead of night." Siris shifted in the cradle of my elbow. "A whole pack of the fiends invaded in a mad rush for people, livestock, even the crops... thankfully, we were here to stop them."

The villagers stopped their processions and rushed over in a frenzy, some with smiles, some with tears, some with reserved grace. One by one, they dispersed... except for one man.

A farmer, heavy set with a grizzled beard and pitchfork in hand, stepped forth and set a callused hand on my shoulder. "Thanks for what you done, stranger," he grunted under his beard. "It may look gruesome now, but you saved us. If not for you, they'd have gotten our animals, our crops, maybe even us." The farmer turned away. "Most of 'em are gonna forget what you did here... but not me."

Siris. I nodded, biting my lip as I did so. *Maybe you deserve my respect.*

Arvel patted me on the back. "Let's get out of here."

We slipped past the crowd and were out in the open country in no time... and before long, we met our destination.

Arvel and I stood at the edge of a cliffside, the breeze funneling up into our faces as we peered down into a network of trees below. The plumes of leaves went on as far as the horizon, filled with leafy umbrellas.

"The Lunar Jungle." Arvel shrugged. "A bit less impressive in the daytime."

I rubbed my chin and surveyed the vast green. "How do we get in?"

"That's the least of our problems." Arvel pulled a bag off his shoulders and delved into it. "You've learned your wings, yeah? Why don't you go fly overhead for a bit and find us a place to camp?"

"Sure." I bent my knees and spread my wings wide, setting Siris on the grass as I did so.

"Hey," Arvel snapped his fingers, "put your helmet on. I don't want to find you with your head splattered like a melon."

I lifted Siris to my eyes. "You going to pull another one of your stunts?"

"No." Siris remained still. "I'll refrain."

"Good."

I beat my wings, and took off over the trees. In seconds, Arvel was left behind.

The jungle was a marvel of natural artwork. Flowers of every kind sprang to life from the sides of moss covered trees, and the chirp of birds rang true. Vines draped from intertwining branches, with tiny, brightly colored insects leaping between them. The place was utopia.

"Siris, I get why you did what you did." I slowed to an easy glide. "You saved those people's lives. As annoyed as I am, you did a fine job of it."

"I already apologized." Siris' voice echoed from all sides. "If that's unsatisfactory, maybe I could teach you a thing or two. Swordplay, perhaps?"

I laughed. "Good one."

"I wasn't joking. That's an honest offer."

I smiled. "You're a bit bodily challenged."

"Well, we won't instruct by conventional means."

"If you're asking to possess me again, then no." I spotted a divot in the trees. "If not, I'm listening."

"Are you aware of the term *muscle memory?*"

"Yeah." I hovered over a small clearing, about a mile away from the cliff. "Freshman year biology. What's your point?"

"If I teach you *through* your body, you'll learn quickly and instinctively. Within a few days, it'll be embedded in your reflexes."

A gap in the trees caught my eye, opening to a small clearing. *Got one. Time to go back and find Arvel.*

"Training from an experienced knight." I boomed off toward Arvel. "Sounds good to me."

Arvel had set himself up a climbing rope by the time I got back. "What's it look like?"

I touched down and pointed out across the forest. "There's a break in the trees about a mile out."

"Let's get moving, then." Arvel grabbed onto his rope and headed to the edge of the cliff. "It'll be dark by the time we get there."

...and he was right on that one. With the moon high above our heads, we set up at a creekside grotto.

"I know you said it was a dramatic change," I refused to blink as I whirled my attention about the area, "but this is fantastic."

Starlight cascaded through the treetops, now awoken with a hot pink glow. Luminous insects the size of birds flittered in the air, and the grass pulsed with a neon glow in the moonlight. The sounds of day... the birds, the wind, the trickling streams, all had been replaced with a bizarre symphony of the night.

"Yeah, the Lunar Jungle's quite a place." Arvel extended his finger to a drifting ball of pollen, bobbing along like a jellyfish. "A whole other world, huh?"

"What do you think, metal head?" I tapped Siris on his iron side.

He grunted. "I've seen better."

"Alright, let's go through this one more time." Arvel pointed to Siris. "You're Siris?"

"Indeed. Knight Siris of Requiem."

"So, if *he's* Siris," Arvel raised his eyebrow and shifted his attention to me. "Who in the name of all that's good and fun are you?"

"Well, it's a little complicated." I reached into my pocket and grabbed my Realm Stone. "My name's Travis Shepard, and I'm from another world. I'm seventeen years old and live with my father."

Arvel said nothing, but his eyes grew distant.

Yep, I lost him. I tossed him the Realm Stone. "I'm something called Exalted. In the simplest terms, a protector of the Realms."

Arvel studied the stone in his hand. "Still doesn't quite explain why he's a glorified lantern and you're in his meat suit."

"I am not a—" Siris growled. "Never mind. I gave my body to this dimwit for a higher purpose than myself. After challenging him, this is how I ended up."

"Wait a minute, you're telling me he made you like this?" Arvel snickered. "Bloody hilarious."

"It may be funny now," Siris hopped onto my lap and looked up to my eyes, "but when I can materialize my full soul body again, there *will* be a round two."

I moved him to my side. "Don't lose your head over it."

"Ouch!" Arvel winced and dropped the Realm Stone onto the grass. "That thing's hot."

My eyes caught the growing shine of the Realm Stone, and immediately my gut lurched. "Invasion."

"Invasion?" Arvel grabbed his bows and stood. "What's that supposed to mean?"

"Something's crossing over into this world." I grabbed Siris and the Realm stone. "If it's like the last one, things are about to go sideways."

A soft red flash rose and fell behind my back.

Arvel notched an arrow and drew. "You tell me, what's it look like... a threat?"

At a glance, I realized I'd come to the single most terrifying moment of my life.

The light of the jungle framed the wide eyes of a quivering, skinny figure with a superior knack for getting into trouble... my childhood best friend.

"Worse..." I started walking. "Chad."

His conscience slipped, landing him on his back with a thud.

I sighed and tapped my foot. "Of all people."

Sixteen

Slow breaths pulled me from the grasp of nothingness. My lazy eyes moved about and pieced the image of my living room, one detail at a time.

A constant hum at my side drew my attention, the sound of Mohandar at work. His hands drifted up and down my disrobed chest, producing a soft lavender glow along the way.

Gotta get a look. I lifted off the couch.

The slice wounds from Ulanog's hooks had closed up completely, with no sign of stitching. All that remained of the brutal lashes were strips of pale flesh.

"Finally back," Mohandar lifted his focus, but continued his practice, "and in good time. Your father was starting to worry."

"Is he up?" Dad stomped in from the kitchen and smiled. "Morning, Travis."

I shifted to stand, but Mohandar refused to budge. "Let me up, will you?"

"Sorry, but no." Mohandar eased me back down. "I need you to stay still for a little while longer. I may have sealed your cuts, but I need to finish fixing you internally."

Dad knelt down beside me. "How do you feel, son?"

I looked over at my elbow. "Glad to see my hand facing the right way."

"Yeah." Dad scratched his beard. "You got beaten up real bad... what did that to you, anyway?"

"Ulanog the Exiled," Mohandar answered. "A hulking brute with four arms and a twisted soul." He moved his hands over my heart. "Many times more powerful than Travis."

"I thought I had him pretty good."

"You were blind to the situation, Exalted One." Mohandar removed his hands and backed off. "Ulanog wore out your Power State without even half of his strength. If I hadn't intervened, both you and your friend would have perished."

"Kate!" The word twisted my lungs in just the right way to send me into a pitiful coughing fit.

Dad opened a window. "Haven't spoken with her since that day. I thought she might—"

I looked around at every clock in the room. *"That day?"*

"I... probably should've led with this." Dad rubbed his forehead. "It's been two days."

"It's Sunday?" I rolled off the couch and stood up. "No wonder my stomach hurts."

Mohandar shifted and stared me down. "Where do you think you're going?"

I started upstairs. "I've got things I need to do."

The sound of flowing water accompanied my exit from the bathroom, but to my surprise, dull voices were coming from my *closed* bedroom door.

I eased the door open, and the murmurs became definite.

A crisp ding came from the direction of my bed. "Hello, Travis."

"You—" I took a few breaths, keeping my temper cool. "What are *you* doing in my—"

With no warning at all, my body was thrown onto my bed by an ecstatic book.

The joyous singing of the Sacred Scripture encircled me, and I leered down the ethereal form of...

Siris.

"As I was saying." I reached out and wrapped my fingers around the Sacred Scripture. "Why are you here?"

"You agreed that I'd be tagging along with you." Siris bounced onto my bedside table and looked at each individual item. "I did mean here *and* Reach."

"Just wonderful." I rolled onto my back and sighed. "Between you and the faceless wonder, my privacy is *shot.*"

"Don't worry, I'm not much of a pain to live with." Siris plopped onto the floor. "After all, I'm—"

He's listing his qualities again... I went to my dresser and pulled out a deep black sleeveless shirt. *Maybe I can sell him to the circus... The Talking Ghost Helmet.* I closed the door behind me as I left. *They probably wouldn't take him.*

I pulled the shirt over my head and made my way downstairs.

Dad and Mohandar turned from what appeared to be discreet conversation as I approached.

"Thanks for fixing me up, Mohandar. I'm going out for a walk."

"You're welcome," he nodded. "Remember, we've got training to do this evening."

"Alright." I headed for the door. "See you when I get back, Dad."

Dad stepped out into the kitchen and cracked open the refrigerator. "Don't hurt yourself."

The front door groaned on its hinges as I pulled it open, and met a warm wall of summer air... and Kate in mid-knock.

The faintest blush flooded her cheeks as her hand retreated to the side of her burgundy T-shirt and slim-fit jeans.

She looked off to the side and tucked her arms behind her back. "Hey."

"Hey." I stepped outside and closed the door. "You want to go for a walk?"

She tracked me as I walked right past. "Huh?"

"Just to the woods." I looked at her over my shoulder. "You coming, or no?"

The Sacred Scripture hummed and danced, beckoning.

"Um..." She shrugged and followed. "Sure."

We started down the long, dusty driveway, in the comfortable quiet of the morning.

I spun the Sacred Scripture with my finger. "How are you doing?"

"Good." Kate smiled. "Better than you."

I moved my restored arm around, still a bit numb. "And a holy miracle, at that. I'm glad."

Kate gently touched my shoulder. "Thank you, by the way."

I raised my eyebrow. "For what? Mohandar's the one who saved you."

"You had *zero* chance of winning, Travis... and still you got up every time that brute put you on the ground." Kate grabbed my shoulders and turned me toward her. "It doesn't matter how strong you are on the outside, what counts is your spirit. Disagree all you want, you've got the heart of a hero."

"Yeah, you could say so." I chuckled as I looked down either side of the road between my driveway and the forest. "How'd you find my house, anyway?"

"We drive by all the time." Kate started to cross. "I see you outside a lot."

"Oh." My eyes widened, remembering my tendency to do yard work shirtless.

We were surrounded by woodland in no time, making our way through deer trails in the forest.

Kate bit the edge of her mouth and looked around with the slightest hint of disconcertion.

I gave her a playful nudge. "You're doing it again."

"Hmm?"

"You look away when you're nervous." I loosened my posture a bit, and tried to smile. "If you want to ask me something, go ahead. We're friends, right?"

Kate turned and looked me right in the eyes. "What are you?"

"Exalted." I shrugged. "My dad was human, my mom wasn't, so now I've been called to be some kind of big-shot defender of the living. I'm not so different now than I was on the last day of school."

"Right." Kate let out a sarcastic laugh. "If you'd beat up those two goons with fists of lightning, I think I'd have noticed."

"Well, yeah..." I counted on my fingers. "There's the Power State, the book, Siris and Reach... but otherwise, same old Travis."

She pulled her arm through her drawstring bag. "Hold on. Are you going to be fighting off big scary monsters *often?*"

"From what I've been told, yeah." I ducked under a spider web. "Why?"

Kate knelt down and rummaged in her bag. "Here. You'll be needing this."

Between her smooth, pale fingers, she held a brilliant piece of metalcraft. It gleamed in the sun, accentuating its defined edges... a face shield of the long-forgotten knights, fixed to a leather binding on the back. Streaks of navy blue paint surrounded the visor, flowing down between vertical breath slits on the side.

"Kate, this is awesome." I accepted her gift and held it closer so I could see. "Where'd you get it?"

"My dad's a pretty great metalworker..." She smiled. "From time to time, he lets me use his tools for some of my own projects."

"You made this?" I ran my thumb along the fine edge. "Kate, thanks but—"

She bounced and let out a barely audible squeak. "Come on, put it on!"

I pulled the straps on over the back of my head, and my bangs flapped over the chilled metal. "What do you think?"

Kate put her hand on her hip and nodded. "The bad guys will never know what hit 'em."

I'm not used to half of a helm, but it's kind of nice. I made eye contact through the narrow opening in the mask. "Thank you, Kate."

"No problem." Kate opened her arms. "Come here."

Hugs? I groaned under my breath and stepped forward just enough for Kate to lock me in a trap of affection. *Why do we have to do hugs?*

"Sorry, I had to torture you just a little." Kate took a deep breath. "Be careful, and keep me in the loop... but I better go home. Your dad might think we're doing more than just walking."

"Whoa," I backed up with stiff posture and golf balls in my eye sockets, "why do you think he'd get that—"

"Travis, relax." Kate raised her hand, cackling. "You know, for a tough guy, you're really easy to embarrass."

"Whatever." I grunted and leaned against a nearby tree.

Kate took one more deep breath. "Let's get out of here."

***

The Observatory gleamed in the starlight. Mohandar and I had come to the surface of a nearby moon, nothing but an empty stretch of rock as far as the eye could see. Asteroids danced below the comets, casting their shadows as they passed.

Mohandar and I faced one another, a few feet of space between us. My Power State, like his cloak, twisted in the celestial wind as I awaited instruction.

"Welcome to space, Travis." Mohandar stretched his arms. "How does it feel to breathe when there's no air?"

"Weird..." My lungs had a strange, dense feeling... I grimaced. "Weirder than breathing water. Why are we here, Mohandar?"

"You asked me to train you." Mohandar looked up at his home. "Until you can control your Power State well enough to use it in the Observatory, we'll do your training out here."

Seems a bit exaggerated.

"Travis, today we'll be learning something crucial to your survival as an Exalted." Mohandar pulled his staff from his back. "The relationship between Soul Energy and your life force. You remember your fight with Ulanog, do you?"

"Of course." My tone lowered. "He wiped the floor with me and you came to the rescue."

"More specific." Mohandar raised a finger. "You pushed yourself with determination, all the way until your Power State collapsed under you. The reason for this, as you'll learn, is the limitation of your Soul Energy." He levitated closer, greeted by the Sacred Scripture. "Earlier, I taught you that your Power State is fueled by the bond between your soul and the Sacred Scripture. The book, however, can only pull so much weight." He backed away. "When your Power State failed in the previous fight, it was because you had exhausted your limits... drawing close to death and placing far too much strain on your partner."

The Sacred Scripture moaned... with a hint of sympathy.

Can't let that happen again. I gave my book a spin. "What do I need to do?"

"Soul Energy is like a muscle." Mohandar sat down, crossing his legs. "To make it strong, you must first break it down... but it's a tricky business. The closer you push to your limit, the more you'll gain. However, if you go too far... your soul will dissipate, incinerating you from the inside out."

Huh?

"This is why it's important to train your Soul Energy diligently." Mohandar opened his palm and allowed his violet aura to dance upon it. "It's far better to have excess strength than run the risk of a grisly end... questions?"

In order to serve my duty as Exalted, I need to get strong... fast. I rolled my hands into fists. "Let's get started, then."

"As you wish." Mohandar straightened up. "Let's practice your shaping... prove to me that you can conjure a sphere."

Like nothing, I popped one out of my radiance. "With all due respect, I think it's time for something more advanced. You said the harder I train, the more my Soul Energy will grow, right?"

"Indeed." Mohandar took a deep breath. "What do you have in mind, young one?"

Memories of my bout with Ulanog, and my fearless teacher soaring to our rescue, came straight to mind. Immediately, my heart was filled with drive... an unavoidable push to be just as awesome as Mohandar.

I smiled and bent my knees. "I want you to fight me."

A long pause of silence set in.

"Pardon..." Mohandar stood, shrugging his cloak to his back. "You want to fight?"

"Yeah." I stretched my arms. "Give it your all, and only stop when I can't fight anymore."

He crossed his arms and grunted. "You continue to amaze me, Travis... as you wish."

Wait, really? Heck, yeah! I watched as Mohandar walked away, stopping with about twenty feet of distance between us.

Mohandar opened his arms. "Is this enough space?"

"More than enough." I raised my fists and allowed my Power State to course through them. "Ready?"

My teacher turned, allowing his cloak to obscure him. "Yes."

Thundering steps pounded as I closed the distance in seconds with a right hook. Mohandar leaned to the side, effortlessly ducking the attack.

"Remember yesterday's lesson." A solid arm spun me around to face my teacher. "Instincts are predictable."

He's fast! I sprang back, drifting through the air along the way. *He's right, though. I need to—*

A fluttering cloak trailed beside me. "You're quite fond of traditional melee combat... unfortunately, it limits you to vertical, horizontal, and linear attacks." A torrent of wind sent me bouncing along the ground. "It also doesn't make good use of your Soul Energy."

Alright, try something different. I focused inward and shaped my Power State, unleashing a swift blast of Soul Energy. *There.*

"Easy." Mohandar raised his open hand and swatted the blast off into space. "Your blast either needs to be more powerful or more creative."

You want more power, huh? I growled and harnessed my energy once more, my forearms shaking from the potency. Snapping electricity raced forth, charring the stone as it raced to Mohandar. Within seconds, the battlefield had vanished, my vision overtaken by cobalt talons of lightning.

I stopped, and my body immediately grew heavy. "How's that?"

Mohandar's voice came from behind. "Much better, but too taxing for you to use at your current level... you can feel its toll, can you not?"

My heart rate's up and it's getting hard to breathe. I turned around, sweat beading on my forehead. "Mohandar."

The Observer was seated with his legs folded, just like he was before we started. His cloak was pristine and glossy, and he showed absolutely no sign of stress... he lifted his gaze. "Yes?"

"I thought the terms were clear." I folded my arms. "You were supposed to fight at full strength, until I couldn't keep going."

"If I could, I would." He took a long, deep breath. "Unfortunately, you don't know what you're asking."

I stomped, and readied a thunder-powered punch. "Mohandar, I just fought against a brute the size of a house, and nearly got myself killed doing it!

How do you expect me to be ready to take on the threats to the Realms if I don't train at the same level?"

I thrust my arm forward, but Mohandar was nowhere to be seen. With a slow turn, I followed his cloak... and beheld his arm coated in hot pink plasma. He bent his elbow and tightened his grip on his staff, the air around him warping.

"You want a taste of my full power... then behold." He brandished his staff, and an invisible force threw me to the side.

The moon beneath us shook as Mohandar unleashed his fury, blazing into the cosmos as a concentrated ray. His Soul Energy took on the form of a comet... steadily flowing and growing brighter by the second. It all finished with a flash, and a distinct thump. Broken pieces of a distant planet drifted in the nothingness, steaming after being split by Mohandar's channeled strength.

No way. My hair was blown back on my head, and my eyes wide at what was before me. *I know I'm supposed to get strong as an Exalted... but I'll never live up to this.*

"That's good for fifty percent..." Mohandar sighed. "The planet was uninhabited, like an overgrown asteroid. It's more useful as a cloud of space dust."

Words refused to form, my brain still petrified.

"Now, Travis. Show me your sphere-making skills."

"Yes, sir."

***

I held the shining mask in the flickering light of fire as Dad and I relaxed in the night, each of us stretched back in a beaten-up lawn chair. Stars passed in and out of view under the drifting clouds, as the air grew colder by the minute.

"Man..." Dad said as he rubbed his beard, digesting the summary of today's lesson. "I didn't think Mohandar was packing that big of a punch."

"I don't think there's any way I'll catch up to him." I rolled my gum around in my mouth, its flavor faded. "Still, I'm gonna get as strong as I can... strong enough to make Ulanog look like a pushover."

Dad leaned over and looked right at me. "You better be careful. Having your soul burn you from the inside out doesn't sound like fun."

"Even if I wanted to be careless, there's no way I could." I sagged into my seat. "Especially since I have to make sure Chad doesn't get himself killed... he's paying a visit to Reach."

"Chad's in Reach?" Dad grabbed the fire poker. "My condolences."

I took a sip of root beer. "I'm not really sure what I'm going to do."

"Hey." Dad stirred up the fire with a grin. "At least he's not a four-armed *overlord*."

"It'd be less work if he was." I shook my head. "...that whole fight really bothers me."

"Travis," Dad sat back down and picked up his drink, "no matter how strong you get, you're still going to fight losing battles. You need to learn from your loss, and look at what it gave you."

I gave him my attention.

"Losing to Ulanog gave you a window of insight into how these invasions work. Think about it... that guy came over here by *choice*. You think he just stumbled upon our world?" Dad took a drink. "Personally, I think there's a bigger force behind this whole sham."

"Yeah," I shifted in my seat. "But who?"

Dad took a deep breath. "We don't know. Life is falling apart, making these invasions bigger and more frequent as we draw nearer to destruction. Son... you're the only chance we've got."

"Okay, Dad..." I trailed off. *Learn from my loss... I understand. So far, I've just been breezing my way through. Ulanog's a warning that time's running out for us all. Reality's fading away, and I need to find a way to stop it. It's time to train hard, time to take things seriously.*

Kate's mask gleamed.

Time to become a hero.

Seventeen

A rvel and Siris were both petrified at the sight of a rag doll of pasty skin and chocolate brown hair... Chad, my idiot best friend, had crossed into Reach.

"What do you mean, *worse?*" Arvel gave me a cold stare. "He's either dangerous or he isn't."

"Three." I stood up and stretched.

Arvel shifted, watching. "You listening?"

I strolled my way to Chad. "Two."

Arvel sighed. "Talking to a rock."

"I understand *completely.*" Siris bounced. "If he doesn't want to hear it, he just—"

"One." I took a knee beside my friend.

Chad's upper body shot off the ground, and we locked eyes. His arm stretched behind him, clinging to the grass as he wheezed to awareness.

"Chad." I extended my hand. "I need you to stay—"

"How do you know my name?" With a disturbingly feminine yell, Chad plowed his sneaker into my face. He scampered to his feet and whipped around, tapping his foot faster at each new sight. "Where am I?"

Arvel chuckled. "Need a hand?"

I rubbed my ringing jaw. "Let me handle this."

"Handle *what?*" Chad's arms shot out, flailing in a ridiculous display. "I hope we don't have a problem, 'cause I don't think you want one."

"It's Travis." My eyes narrowed. "You've never won any fight you were stupid enough to step into."

"You know my friend's name, huh?" Chad raised his chin. "What'd you do to him? Kidnap him, throw him in a bag, and release him into some weird... glowy place?" He laughed. "You had to, he hasn't texted me in a *week!*"

All expression left my face. *Unbelievable.*

Chad raised a fist, nostrils flaring. "Well, I don't care what kind of secret government agency you're from. I'll beat you to a pulp and get Travis out of here!" Chad bounced on his toes and stretched his arms. "Come on, hit me with all you have... *chicken wings.*"

I looked at Arvel and pointed to Chad.

"Yeah." He nodded. "Definitely worse."

Chad stomped his feet. "Come at me, I dare—"

"I can't believe you're making me do this." I cranked my arm and heaved forward. "Sorry."

Chad squealed and took off in full sprint. "You're a lot bigger up close!"

I beat my wings, cutting Chad off. With a ping off my armor, his big nose became acquainted with my chest. He tumbled backward and splashed into the shallow creek.

"Enough." I took slow, patient steps and got down on eye level. "You ready to act like an adult?"

"Look, whatever you've done with my friend..." Chad lowered his head, "...just—"

"It's me!" I grabbed him by the shoulders and shook him. "I get that the wings have you confused, but I'm Travis Shepard. You pull any more of this crap with me, I'm gonna give you a right hook just like I gave Joey Daniels after he stole the Valentine's Day card you wrote for that cute girl in third grade!"

Chad stopped struggling and studied my face.

"He ran off crying. You remember what you wrote in the card?" I let him go and stepped back. "Ch—"

"Ched Davis." He laughed. "I was so nervous I misspelled my own name... you know, you government guys—"

Chad's cheeks rippled as I gave him a frustrated wallop to his jaw.

Chad rubbed his face and smiled. "Hey, Travis."

I shook my head and extended my hand. "I swear, you're the biggest pain in *two* worlds."

Arvel stood, with Siris on his shoulder. "From yours?"

"Yeah." I pulled Chad out of the water. "Stuck with him for about ten years, now."

Siris turned and gazed at the newcomer. "We ought to fill him in."

Chad froze at the sight of Siris.

"Never seen an animated helm before?" Siris chuckled. "Believe me, I'm not the scariest thing you'll see in this world."

Arvel brushed Siris off his shoulder. "Can it."

I gave Chad a nudge. "Before we get into it, you remember anything about how you got here?"

Chad visibly thought. "Not much. One second, I was on my computer, then there was this big red flash."

"Okay..." I tapped my fingers against the sides of my armor. "Alright, now about me."

Arvel, Siris and I gave Chad the basics... a few times. When he finally grasped the idea, we crashed and called it a night.

Wasn't long until my eyes shot open. Aside from Chad's snore erupting from my tent, the jungle was eerily quiet.

"Travis."

Of course. I rolled against the ground, my wings thudding along the way. "What?"

"Quiet." A faint, echoing whisper arose. "Don't move, but look... in the bushes."

"Siris... what are you doing up?" I nudged him aside. "Go back to—"

"Travis, stop talking."

"Alright." I shrugged and looked out ahead, across the brook. *What the—*

A cluster of six small eyes drifted in the distant bushes. The specks loomed in the darkness, a constant reminder of our vulnerability in this alien world.

What is it? I rubbed the sleep out of my eyes. In a literal blink, every inch of my body froze.

A figure bathed in fluorescence loomed in the open grass. A mantis, slender and long, held a statuesque pose ahead of our camp. It simply gazed in the stillness, almost bowing to me and Siris as it held its talons for arms to its thorax.

My eyes beat shut for another fleeting second, and the faint clicking sound of an insect's breaths set in. I remained motionless as I gazed deep into each individual abyss of an eye, now within an arm's length.

The mantis stretched high on a net of legs, its imposing height setting in. Still, the picture of majesty remained neither aggressive nor hospitable. The thing was just... here.

Talk about huge... I focused on keeping my breaths slow as I wrapped my hand around Siris' crest. *This thing's seven feet tall.*

A fidgeting antenna brushed against the edge of my face when the visitor lowered its body to the grass, taking its royal time as it did so. The sheer formality of the insect's visit set my suspicions at ease... until it took interest in Chad.

I read this in a book... I tightened my grip on Siris. *Mantids are ambush—*

In a blur, the withdrawn claws of the mantis flared out and seized Chad's leg, just barely exposed from the tent. Chad yelled as he became ensnared in a chitinous prison, sped away on the creature's scuttling legs.

I pulled Siris over my head and surged forward on my wings. "You let go of my friend!"

A flow of chills pulsed through my brain as I instinctively reached for the sword on my back and delivered a seamless slash to the kidnapper's forelegs.

The insect toppled to the grass, spilling Chad from its clutches.

"Siris." I instinctively raised the sword to my folded elbow, straight out to the recovering predator. "That cut... your doing?"

"Yes." Siris' voice bounced through the corners of my head. "Let's take it on. *Together!*"

The mantis squared its body off to us, presenting its scythe-like arms as wings of aurora unfolded from its back. With a hiss, it started circling, stumbling on its injured legs.

"Alright, Travis." My helm flashed as Siris spoke. "Sword training starts now."

The mantis lunged forward, its hungry talons stretched like giant fangs. My sword met them in the air, guiding them to the side. Like flowing water, the bug contorted and came in for another.

"Your blade is your defense." My wings forced forward and rocketed me out of the way. "Wait for your opponent to strike first." The phantasmal grip on my body released, and the body of the mantis rapidly closed in. "Parry, now!"

I consciously gripped the handle of my blade and met the ravaging claws of the reaper, giving them a hard shove.

"Now, counter!"

I heaved my body weight behind my blade and delivered a harsh slash to the joint of the mantis' arm, a mist of juices spurting from it. The mantis lowered its head and retreated, convulsing.

"Thanks, Siris." I smiled and pulled my sword back. "Might as well finish—"

A powerful hum pierced the night as the bug's wings flared, unleashing a stream of hot pink moonlight. The searing radiance bored through my armor, and the breath rushed from my lungs when I met contact with rough bark.

"What a creative attack!" Siris shuddered, rattling both sides of my skull. "Never seen that one before."

"Yeah." I pulled myself to my feet. "*You* didn't take the hit."

The mantis spread its wings and leapt in to finish the job.

"No matter." My sword raised straight ahead. "We've already won."

With a clean whiz, the mantis flew straight into the blade of the sword, sealing its own fate.

Silence returned to the night.

I pushed the limp carcass off my blade and shook off the blood. "That's a nasty kabob."

"*Never* leap toward your target if you can't stop." Siris popped off of me and pinged onto my shoulder. "Overextending is synonymous with suicide."

"Thanks, Siris." My eyes caught Chad, huddled up in the distant brush and quivering. I knelt down beside him. "Chad, are you alright?"

"There was a knight."

"Easy, bud." I put my hand on his shoulder. "You're all stressed out, you're not thinking straight."

Chad's eyes met mine, welled up and shaking. "This big freaking rip in the *world* opened up, and a knight came out of it. He... grabbed me."

"You're safe, Chad." I helped him stand. "...Thanks for telling me."

I spent the rest of the night in Chad's tent, sleep-forsaken as I peered out of the shelter's entrance over and over again.

Chad... the last thing I'd expect to come out of a cross-reality portal. My wings curled over him protectively as I kept watch. *Guess it's better, though. Thanks to him and Dad, I've got a lead... Invasions look like a rip in the air... knights traditionally carry weapons with blades. Could this knight Chad's talking about be cutting worlds open?*

Chad stirred in his slumber, and I stepped out of the tent... surveying the night.

I can't let him die here.

EIGHTEEN

The chill of a fresh root beer fizzed in my hands, paired with the crisp crack of an opened can. "Hey Siris, how're you getting back and forth between the Realms *with* me? I know you told me you were invading, but the signs point elsewhere."

Siris clinked against the armrest of my living room's leather recliner. "You know how I said I *partially* fused our souls?"

"Yeah." I paced by and set my soda can on a small stand beside the couch.

"It's kind of funny..." Siris let out a well-restrained laugh. "It started small, but that tiny little bond has become... well, not so tiny."

I stared down the ghostly helm, ignoring the fact that the Sacred Scripture was yipping away flinging couch cushions all over the place. My eyes narrowed. "*What?*"

"Don't get so flustered." Siris popped off of the chair and onto the carpet. "We're *connected*. When you leave a realm, so do I. It's really that simple."

"My body is my body, and it's going to stay that way." I eyed up the Sacred Scripture. "Now, if you'll excuse me..."

The Sacred Scripture halted its frenzy at the snap of my finger, leering at me with a full-sized couch cushion in its grasp.

I pointed at the book. "We've been at this since day one. You can't destroy *everything*, okay? If you want to, I'll play with you. Heck, even *Siris* may want to."

The Sacred Scripture barreled into Siris, the collision echoing through the house and initiating a battle of miniatures. Shelves rumbled, the chairs rocked, the floor vibrated as a tiny, ghostly helm did battle with the rambunctious godly text.

"Travis!" Amidst the calamity, Siris' voice arose. "You get in here and deal with your infernal pet!"

"I did." My phone started rumbling in my pocket. "And it's not my pet." A familiar name on the phone's screen pulled my focus. I lifted my cell to one ear and closed the other. "What's up, Kate?"

"Um... yeah, Travis?" Her voice came out horribly muffled. "I think it's time for you to power up again."

"Huh?"

"Turn on the news." Kate's voice wavered.

I snagged the remote and turned on the TV. "Jeez... can't say I expected that."

The broadcaster's voice permeated the room. "Unidentified terraforming occurring in London incites mass chaos. Destruction levels are worsening by the minute."

Before me was the very scene shown to me by Mohandar... only far more grim. Reach had begun to crawl into Earth.

It's actually happening. I stood and paced, but my eyes remained glued to the screen.

"What are you gonna do, Travis?" Kate's voice grew stern. "You better not get yourself killed."

I separated Siris and the Sacred Scripture. "What else is there to do? I'm headed in."

Kate's steel mask gleamed in the windowsill, the mark of the hero within.

"Don't do anything abnormally stupid, alright?"

"Alright." I fixed my mask on. "Thanks, Kate."

Siris, the book, and I all bolted outside.

The complete tranquility of the rolling hills and my dusty driveway siphoned all the thrill out of the moment... slowly, I cradled my now ironclad forehead in my palm. I grunted, "Siris."

"What?"

"Unless you expect me to call in a private jet, I've got no way to get to London."

"Are you kidding?" Siris bounced. "Sure you do."

"What're you talking about? You got some spirit airliner or something?"

"No, you fool." Siris sprang up onto my shoulder. "You've got wings!"

I slowly raised my eyebrows. "Does this look like Reach to you?"

"Think about it," Siris sighed. "Your Power State plus my Winged Knight knowledge equals..."

I slammed Siris down over my head, and he seeped into my mask as a gush of blue flowed out of me from within. With the rush of awakening, my aura flared to life. Wings of spirit, laden with innumerable wispy feathers twisted outward. At last, the wall between myself and the endless sky was shattered.

"Wings." My newfound limbs bared for takeoff. "Genius."

With a reverberating boom, the grass around me writhed. Enveloped in a divine sapphire blaze, the Sacred Scripture and I broke through the clouds.

Turbulence blasted my face as I took on the aspect of a fighter jet headed for the fray.

"Travis." The inside of my visor flashed as Siris spoke. "You've gotten stronger since your last appearance, for sure. Even so, what do you think you're going to do once we get to the crossover site?"

"Help." Sandy beaches blew by from underneath, and gave way to open water. "Holy crap, how fast are we going?"

"Trust me, you don't want to know," Siris laughed. "Fast enough to cross the Atlantic Ocean in... well, now."

A blur of violet rushed in front of me.

Sudden collision numbed my shoulder and threw me aside, spiraling. I straightened my body out and regained control. *Relax. Keep your thoughts straight, and your wings will be, too.*

I arched back and shifted to hover, greeted by the flowing cape of my teacher.

"Glad to see you've made it." Mohandar stretched his arms out as he seamlessly levitated. "I hope you're ready, because the two of us have work to do."

My mask pulsed. "I'm here too, Mohandar," chimed Siris.

I raised my open hands to Mohandar. "I know you teleport, but since when do you *fly?*"

"Always." He rotated and sped forward. "Spacial jumps are too taxing to be used on a whim. Now, onward. We *must* take action."

I accelerated and matched pace. "How close are we?"

"Take a look."

Trees, laden with vines, twisted as they broke their way through ages of architecture. Blinding flashes pulsed through the area, in sharp contrast to the billowing clouds above. Before long, the horizon was gray against the lurid forest of chaos ahead.

The world shook as the sky pulled apart and became a deep, sinister red. Thunder rumbled, and darkness fell upon the world.

"Invasion!" Mohandar took a dive. "Travis, you need to get a move on for the Shards, or we're as good as dead!"

"I can't do a thing about the Channeling Crystal until I get back to Reach." We took to the streets and blazed over the heads of the fleeing populous. "What's our plan for *now?*"

The Invasion Scar contorted as a reptilian head the size of a bulldozer emerged, with a long snout and a frill of luminescent tufts surrounding its granite-colored neck. A stream of onyx scales glimmered behind, an endless flow which twisted and turned as the great reptile glided into the skyline of our world. Finally, a tufted tail fin emerged from the gash in space, and the endless serpent twisted over the city.

Amber eyes squinted shut as the lizard opened a maw full of scythe-sized teeth... and released a waterfall of ice.

"We need to engage together..." Mohandar glanced over his shoulder at me. "First, you and Siris need to help get the people out."

"On it."

Mohandar thrusted forward and pumped his fist back, coated in the lavender glow of his soul. "I'll buy you some time."

A violent boom on par with an explosive detonation reverberated through the city.

"Everyone, head for the beach!" I hovered over the swell of fleeing citizens, from cars to pedestrians and bikers alike. "Quickly, go!"

A sum total of about five people listened, while the rest kept on moving.

Well, vocal guidance isn't going to do anything. I turned my attention skyward. *At least I tried.*

The dragon bellowed its voice of thunder, and rushed Mohandar with an open jaw. Mohandar seamlessly ducked to the side and fired off a ray of plasma in return, but his foe immediately countered with a gush of frost. The grasp of winter missed my teacher, but managed to eat into the rising trees, shattering them like glass figurines.

My mind melded with Siris, and together we functioned as a single powerful unit. *We can do this... just stay focused*

My spirit expanded, forming a burning canopy above the fleeing civilians. Each second it grew bigger, catching more of the falling razors and locking my muscles tighter by the second... until every last person was safe.

"Looks like the last one." I wiped the sweat off my forehead. "Siris, thanks for—"

The windows of a corporate building shattered as the speeding form of Mohandar crashed through.

The ruler of the sky reared back and let out a victorious cry, cut short by a fleeting pale lance.

Mohandar's cloak blew about in the wind as he closed in on the stunned beast. Gashes, burns and rips had ravaged the fabric, making it more fringed than whole. His staff pulsed with inner power, visibly energizing the very air as he gripped it tight with vigilance.

The dragon rushed forward, plowing Mohandar back *through* the building. In a hail of rubble, my ally's limp body plummeted to the ground and landed hard on his back.

This time, the predator didn't hesitate. It immediately turned toward the earth and snapped its jaws open... burying Mohandar in a prison of unyielding cold.

Mohandar! My chest kicked as my heartbeat accelerated. My muscles grew loose under constant shivers racing up and down my spine. *That's it... my turn.*

In mere seconds, the battlefield was under siege of violent thunder... the sky boomed and dropped its sovereign lances upon the city. Soon the storm raged upon me as well... in the form of the Power State.

My eyes narrowed on the turning gaze of the gigantic lizard before me. "You just made a horrible mistake."

My enemy roared as it accelerated with incomprehensible speed, upon me in the blink of an eye.

Sword. I clenched my fist and the blade of my soul was summoned. With the tiniest thrust to the side, I ducked the serpent's lunge, and countered with a brutal cut to its entire face. "You know what you get for hurting the people I care about?"

Tenacity raged as the beast re-engaged, spewing its chilling breath.

My body stiffened as the grasp of winter ensnared me... the ice tried, but couldn't stop my burning fury. Instead, my body grew smoldering with raging sparks. With a thunderous burst of fury, the frozen capsule shattered.

I smirked. "You'll have to do better than that."

My enemy turned tail and fled as I loosened my sword arm.

"You were enough of a jerk to attack these people." I closed in with a vengeance, blocking his retreat. "You really think you can get away?"

I raised my blade high, and a pillar of lightning descended upon it. My body kicked with an overdose of raw electricity, transforming my sword into the divine armament of a deity.

"Eat this." I threw all of my body weight forward.

The sky shook, the earth rumbled, and the wind howled as the blade came down, silhouetting the overgrown city with a neon blue explosion. Fragmented bone and splintered scales danced as they fell to the brewing pool of blood below.

My knee struck the ground, followed by two separate thuds... one for each half of the dragon. My mask gleamed as the clouds parted, and the sun reigned once more.

The area was quiet as I paced over to the fallen beast, its stench spreading.

I sighed. "You've got a bad habit of watching rather than participating, Mohandar."

He sighed. "How did you know?"

"Like this thing could've beaten you?" I gave the lifeless body a shove, and it toppled. "Please."

Looking up, the gravity of the situation finally set in.

Trees, the very same ones out of the Lunar Jungle, towered over what little remained of the great city. Vines hung where power lines used to be, weeds crackled through the asphalt, and alien flowers sprouted in every recreational garden. All that remained of London were echoes and rubble... overtaken by another world.

"Well... what do we do about this?"

Mohandar ran a hand along his tattered cape. "Get hold of a Crystal Shard, and quick. If we don't turn back the clock now, time will stop... both here and in Reach. Locate the shard, give it to the Sacred Scripture, and these worlds will be pushed off one another... at least for a while."

A stray breeze blew against my body. "He's not lying."

I looked over my shoulder and beheld the turned back of a mystery.

Black hair flowed in the wind, mounds of it trailing behind a body armored in stone and adorned with worn rags. The unidentified one stood silent... as if waiting for something.

"Listen to Mohandar," a deep male voice answered. "From your campsite in Reach. Two miles north, one mile east. Your shard awaits there."

"Who are you?" I turned... only to find nothing. All traces of the visitor were gone.

Mohandar took a deep breath. "I can't believe it's him, after all this time... Palatharx."

I looked at the Sacred Scripture and awaited explanation from Mohandar.

The Realm Stone grew burning hot in my pocket... sending me to Reach without the faintest clue to who this *Palatharx* was.

My only option was to have faith in a complete stranger.

NINETEEN

The Lunar Jungle was an absolute disaster. Trees laid groaning on their sides, with shattered asphalt hanging from their branches. Flowers were buried by rebar, and rocks had been split by girders... former beauty now buried under the echoes of industry.

"When you told me about Reach and Earth crossing the first time, I can't say I believed you." Arvel's cape shifted as he swung his leg over a chunk of highway. "This is serious."

My wings tucked in upon contact with the smoldering door of a minivan. "We need the shard before the end of today... Like it or not, this tip-off's all we have."

"I'm not too sure, Travis." Chad twisted his body to avoid contact with a spider web. "You just got done fighting at an invasion site and there happens to be someone there to help you fix the damages? Doesn't that seem a little *too* convenient?"

"Chad, when you've got the weight of *two* worlds on your shoulders, you can call the shots." I glanced back. "Just stay close."

A flicker of red and orange raced across my field of view. A butterfly, flitting about, twirled in the air and landed on my shoulder.

Arvel rolled his shoulders. "How much farther?"

"One more mile," Siris piped up. "We're nearly there, wherever *there* may be."

I gently brushed the butterfly off. "Good. I've got a feeling we're running out of—"

A low pulse, like the sound of a drum, echoed through the overgrowth.

A soft numbness spread through my body. *Time.*

The breeze ceased to stroke the backs of my wings, the songs of the birds and the flowing water hushed, and the flitting butterfly was now petrified... trapped in a real-life painting.

I turned around to Arvel and Chad. "Man..."

Arvel's body refused to budge, frozen mid-leap above a fallen log. Even in pure stillness, he reminded me of a fabled renaissance hero.

Chad was... quite stellar. He'd been fortunate enough to be caught in the middle of his bout with a low-swinging vine, his arms flailing into the air with squinted eyes.

They're petrified... but shouldn't I be, too? I can't think about it now, I need to get to the Shard.

"Alright." I pushed onward, unfurling my wings. "Looks like I'm alone."

Siris laughed inside my helm. "Nope, you've still got me."

Great. I soared high and burst through the trees. "I was looking forward to some quiet."

"This isn't quiet enough?" Siris' inner light flared. "Time's still, let's move!"

Soon, we met our destination.

A dilapidated clock tower sagged in the silence, hollow and forgotten. Relentless wilderness had choked it from within, erupting in blossoms of foliage. Bricks lingered in the air, ignoring gravity itself.

"Two miles north, one mile east." I slowed as we approached the building. *Just like he said.*

A wisp of flowing black hair fanned out from the very tip of the lightning rod, accompanied by a blinding white light. The figure stood tall, watching me all the way in.

I beat my wings and held position. "We're out of time, where's the shard?"

"I am well aware of the circumstances." The strands of ebony parted, revealing a scarred face and a faded brown rag wrapped around the pale white chin of my unknown assistant. His irises were blood red... emanating an unnerving aura. "You'll get it, don't worry."

I crossed my arms. "If you *understand,* why are we chatting?"

"Relax, I have it here." The stranger reached behind his back with a sigh. "You Exalted always were *impatient.*"

His stone armor brightened under the soft white glow of a true treasure... a bowling ball sized bundle of mineral. Its inner glory paralleled the sun, surging forth and bringing a beam of hope into the lifeless world.

He bounced the Crystal Shard in his palm. "My name is Palatharx, and I'm looking to make an offer."

"Sorry, but I think this can wait." I raised an arm to block my stinging eyes from the crystal. "People are on the brink of dying. That outweighs this conversation."

"It's a shame how they work, is it not?" Palatharx stepped across the lopsided roof and came closer. "The Realms... home to all life, truly the single most flawed system in existence. This very moment is clear-cut proof."

"Yeah, they're not perfect," my impatience rumbled, "but there's no changing how the Realms work."

"Not exactly." Palatharx extended the jagged mass to me. "What if I told you there was a way to forge a *new world,* where innocent souls aren't suspended in motionless prisons every day... where evil ceased to roam the hearts of men... where everything doesn't fall apart when one stupid crystal breaks?"

My helmet nearly popped off as it flared bright. "None of this racing around like a madman? Count me *in!*"

"Shut up, Siris." I folded my arms. "Palatharx, I don't know if you've realized... you can't create a new world when there's already one here. *What are you getting at?*"

Palatharx's eyes narrowed. "Don't question the one handing you an olive branch."

Dense crystal dinged on my breastplate. *About time... now we can help the people at home.*

Palatharx nodded with a grin. "Take it."

And Chad thought we couldn't trust this guy. "Trap?" Yeah, right.

"Thanks." I wrapped my hands around the Crystal Shard, and my gauntlets immediately heated through. "I owe you. Without your help, we wouldn't have—"

A sharp, clawing pain latched onto my chest... tearing me from the sky.

"Travis!" Siris' consciousness bored into mind.

My iron body thudded against the grass, as my eyes focused in on the Crystal Shard... A surging beam fired from within, ripping through my armor and searing into my chest like a drill.

Palatharx barely made a sound as his feet touched the burnt grass. "You should do more research before rushing into your missions."

"The man's right... it's my fault." Siris rattled on my head. "Mohandar told me I wasn't supposed to let you *physically* touch it!"

"Would've been nice to know before I already did." I fought to get off the ground, to no avail.

"Exalted have one true weakness... Ancient Energy. Something as old as a crystal shard will quickly break an Exalted from the inside out." Palatharx opened his palm, and a machete-like weapon manifested in his grasp. "Did you really think I was here to help you save your precious world?"

"Deceptive coward." Siris' presence moved forward. "Show some honor."

Palatharx rubbed the false edge of his weapon... a blade the length of a greatsword, with a single jagged edge. Ruby plating encased its guard and backing, protruding into hooked fangs.

Travis, you idiot! My arms buckled, and my wings collapsed under the weight of an invisible elephant. *Why didn't you pay more attention?*

Palatharx planted his stone boot beside my face. "Creation cannot come without destruction. Think about it, Travis... maybe you'll have a change of heart."

"Hate to tell you..." I flared my nostrils and mustered all of my fading focus. "It ain't gonna happen."

"Shame." Palatharx sighed and tightened his grip. "Now you have to die."

I stared him dead in the eyes as the weapon came down... followed by a distinct metal clang, ringing through the trees.

He got me... my eyes dried out from the heat. *But how?*

Burning flames, pale as the moon, wisped around my body, convening at the edge of my executioner's machete.

A fleet of orbs the size of lightning bugs gathered above my body, joining until they formed a figure wrapped in heat waves. Wings of vengeance spread wide, unveiling a massive plated body and the familiar crested helm to go with it.

Siris had gotten bigger since we fought, every plate of armor denser and more imposing... every inch of him echoed the heroes of legend.

"This is your only warning." With a single forceful shove, Siris pinned Palatharx's blade to the grass. "Flee before I reduce you to ash."

Palatharx lifted his weapon to his shoulder. "Making this a nuisance, are we?"

Siris widened his stance and became an unmovable wall.

"Step aside." Palatharx loosened his posture. "You can't defeat me in battle."

"Words." Siris cocked his elbow and raised his stance as his blazing longsword manifested. "I'll not stand by to let you harm my friend."

Palatharx fixed both hands to his blade and sprang forward. "I'd hoped to make allies today. I'll settle for crushing a worm like you!"

"If fate serves..." Siris shifted to the side and parried the downward slash. "So be it. Bring me the *glory* of battle!"

Palatharx hooked around Siris and kicked him into the surface of the clock tower, causing it to groan and sag down toward us. The deceptive menace spared no time, leaping after his prey immediately.

Siris blasted out of the way, retaliating with a slash strong enough to pierce his foe's stone armor.

The earth trembled under constant and ominous shockwaves.

"You're too late." Palatharx cracked his limbs as he stood, laughing along the way. "Reach is collapsing."

Siris spread his wings and collided with the enemy. "So long as there's ground to stand on, there's hope."

The two rocketed into the sky in a deadly embrace as fists pounded against one another. With a raging burst, they separated.

Dull murmurs barely scratched the edge of my fading conscience.

More battle chatter. My body bounced under the intensifying tremors. *This is getting bad. Why hasn't the Crystal Shard restored the flow of time? I have it, but...*

My eyes popped wide as I recalled Mohandar's instructions.

Locate the shard, give it to the Sacred Scripture, and these worlds will be pushed off one another.

A grim realization set in.

No, no, no! I scoured the area, desperately searching for my literary companion. *How am I supposed to give the Crystal Shard to the Sacred Scripture when it hasn't ever been to Reach?*

A surge of scarlet mist came from above as the two specks that were Palatharx and Siris engaged in a frenzy of fast, hard collisions.

"You've done well so far, Knight Siris." Palatharx's voice sounded as if it were through a loudspeaker. "Feel my unburdened power!"

Flashes of energy, the swift union of red and white souls, pulsed against the frozen world, lighting the disasters below. Pebbles beside me began to rise against gravity, and cracks burst forth in the grass as I lay motionless.

Come on, Siris. My breaths shortened, the edges of my awareness giving way to black. *You've got this.*

A streak of flame plummeted to the earth beside me, followed by the impact of its pursuer. Inferno raged, spiraling around Palatharx.

Distant clicks whispered in my ears as the two adversaries met once more.

Palatharx's lips curled into a smile beneath his sinister guise of red... every inch of ruby in his machete mirrored avarice as he leered at Siris.

Siris clutched his sword arm, whose blade was lagging below. Wisps of pure spirit cascaded out of him from fine cuts in his manifestation... his very life force dispersing.

The horizon grew dark, spreading its lurid influence on the scene ahead of me.

"You're holding back." Palatharx stepped forward, the cloths around his armored body fluttering as he did. "You shouldn't be."

Siris tucked in his wings, and his chest grew bright enough to rival the sun. The divine radiance crept throughout his body, transforming him into the embodiment of light itself... a clean ring came forth as his burning blade grew, becoming as tall as its heroic wielder.

"I am Knight Siris..." Siris lifted solar wings high. "Perish, you corrupt scum!"

With one incredible stroke, Siris' attack grew... and grew... and grew. The darkness of the sky faded away, and the air roared like a collapsing tsunami under its might. The Talon of the Heavens seared through all in its path, overloading my eyes until it fizzled out.

To think he'd been hiding such— My eyes shot wide. *No.*

A menacing grin emerged from the aftermath. "Such an attack may have killed Ulanog or a world-devouring dragon, but me?" Palatharx tightened his grip on his weapon. "What a *joke.*"

Siris' radiance grew weak, and his knees wobbled. "Guess I'll just have to find another way."

Palatharx paced forward, his cold manner unbreakable. "Still think you can pull through? You hero types disgust me."

"As long as I have breath in my lungs," Siris snickered. "Well, I don't have lungs... but you get the expression."

Siris heaved his body into an upward slash of his blade, effortlessly evaded by Palatharx. A horrible screech immediately followed.

The limp, lifeless form of a great wing hit the blackening grass, dissolving into a flurry of tiny sparkles. Amidst the shimmering farewell, the wing's partner also fell... accompanied by Siris' left arm. Siris hunched over and coughed... a stream of undulating aurora pouring from his ravaged body. With the single limb remaining, he boldly attacked the menacing form of his adversary.

"Fool." Palatharx raised his open palm and caught Siris' blade. "You should've just let me kill the kid." His fingers curled in and sent the splintered remains of Siris' astral weapon into the air. "It would've been faster."

Siris, don't be stupid... I pushed all of my will against the pressure of the Crystal Shard. *You'll get yourself killed!*

Palatharx watched my defeated friend collapse to his knees.

"Travis..." Siris turned to me. "I'm sorry."

With a single brutal swing of the ruby blade, Siris, my friend... became nothing but a memory.

"Siris!"

A quick blur of blue passed through the edge of my vision, and the grasp of the Crystal Shard released.

The Sacred Scripture had arrived, just in time.

The book glowed bright as the source of my torment dissipated and seeped into the book's pages.

Breath filled my lungs, focus blasted into my mind, and my composure shattered as I took off toward the powdered remains of the fallen warrior.

All-consuming fury rushed through my body, taking control of every inch as my Power State roared to life. The broken chunks of dirt levitated with my rising cry, surging skyward as my soul intertwined with the Sacred Scripture. "Palatharx..."

"Things are getting a little too heated for me." Palatharx brushed the ghostly powder from his weapon. "I think I'll take my leave."

"Stay where you are, you heartless piece of trash!" The wrath of the tempest ensued me as I launched to Palatharx, my blade hungry for vengeance. "I'll make you pay for what you've done!"

My sword shot forward... but its target was gone. Blinding white light poured from the sky, hushing the earthquakes and replacing them with gentle wind. As the light died down, my eyes found no sign of Siris' murderer or Earth's influence on Reach. The clock tower, the debris, all of it... completely gone.

I'll make this right, Siris. I knelt down amidst the ashes. *I swear.*

TWENTY

Frozen wind pierced my sweatshirt as I rested on a thick mat of snow. Mountaintops went out as far as I could see, dawn creeping between their valleys. Snow danced as it fell, collecting on the edges of my iron mask and the chilled denim on my legs.

Mount Everest. I took a deep breath. *Quiet, still, and way too far for anyone to follow me... perfect.*

I bowed my head over the mask, which seemed hollow without its bold personality.

"Siris..." I brushed the snowfall from my arms. "Why'd you have to go and get yourself killed?"

The mask shimmered in the gentle touch of the sun, just barely lighting the edges... and an invisible stone slammed into my heart. I rose and collected my thoughts.

"You should've just let him kill me." I stomped off, turning my back on the horizon. "Why throw your life away for some teenage idiot like me? You were a knight, a spirit, and a hero... you could've gotten the stupid Crystal Shards put together by now, and instead you chose me." My skin began to spark. "What reason did you have to choose me? I should be the one who dies so somebody else doesn't have to!"

The mountain shook under the fury of my awoken Power State, my screaming anguish taking on the form of vicious lightning. Thunder rolled, skies darkened, and snow melted underneath the hurricane of emotion.

Why do people keep dying on me? What am I doing wrong? Why was I so stupid to pick up the Channeling Crystal? My fury burned as my eyes went to the sky. *Someone answer me!*

I froze, as faint echoes of my lost friend bounced in my soul.

Travis, when I look at you... who you are... it reminds me of something my father once said to me.

A salty droplet rolled down my cheek... warm against the wind.

A man is not judged by what he lives for, but who he dies for... Travis, I died for you because I knew you'd do the same for me.

The air grew cold against my skin, rushing faster with each second.

Siris, if I hadn't made such a bad decision, you wouldn't have had to die. The snow melted away as I dropped to a knee. "...It's my fault."

Snow crunched behind me, and the fluttering shadow of a cloak caught my eye. "Siris' death wasn't your fault, Travis."

"What do you mean, Mohandar?" I looked over my shoulder, tears streaming from my eyes. "I'm the one who trusted Palatharx and got paralyzed, I'm the one who put Siris in danger, and I'm the one who was too helpless to fight... how could the blame go to anyone else?"

"Because it's mine to take." Mohandar looked up to the sun, breaking through my storm. "You didn't fail Siris as a friend... I failed you as a teacher."

The clouds parted, and light trickled onto the peaks. "You took an ordinary kid and made him into an Exalted. Where's the failure?"

"I taught with speed instead of depth." Mohandar's steps crunched as he walked past. "I was so afraid to have you unprepared that I left out critical points of information... the points making a difference between victory and defeat."

I remained silent.

"You cannot blame yourself for this tragedy, Travis..." Mohandar extended his hand. "I know it's hard, but all we can do is keep going. No more cutting corners, no more slacking... next time, you'll be ready."

"Next time?" I beat my fist against the rocky surface of the mountain. "Mohandar, there can't be a next time! What if Dad ends up under the gun, or Kate, even? What if it's the entire planet, and I can't stop it because I missed a little technicality?"

He backed off, but didn't speak.

"Siris is *dead,* Mohandar..." I rose, and turned away. "I came here because I wanted to deal with it, and I didn't want anyone to follow me. Please, Mohandar... just let me do this alone."

Mohandar's posture loosened, and he pulled his cloak across his body. "...I understand."

He disappeared in a blink, leaving me in solitude.

The radiance of the risen sun cast its blessings upon my mask, gleaming from under its dusting of overturned snow. Taking it in my hands, I sat down and swung my legs over the cliffside... hanging on the edge of the world.

***

With a thump, I landed in the dusty driveway, and my Power State faded. I looked around and found an unexpected guest on my front porch.

Kate lifted her gaze from the ground, her long hair flowing with the rhythm of the breeze. Her ever-present smile was far from sight, replaced by slow breaths and a heart-melting gaze.

Dad must've told her about Siris. I sighed and straightened my sweatshirt. "I'm in no mood for company, Kate."

She looked away, eyes low. "I thought you could use someone to talk to."

I took off my mask and had a seat next to her on the stairs. "Thanks, but I'm fine."

Silence framed us as Kate drew lines in the dust with her boots and I rubbed my hand against the grainy surface of the porch... scouring for the right words.

I rose to leave... but the second my hand met the doorknob, a soft touch descended on my shoulder.

"I know how you feel." She gently tightened her grip on my sleeve and eased me back to her. "No matter what you tell yourself, or what the situation was, it's somehow still your fault. Deep down in you, it just boils. Anger, sadness, confusion, it all just snowballs into one ugly beast."

I took a deep breath and gave a slow nod.

"So don't let it, alright?" She looked me dead in the eyes. "How could it be your fault that Siris made the decision to give up his life for you?"

I tapped my foot. "Because—"

"No." Kate shook her head. "Whatever excuse you have to blame yourself is pointless. Siris made his decision for your good. He wasn't chosen to be Exalted... you were." She laid her hand on the center of my chest. "And I see it in you. You're a man fit to be Exalted. No matter what life throws at you, you never give up." Her eyes began to glisten. "You *can't* give up. This world and Reach need you, Travis. This is a tough loss, I know, but you can't stay down... we're all counting on the Travis who rises every time he's put on the ground. If you don't get back up... no one will."

A flame of revival kindled in my soul.

"So," Kate gave me a playful shove. "You're gonna quit feeling sorry for yourself and get to work, got it?"

I smiled. "Got it."

"Good." She turned to leave, with a smirk across her face. "If you need anything, you better—"

I tugged her hand and wrapped her in a quick hug, getting a small squeak in response. Her posture loosened against mine as she slowly returned the embrace.

"Thanks, Kate." I backed off. "I really appreciate it."

She brushed a strand of hair out of her eyes, a faint blush on her cheeks. "No problem, Travis... it's my pleasure."

With a wave, she descended the stairs and headed down the driveway, the sunset framing her as she left.

I won't let you down.

TWENTY-ONE

The Lunar Jungle sang once more, freed from the grasp of disaster. With all echoes of Earth gone, the overgrowth flourished... like nothing even happened.

My wings curled over my head, bobbing along with my torso as I sifted into the dirt. One stroke at a time, I made a nice two-foot hole at the base of an isolated tree.

My iron knees scraped against the ground as I spread the powdered remains of my winged friend underneath the tree's roots. "He did a fine job."

Arvel looped his Eagle Amulet off and wrapped it around his palm. "Thanks for including us in this, Travis. You mind if I lead?"

Chad glanced over at me with big eyes. "Travis is the only guy here who actually—"

"It's fine by me." I stood, looking down to the wispy remains. "I'm no reverend."

"Thanks." Arvel extended his arms to us, his voice dropping as he did. "Let's bow."

I hooked my fingers under my helm and cradled it in my elbow. Soon after, my eyes closed and my neck dropped down... opening the path to silence.

Arvel cleared his throat. "This world isn't meant to be permanent. In fact, our lives are only a test run for what's to come. I didn't know Siris well, but he seemed like a truly good man. He fought to the moment he dropped, meeting his end in the defense of a dear friend. May his soul find peace and purpose in the chapter to come." Arvel set his hand on my shoulder. "Travis, I need your help for the next part."

I rubbed my hands. "Sure."

"When we did this in my hometown, we'd burn the remains." Arvel shrugged. "Could you do the honors?"

I nudged the Sacred Scripture. "Want to give it a shot?"

The book faced me, and its soft blue glow intensified.

"Alright." I locked my knees and reached within.

Here goes. My first power-up in this body.

With unspoken grace, my Power State spread from my chest into every feather of my wings. My skin shed its pigment to become pale as the moon, and my veins illuminated within.

Chad's mouth hung open. "That's *awesome*."

"Now, there's an Exalted." Arvel grinned. "Go ahead, Travis."

Just like we practiced. I focused my inner thoughts, and recalled the essence of the flame. The flickering cinders, the gentle heat, the softness of its company... they all twisted together until the spectral image of a dancing pyre locked in my brain. *Visualize and produce.*

My ironclad palm's light laced itself together, and blessed us with the presence of a gentle, swirling ember.

I lowered to the grass and released the flame. "Rest easy, my friend."

The two phantasmal forms met in a cloud of whirling shimmers, each one dissipating as they rose to the sky. In a few graceful seconds, the final memory of the winged warrior had moved on.

I sighed as I watched the last one go. *Bye, Siris.*

After a few minutes of reflection, the three of us packed up and shipped out. We traversed the mountains, valleys, and forests of Reach, headed to our next destination... the Stairway to the Stars. With enough determination and perseverance, we found ourselves there, at the base of a titan.

Arvel, Chad and I stood with necks craned all the way back in absolute admiration.

Clouds parted in the face of the earthen giant, blocking its distant peak. The mere sight was enough to solidify its title as the *Stairway to the Stars.*

Chad spun around and headed the opposite direction. "I'm going home."

"Good luck," Arvel sneered, catching Chad by the arm. "You're a cross-realm invader. Unless we kill you, you're not going anywhere... besides, it won't be so bad of a climb."

The ice-ridden heights of our obstacle burned through my mind.

Chad has a point. I rubbed the bottom of my chin. *There's no way he'll survive the way up... especially in jeans and a T-shirt.* I sighed. *Of all people, why him?*

"*Won't be so bad?*" Chad threw his arms toward the mountain. "Look at it! Ice, stone, wind, angles *over* ten degrees? We've gotta be at least a mile away, and I can't even see the top!"

"You'll need to toughen up if you're tagging with us, kid." Arvel looked down at his amulet. "Clock's ticking, and we can't wait for a straggler."

Hold on... with my Power State, I've lifted and thrown things five times my size and about two hundred times my weight. Who's to say we need to climb at all?

"Oh, I'm the straggler?" Chad grunted and raised his fist. "What've you done to help the team? Yeah, you help shoot us out of the small situations, but when are you gonna do anything *really* spectacular?"

Dang it, Chad. I looked over at the Sacred Scripture. *This is why I get into so many fights...*

Arvel reached for his bows. "You better watch your mouth, shrimp."

That's about all it took to start a full-fledged battle of the idiots.

I smiled at the Sacred Scripture. "You ready?"

The Scripture lowered its cover, as if to nod.

"Alright." I flared my Power State to life and spread my wings wide. "Hold on, guys."

With the force of a rocket, I combined the thrust of my Power State into a single hefty flap of my wings, snagging Chad and Arvel in my arms. I was blazing skyward, with a screeching wise guy in one arm and a silent, but clearly nauseated assassin in the other.

Arvel's face flapped in the turbulence as we ascended higher and higher. "If we survive this, you're *so* dead."

The Sacred Scripture corkscrewed around my body, singing.

"How come you're so happy?" Chad's words were staggered between his heaving breaths. "I can't... even... breathe!"

The Scripture hovered in front of him for a brief moment before zipping off.

"You guys alright?" My gut jabbed me as I laughed. "I wanted to run this by you, but your conversation sounded too important to interrupt."

In unison, they yelled, "Shut up, Travis!"

I raised my gaze to the dense layer of clouds ahead, broken apart by the spire of stone and frost. "Love you guys, too."

With a quick barrel roll, we burst through the clouds. The entire world had faded away, leaving only us, the mountain, and the snaking aurora above.

With a resounding thud, I touched down at the peak of the mountain. "Thank you for flying with Exalted Airways."

"Well, thanks." Chad collapsed to the moist, snowy surface of the summit. "What do I owe you for my ticket, captain jerk face?"

"Don't worry about it. Idiots fly for free." I laughed. "If you have your platinum card, I'll upgrade you to first class."

"You say that like we're gonna do it again." Chad snorted. "It ain't gonna happen."

Arvel brushed out of my grasp. "How else are we getting down, Chad?"

"Dang." Chad's face fell. "Guess we're onto the real question now... where do we go from here?"

Ahead was a frost-coated archway, ageless and absolutely magnificent in design. Statues of bizarre humanoid heroes gazed into the endless cosmos off the cliffside. The only thing separating us from what rested within the inner sanctums of the gate was a long, gradual set of stairs.

"I'll say..." I took my wind-chilled helm off. "Temple."

Arvel snickered. "Glad you're so observant."

Chad let out a giggle, the only thing needed to set off a domino effect of three fools cackling their faces off. We'd have probably gone for hours, had a lone figure not silenced us all.

In a tiny moment of observation, I picked out the seated figure of a living enigma... the White Wolf of the Exalted. He awaited us at the mouth of the temple, shrouded behind a veil of dancing snowflakes and twisting aurora. His glacier eyes burned into mine, and I found every inch of my body petrified.

How does he do this? I fought within the carnal prison of my body. *I can't move!*

"Alright, then why don't we go ahead and—" Chad's body language flipped on itself upon seeing me. "You okay, Travis?"

My veins bulged out of my neck and sweat streamed down my face as the wolf's stare grew more intense by the second. *What do you want?*

In a mere breath, his seated figure was within an arm's reach. With a flip of his black-marked ears, he engaged my view once more... this time sending a single, reverberating phrase throughout my mind.

Prepare yourselves.

With his purpose spoken, the fur-covered sentinel averted his gaze. My body released, a wave of ecstasy coasting through it.

It was then, in that very second, when Chad shifted his focus and came eye to eye with the embodiment of mystery. With a gasp, he scrambled backward and right into Arvel's plated leg.

"Cut it out, will ya?" Arvel gave Chad a light shove. "What's wrong with you?"

"Wolf..." Chad's breathing hastened. "Wh-white Wolf."

Arvel looked about, clutching his bows. "I don't see anything, kid."

I blinked and studied the snow... not a single print or track remained. The only sign of the wolf's presence was Chad wheezing with a face pale as the chilling powder around him.

"I'm going to scout ahead," Arvel sighed. "We don't have time for this."

Arvel started toward the temple grounds. In the cold silence of the summit, I knelt down beside Chad.

"Hey." I put my hand on his shoulder. "It's alright, he's gone."

Chad's eyelids drooped. "No, he's still—"

"Three, two, one..." Chad's eyes rolled back and his torso thudded to the ground. "Touchdown."

The Sacred Scripture murmured and prodded at Chad's limp arm.

"Yeah, I know." I hoisted Chad over my shoulder. "Good thing he's not the one in charge of saving the world, huh?"

Soon, the resounding footsteps of Arvel and I bounced off the ancient stone walls of the mountain temple. Within the gateway were the openings of a timeless marvel.

An open garden overtaken by powdered snow awaited us within. Flowers, bushes, and leafless trees formed the work of an artist, each piece encapsulated within its own personal shell of ice. In the center of the courtyard was the pulsing glow of our prize.

I scratched my head. "If it weren't for that big glowing gem, I'd be expecting Santa Claus."

"Can't say I know who that is." Arvel's cape flapped in the gentle breeze. "Let's get this thing and get out while we can."

"Right."

The snow faded when we drew close, melted away by the steady heat of the bizarre gem which rested on the surface of newly exposed grass. With a gentle, phasing glow, it pushed away the grasp of winter and welcomed newborn flowers around its slick, glassy surface.

The Sacred Scripture zipped around the Crystal Shard and hummed, hovering just a few feet away.

"Alright, scripture." I nodded. "Do your thing."

A soft blue glow coaxed the edges of our armor when the Sacred Scripture let loose a net of spirit-forged tendrils and wrapped its target... with a graceful wave, the gem turned sky blue and dissipated into the surface of the book.

With a final cheerful hum, the book returned.

I took a deep breath and looked to the sky. "Two down."

"I don't think I'm gonna get used to that." Arvel stepped back. "A floating book I can do, but when the thing starts eating—"

"It didn't eat the crystal," I chuckled. "I think *absorb* is a better word."

"What, with its little glowing tentacles?" Arvel gestured to the happily hovering Sacred Scripture. "It ate the thing!"

"What's your point, Arvel?" I gave my book a spin. "The shard was there, and now we have it. Isn't that the only thing that *really*—"

A sudden shift under my steel boots sent shivers up my spine... and a growing heat rose in the side of my armor. The Realm Stone was burning... and in an instant I knew, fun time was over.

TWENTY-TWO

Half of the Observatory's library was piled on my desk, bed, and floor as an ocean of paper. The Sacred Scripture danced among the literary chaos as I paced with a single text in my hand, titled *On Creation and Destruction*.

Dad sat cross-legged in the corner of my room, his neck hunched over as he studied. "You know, I haven't seen you read since you were eight. This is a bit... extreme."

"I haven't had the chance to go back to Reach for a week, and there's work to be done." I snapped the material shut. "From what it says here, there've been mavericks like Palatharx before... guys who want to exploit the Realms' self-destructive nature to destroy them. Thing is, none of them have ever made it past theory."

Dad rubbed his forehead. "He's already got them one-upped. If you ask me, there's no room to compare 'em."

"You're right..." I glanced about the room. "Where's the one about the—"

The Sacred Scripture chimed and rushed over, with *The Specifics of the Channeling Crystal* in its grasp.

"Thanks." Pages sifted under my fingers. "As I see it, our biggest problem is this. Even if we manage to put the Channeling Crystal in Reach back together, Palatharx is just going to break it again."

"So you're saying, *he's* our problem." Dad rolled his shoulder. "Recovering shards will patch the damage he's doing."

I cracked open a box of gum and popped a piece in. "That's our best bet, but I still have to find a permanent solution."

Dad tugged at the folds of his jeans. "Thought you told me you couldn't handle the shards. Something about it burning you on the inside?"

"Like a fire poker... then throw some rubbing alcohol onto the wound." I shuddered. "Not a problem, though. The Sacred Scripture absorbs them, somehow."

"I read something on it a while ago." Dad picked up another book. "Right here... the godly scriptures are the *only* things capable of recombining Channeling Crystals, and they do it inside themselves." He shifted and sat up. "How do you think you're gonna get rid of Palatharx?"

"Thinking about punching him." I cracked my knuckles. "Only problem is, I haven't seen that devil since he murdered my friend."

"Yeah, I'm guessin' it's because of those big red things... Invasion Scars." Dad snapped his fingers. "When he left London, he left through one of those."

"He did," I nodded. "Chad said he saw a man in one when he got pulled to Reach. You think Palatharx lives between the Realms?"

Dad froze. "Chad's not *still* in Reach, is he?"

I nodded my head with a grimace. "Sure is... it's been a week, but he's alive and frozen."

"If his parents come asking about where he is, I'm not gonna know what to tell 'em," he chuckled.

"The truth." I shrugged. "Tell 'em he went to buy a video game and never left the store."

"For a week?" Dad smirked. "Seems like Chad... what do we really tell them?"

"He and I went out camping, and we'll be back soon."

"Got it." Dad scratched the corner of his nose. "What's the book over there?"

I turned and beheld the single untouched book of the mass, pristine and shut on my desk. It had an aged, blackened leather cover and pages which crackled when they turned, each marked with a bizarre, indecipherable language.

I stepped carefully between the labyrinth of information and lifted the mystery text to my eyes. "Let's find out."

Silence fell.

Heck, is this thing in Japanese? I sighed and flipped more pages. *This picture looks cool.*

The frozen imagery of two warriors in combat was scribbled onto the ancient paper. Their fists of ink barreled at one another, each closed in for a hefty punch.

I brushed off a layer of dust, and my breathing halted. Wait.

The fighter on the left side of the page was adorned in a modern-day hooded sweatshirt... and his opponent had a mound of blackened hair which trailed behind him like a tail.

Is that... Palatharx and me? My hand shot into my pocket. *There's a caption. I have to figure out what it means.*

Dad looked up from his studies. "Thought you were reading?"

"It's in another language." I punched a few digits on my cell. "Gotta call the big guns... Kate?"

"Hey, Travis," her chipper voice answered. "What can I do you for?"

"Huh?" I tapped my finger against the desk. "Uh, you take Latin, right?"

"Umm... yeah," she paused. "Why?"

I stroked the edges of the book's faded cover. "I've got something that looks kind of important, but I can't read it. Latin's the root of most languages, so..."

"Sure thing." Thuds came from the other end of the line. "I'll be right over."

The Sacred Scripture yipped and circled to my side, extending a screen of neon light to the picture's captions. The ink slowly began to warp.

"What do you think you're doing?" I pulled the material away from the Sacred Scripture, but couldn't shake it off. "We have to read it, not destroy it!"

In a matter of seconds, the chicken scratch under the picture had warped into clean, easy English.

"Nice job, Scripture... high five." I held up my hand to the Sacred Scripture, and it met me with an extension of its glow. "Kate, don't worry about it. Just stay—"

She'd already hung up.

"So be it..." I hunched over the aged paper. "What've we got here?"

Change. Preservation. The two go hand in hand, yet at the same time, fist to fist. Only their fated battle will decide the future of the Realms. Be wary of the scars, for they mark the gateway between these destined enemies.

I shut the book. "That's it!"

"Fifth time you've said that today." Dad flipped his page and rolled his eyes. "Let's hear it."

"No, Dad. We've actually figured it out." I snapped my fingers. "You know the Invasion Scars? The big rips in the air that happen when a powerful individual's coming over?"

He nodded, slowly.

"This caption calls them the gateway between two destined enemies." I paced about, picking up the mess. "Chad said he saw Palatharx in one... I witnessed him show up alongside one... he's definitely connected to the Invasion Scars."

"We've been over this..." Dad chewed on the edge of his lip. "Recently, matter of—"

"Yeah." I held up my finger to silence him. "Invaders come from somewhere, right? Then by default, Invasion Scars are two-way streets."

Dad's eyes lit up.

"If Palatharx is always where an invasion happens, I can cross through the portal the opposite way..."

"And take the fight to him!" Dad let out a hoot of victory. "It's like we've won already."

I took a deep breath. "Let's not get ahead of ourselves... Thanks for helping, Dad."

"No problem." He stood up, stumbling. "My leg fell asleep... but it was nice to be able to pitch in for once."

"Pitch in?" I raised my eyebrow. "You put a roof over my head, clothes on my body and—"

"You know what I mean." Dad groaned and rubbed his forearms. "Now, you better get downstairs. Kate's gonna be here in..."

A firm knock sounded against the front door.

I headed for the stairs. "Should've known."

When the door creaked open, I froze.

A silent figure of snow white fur awaited, seated and patient. His eyes locked into mine, and the world turned upside down.

***

In a flash, the gentle breeze and light of the sun were long gone. My front porch was replaced by an inter-dimensional roller coaster. After a bit of tossing, I found myself pinned to the ground with the air squeezed out of me.

Stupid wolf... greet me at the door, and now we're on an adventure again.

My eyes opened with a long breath. Pure blackness surrounded me, as if I was a toy shut in a box and forgotten.

Time to find out where I am. I sighed. *I need a light.*

A growing sting in the pocket of my jeans snagged my attention, and I immediately pulled out the source. The Realm Stone, Mom's gift, was burning bright... and absolutely scorching to the touch.

I fired up my Power State, and my pain threshold increased. *An Invasion Scar's nearby.* With a slight turn, the stone became a blinding white. *That way.*

Phantom wings of pure blue carried me toward the source, my speed climbing with each second... until my body smashed into an invisible wall. I toppled through, sending ripples of pain coursing along my torso.

Now I know how the birds feel. Weightlessness set in. *Hold on, what?*

Cloudy red mist trailed behind my luminous skin, dissolving as it spread. Cold ensued, accompanied by the gentle sway of my clothing. With one long exhale, the final piece of the puzzle fell into place.

A swarm of bubbles surged from my nose.

I clutched my forehead. *Great, we're here again... the place that started it all.*

Pulsing water rippled through the sunken caverns, filled with a neon city of coral and abysmal creatures. I found myself at the start of the road to a godly temple... where my journey as an Exalted began.

The Realm Stone's aura pointed deeper into the twisting path.

Strange. I took off with my Power State, becoming a living torpedo. *Of all places, why here?*

Schools of fish blazed by, twisting to duck out of the way of an Exalted on the move.

With a few high-speed turns, I found myself at the peak of my memory.

Ahead was a field of tangling kelp, and above was the silent and menacing guardian of the sunken temple... a gigantic, battle-scarred shark. The gargantuan beast's eyes snagged my glowing body in an instant, and turned in response.

Well, hello.

Before I knew it, the terror of the sea was closing in at a breakneck pace. With a quick thrust of my arm, I redirected the biological equivalent of a school bus and made a beeline for the temple's open entrance. In seconds, I'd smashed through doors, walls, and the like... until my body was flung out onto dry stone.

So much for self-control. I gagged as I heaved out a bucket load of water. *Keep it up, and this whole place is gonna end up—* I lifted my eyes to the inscriptions on the walls. *Redecorated?*

No heroes walked these walls, and not a single crystal dared show its face. Instead, stories of great empires and the punishment of the wicked reigned true, heralded by a deity who carried a battleax in one hand and a massive bundle of grain in the other.

Am I going nuts? I headed down the hallway. *Is the book's room the same?*

The ancient doors rumbled open with a solitary thud of my shoulder, unveiling the truth.

The ageless eyes of a stone deity leered down at me from stories of height. His mere presence commanded the room, paired with his massive weapon. Beneath a flowing cape and a set of bulky, war-scarred armor, a thick pedestal stood proud.

Lord Grrogum, bringer of Judgment.

A circular stand about the size of a dinner plate rested at his feet, graced with the presence of a parchment scroll.

This is where the book should be. Without a second thought, I picked up the paper. *What have we got, here?*

Travis,

"What?" I froze, but my eyes pushed on.

I've heard from Mohandar that you'd divulged a plan to slay Palatharx and end his campaign on the world. Well, I have the same plan. This area, as I'm sure you've noticed, is highly unstable... like ice, it only stays together if you tread lightly. Fire up your Power State to about fifty percent, and an Invasion Scar will open to Palatharx's world.

Hope you're ready for a heck of a fight.

~A Friend

"A bit rash, but..." I looked around at the room one last time and took a deep breath. "I like rash."

With a bit of focus and willpower, a powerful snap bounced off the walls... and the gates to another world opened.

I sprinted and dove head-first into the Invasion Scar. *Palatharx... I'm coming for you.*

TWENTY-THREE

Tremors rippled through every inch of the frozen garden. Icicles fell, flowers quivered, and trees crashed as Arvel and I sprinted for the gates.

"What's going on here?" Arvel leapt over the frosted edge of a flowerbed. "I thought getting these Crystal Shards was going to *fix* the problem, not make it worse!"

I heaved Chad's limp body on my shoulder. "We can figure it out once death's not a looming possibility."

With a roar, the stone arch marking our escape collapsed... the door to safety had slammed shut.

The magnitude of destruction ceased, leaving only ruins of a once beautiful work of architecture. Lurid stillness filled the garden. Nothing dared make a sound.

Arvel wrapped his fingers around his bow. "Something's not right."

How observant. I looked for another way out. "All the more reason to get Chad safe."

A torrential shockwave threw us to the ground before another word could come out. Chad spilled out of my arms as I locked gazes with the source of the disruption.

Two pale eyes burned their way through an impermeable wall of steam. With a flare of intensity, they narrowed... accompanied by the bellow of a titan. "Travis Shepard. Give me the shards."

The only thing left to keep these worlds from ripping one another apart? I broadened my stance. "I don't think so."

A quick, intense gasp caught my attention, followed by the wide-eyed gaze of a freshly awoken Chad.

"Morning... already? I went out hard, didn't—" His entire body jolted when he fixed his eyes on our adversary. "Holy crap!"

The mist cleared, like an ethereal curtain. With a low groan, the joints of a granite body the size of a house lifted a boulder of a torso up... towering over us. His head tilted down and leered at us from another atmosphere.

"You're blind..." The unnamed giant rolled his earthen shoulders and curled each and every pillar of a finger. "It didn't have to be this way."

I shifted my helm. "Still doesn't. Talk."

Shattered bricks soared through the air under the deadly impact of a stone fist. By pure instinct, I thrust to the side on my wings and plowed into Chad.

Chad squealed and grabbed on tight. "Doesn't anyone use their words anymore?"

I set him down at the far corner of the courtyard. "Stay out of the way. I don't want you getting stepped on."

"Well, I guess I'll just sit on the sidelines, then?" Chad threw his arms around himself. "Hey, where are you going?"

"This guy just tried to make a pancake out of *two* of my friends." I spread my wings and started a full sprint toward the colossus. "I'm gonna pound him back into whatever hole he came out of!"

Power State. An electric aura of strength encircled me. *You know, it really ticks me off when people bust into your business out of nowhere and start throwing punches.* My eyes shot wide. *Man, I'm a hypocrite.*

Thundering impact sent us into the archetypal struggle of titan against man. The grainy, rough surface of the golem screeched against my armor, emitting sparks as I plowed him onto his back.

I sprang back and widened my stance toward the rising colossus. "You gonna explain yourself or what?"

A long pause of silence rested between us.

The giant stretched a long arm behind his skull and popped the joints of his neck. "My name is Kharadin. I come with a warning."

"I'm Travis." I loosened my posture, and my wings gradually relaxed. "Warn away."

Kharadin knelt and stared down over me. "You're working with the enemy. You do not, and *will not* see it until it's too late."

Working with the enemy... I narrowed my eyes. *No way that's true. He just fell out of the sky and tried to flatten Chad. Not exactly screaming trustworthy.*

"The Channeling Crystal isn't broken, Exalted One." Kharadin pointed to the Sacred Scripture. "The Shards you've been collecting are a trap. Carry them any longer, and you'll end up accidentally waking something that actually *will* consume the Realms."

Arvel gave me a cold glance.

I'm not feeling it either, Arvel. I groaned. "Thanks... but I beg to differ. I was put on this mission by Mohandar, the Observer of the Realms... and I trust his judgment. I won't stop now."

"I'm trying to help." Kharadin lowered his car-sized palm to my feet. "Give me the Shards and save yourself."

I looked over to Arvel one more time, as he slowly shook his head. "I'm sorry, Kharadin. I can't."

"How unfortunate." The great warrior of stone pumped his other fist back. "Farewell, Shepard."

A gust of air ripped past my face. By pure instinct, my open palm surged forward as the force of a wrecking ball plowed into it. My eyes shot wide, but I found myself... steady.

How about that? A smirk crossed over my face. "See ya."

With a firm shove, Kharadin stumbled back. Immediately, my wings snapped open and I went on the offensive.

My body lurched with the pure force of a wing-boosted jump. "Back me up, Arvel."

"Already on it, bud." A blur of white and silver flashed through my field of view. "This one calls for the special package."

An arrow lodged itself into the stone giant's chest, along with a fountain of embers burning from a fuse. With no more than a few seconds' delay, a violent explosion reverberated through the open air.

Kharadin rushed forward with a hefty swipe of his arm, bursting from a glaze of flame. My entire body whirled to the side, smashing against a snow-coated tree. Kharadin closed in with earth-shaking strides, just barely missing me with his continued assault.

Close one. I slid through the legs of my foe. *Guess I can't take any chances.*

Another explosive arrow cracked off, dazing the enemy just long enough for me to intercept.

Seconds transformed into minutes through my adrenaline-filled eyes... each snowflake danced along my view as I climbed higher and higher, soaring toward glory.

With both hands on my blade, I closed in. *Let's see how you like a rush at full power.*

My body heaved back and forth under the sheer force of heroic strokes, each cut resounding like a bell. With a mighty upward slash, a torrent of raging plasma sent an electrified mass of stone into the clear moonlit sky.

That's right. I intercepted in a flash, locking eyes with my helpless foe as I spiraled over him. *I pack a bit of a punch for my size.*

The mountain shook as my soul flowed through my arms in a devastating gush of superheated energy, roaring with the force of river rapids. Kharadin's plated chest cracked upon impact with the ground, a fine hole burned straight into his inner workings.

"And that..." I descended beside my fallen enemy, the intense heat of my Power State mellowing, "...is how we take down a giant."

"Gotta say, that's impressive." Arvel jogged over and put his bows on his back one at a time. "...What's wrong?"

"Nothing." I leapt down to my friend. *Can't help but wonder... was he telling the truth?*

A sudden rumble behind me caused my body to freeze. "You let your guard down."

I did it again... My senses dimmed, and I found myself limp against the biting surface of a brick wall. *When am I gonna learn?*

"You should take your own advice, big guy." Arvel sprang back and nocked an arrow with blinding speed. "You've still got me to deal with!"

Arvel's arrow dug into the joint of Kharadin's shoulder, its explosive payload blasting each piece apart. Kharadin roared and retaliated with his other arm, only to be expertly evaded by my archer friend. The second swipe, however... was a different story.

A gruesome crack split the air of battle, and Arvel took a knee. The limp, flopping form of his leg dragged across the snow, leaving a trail of red in its wake.

Don't worry, Arvel. My awareness rushed back, and I stood once more. *I'm on my way.*

"Your energy's depleted." Kharadin's head rumbled as it rotated to me. "You're as good as defeated."

Not so long as I'm still breathing. With purposeful, firm steps, I raised an open hand. *Back at it, here we—*

"Travis, that's *enough*." A firm grasp set upon my shoulder and pulled me backward. "Some days, you make me *sick!*"

"Chad." My cobalt glow flickered. "I told you to stay back. You're not—"

"Shut up." Chad gave me a nice shove. "This happens every single time you get in a fight. Know when to quit! You heard the big guy say it, and I've *seen* it. You burned up most of your power on your first attack, and it didn't even scratch him." He rubbed the stubble on his chin. "It's a matter of science. Blunt force and electrical shocks aren't going to do a thing against someone made of stone."

Kharadin's voice bellowed, "How observant."

"Did I ask for your opinion, wise guy?" Chad bit his lip, eyes flaring wide. "Travis, you listen to me. You're gonna give this a rest and *negotiate* right this second. Arvel's got a broken leg, and you're headed for the same level of punishment. For once in your life, do us all a favor and—"

A swipe of Kharadin's arm cut him off.

Chad thumped across the snow, a trail of blood following.

"You leave him alone!"

A storm of pain ravaged through my body as every cell surged bright once more, each one shattering its previous limits and becoming, by nature... truly Exalted. A furious shout erupted from my lungs under the powerful agony, until the flame of my spirit was burning bright once again.

That hurt pretty bad... I clenched my fist. *I can't pull this off much longer.*

Chad's arms trembled as he pushed onto his knees. "Show him who's boss, Travis—"

Brutal judgment descended on Chad for the second time.

No.

The world stopped spinning.

The snow lost its bite.

Not again! My legs wobbled under me. *How could I have?*

My breaths grew heavy... my mind slowing.

Chad... My fading aura silenced like a quenched candle. *I'm sorry. I...*

"You should have listened to your friend." Kharadin twisted his fist in the mess of rubble and earth. "He wasn't blind like—"

A tiny chime tickled my ear... and a unique, surreal warmth spread onto my skin.

What?

A warm golden radiance coated my face. From between the great golem's fingertips, more and more rays of dawn burst forth, growing stronger until my eyes stung from their pure glory.

My heart pounded like war drums. Right before us, Kharadin's brutal grasp took on the red of a ladybug, shattering under an uncontrollable explosion.

The cataclysm subsided... revealing an event *far* beyond my comprehension.

A small, pale fist clenched tight and emitted a mist of embers. A book, dense in pages and mirroring its companion's fiery aura, spiraled into view. Sweltering air erupted from Chad's illuminated body, making him look more like the king of the sun than a rambunctious teenager.

Chad smirked at Kharadin as he stepped out of his crater. "On second thought... What's negotiation ever done for people like us?"

No way, it can't be... is it? I studied Chad's blazing form and companion book. *He's in full-on Power State!*

Arvel groaned, "Well, slap my butt and call me Sally."

Passed out one minute, fully Exalted in the next. Talk about irony.

"Travis." Chad turned and looked at me with an ear-to-ear grin. "You still got fight left in you?"

"Yeah, but not much." I took my stance, the remnants of my reserves firing up.

Kharadin raised what was left of his only remaining arm, and lurched forward.

"Alright..." Chad planted his feet, and a raging cyclone encircled him. "Let's turn up the *heat!*"

TWENTY-FOUR

My torso thudded against firm stone after passing through the Invasion Scar, bringing about an entirely bizarre world characterized by a crimson horizon and massive chunks of earth levitating in formation. In the distance, a tower of slate stretched to the sky.

A soft laugh came from my side. "You actually decided to show."

A tall, dense figure extended his hand, covered in a black leather glove. A bulging tank top and a pair of baggy cargo pants concealed a bodybuilder's muscle tone. His eyes were the color of gravel, and thick bangs of sandy blond hair hung over his face.

"I'm Drew, Exalted under Grrogum." The scarf around his chin muffled his voice. "I'd go into more, but we're a little pressed for time."

The Sacred Scripture rushed to greet Drew's book, yapping away. It raced around its counterpart, who sported a deep orange glow... and seemed rather unimpressed. It gave a droning moan and retreated to its master's side.

Something about Drew seems familiar... but what?

"Name's Travis. Exalted under Alcyon." I rolled my shoulders. "What's the plan?"

Drew turned his head, revealing a massive scar across his cheek. "Simple. We need to take down Palatharx before he puts us in checkmate."

"So, we're here to beat his face in." I pulled my glistening steel mask over my head. "I like it."

He adjusted his scarf. "When you put it like that, it sounds like we're the bad guys."

A dense cloud of dust kicked up just ahead. The smokescreen peeled away like a curtain, revealing a cold grin and the stone armor to go with it.

"Well, well... I count not one, but *two* Exalted." Palatharx, the realm-wide menace, slowly hoisted his weapon to his shoulder. "To what do I owe the pleasure?"

Drew puffed up his chest, and the air immediately grew humid. "You're tampering with things beyond your level, Palatharx. Your games end here."

Palatharx spread his arms wide and smiled. "Go ahead and *try*."

That's it!

I tightened my muscles, and extended my soul to the Sacred Scripture. Raging spirit gushed out of me, transforming my thin teenage body into a universal warrior. My veins pulsed with the flow of cerulean Power State, and my legs surged into action.

"You're cocky, Palatharx." Wings of moonlight spread wide on my back, rocketing me toward my adversary. "Quite frankly, I'm sick of it!"

My right hook was effortlessly evaded. With just two fingers, Palatharx redirected my momentum and sent me spiraling by.

Rookie mistake. I righted myself in the air. *Don't let your opponent get in your head, Travis.*

Drew spun the sunset orange cover of his book. "Well, so much for your reputation as a calculated, *disciplined* fighter."

The ruins around us trembled as a blast of citrus light overflowed the area. Drew planted his feet, and his body became encased by a burning aura of dancing embers. Through it all, he never broke his laid-back attitude.

"Guess there's no time left to negotiate." Drew spread his fingers, and the air warped around them. "*Let's turn up the heat.*"

My mind went blank for a brief second. *Didn't Chad say that when he went into his Power State?*

Drew blasted into Palatharx with a solid blow of his shoulder, sending Palatharx airborne.

No time to think about it. I glided into action. *We're in this together.*

Palatharx took a heavy swipe with his machete, following up with a sharp uppercut to Drew's jaw. "Come on... give me something I can work with."

I focused my Power State and fired a dense energy blast into Palatharx's side. In seconds I was upon him, relentlessly battering his gut with my bare fists.

With a final, heaving blow to the torso, I forced Palatharx back. "I'm stronger without your shameless gimmicks, huh?"

"Indeed you are." Palatharx straightened up, only to meet a rush of burning, luminous heat to his face. "It appears the rumors of your kind have some truth behind them."

"What rumors?" I buckled at a sucker punch to the stomach. *I shouldn't be talking.*

"Exalted get stronger when they fight alongside one another." Palatharx snagged me by the face and slammed me down. "So *satisfying!*"

The air rushed from my lungs under violent contact with the ground. Palatharx was immediately over me, his fanged blade descending.

"Give up." Palatharx's eyes narrowed. "I'm still under half of my—"

Drew's radiant silhouette flashed between us. "Come to think of it, I agree with Travis." A spectral chime echoed. "Your yammering's starting to get on my nerves." A constant flow of golden light surged from Drew's forearm, bending to form a radiant cavalry saber. "No more games." Drew twisted his wrist and deflected Palatharx's strike with grace. "If you won't take this fight seriously, we will."

My ally's arm whirled like the wind, his burning blade chewing more and more into the armor of Palatharx with each elegant slash. A final thrust sent our enemy soaring in a gush of searing light.

"Get up, Travis." Drew winced. "The hard part's yet to come, so I need you to listen up."

I pulled myself off the ground.

Gruesome horror set in as I looked at Drew's shoulder, covered in fresh lacerations. His breathing had weakened, and he struggled to hold a brave facade. "Palatharx is about to use his Power State." Drew dropped to his knee. "Once he does, he'll have us outclassed by a landslide."

I pointed. "Your arm."

"I know... but I'm not quitting yet," he pulled his scarf off his neck and wrapped it around the wound. "Just taking a little breather."

"Okay."

"I need you to go on full-out offense." Drew looked up at me. "Give him everything you've got... by the time you're worn out, I'll swoop in for the finish."

"No problem." I spread my wings, and my aura intensified. "I've got you covered."

"And one more thing," Drew chuckled. "Just slow down and think, alright? You've got a bad habit of fighting angry... which makes you predictable."

He put my patterns together that quick?

"I'll do what I can." I surged to the sky, with the Sacred Scripture in tow.

Drew's hurt bad... acting like it's nothing. A few more cuts like that, and the guy's going to bleed to death. For his sake, I have to take Palatharx on my own.

The soles of my shoes boomed upon landing, and I found myself staring down at a tomb of rubble.

Palatharx groaned as he twisted free of his prison. "You do know I'm holding back, right?"

Remember Siris. I remained silent. *He let out everything he had in the first rush and lost... just like I did with Kharadin. I have to play this smart.*

"Quiet now, are you?" Palatharx stepped forth and outstretched his arms. "You think you can end my plan... win, shall we say, by killing me? Look around. Do you know where you are?"

If I get him talking... I didn't look at him, but glanced around the area through my steel mask. "Can't say I do."

Timeless masonry formed a helix of symbols all the way to the epicenter of a massive stone platform.

Three pillars bent overhead in the framework of a dome. If I concentrated, I could pick up on a steady murmur from below.

"Time for a lesson." Palatharx took a seat on a crumbled fragment of the pillar. "History with Palatharx... what do you think, is that a good title?"

Keep your guard up, Travis. A thundering longsword manifested in my grasp.

"Suit yourself." Palatharx set his machete aside and cleared his throat. "The very first generation of Exalted rose in a time of great peril... the Realms were being torn asunder, just like they are today. However, during their time, the revolutionary wasn't such a dashing specimen as myself... rather, he was a mad deity."

Guess there's worse ways to spend time with a villain.

"According to legend, the three defenders of the universe banded together and put an end to this malicious figure." Palatharx tapped the side of his head. "But the thing is, history's not always what it seems."

I looked over at the Sacred Scripture. "So, even deities can be bad?"

"The term *bad* is relative..." Palatharx paced on his stage. "But I guess to you, the answer is yes." He shrugged. "According to history, the Exalted fought and imprisoned the Lord of Domination... but the truth is, Yaris is imprisoned beneath our feet."

Yaris, Lord of Domination... I've heard that name before. Still, why is Palatharx taking all this time to tell me a conspiracy theory?

"Enough fluff." I bent my knees and pulled my sword back. "What's the point, Palatharx?"

"The point is," Palatharx's voice vibrated with frustration, "Yaris and I share the same ideals. Both of us want a new world free of suffering." He slowly retrieved his fanged weapon. "Travis... don't you wonder what the big pillars above us are for?"

An eerie silence set in as Palatharx's entire body stiffened. By mere posture, his very being shifted from casual and cocky to the cold demeanor of a hunting panther. His eyes filled with a ghoulish haze as his teeth slowly flashed in a menacing grin.

Fun time's over. My heart pumped harder, spreading a tingling awareness through my muscles. *Remember... fight smart and stall.*

"Think of them like locks, each of them requiring their own respective key." He reached behind his back and presented a shimmering white object the size of a football. "Get it?"

My eyes shot wide. *How?*

Palatharx's stone-clad fingers clutched the glossy surface of a Crystal Shard... the last one needed to complete the task at hand. The two of us faced one another, a fated duel for the right to claim our own separate destinies.

"To open this gate, one must split a Channeling Crystal into three equal pieces, and place them on their pillars." Palatharx tucked the Shard away behind his back. "Thank you for so kindly bringing me the other two."

My arm pushed forward in a flash of adrenaline-fueled instinct, catching Palatharx's descending blade in a rush of raging electricity.

"Ah, how nice." Palatharx smiled as embers began to dance along his skin. "An adversary worthy of facing my true strength. You'd have made a fine ally."

I forced my soul-forged sword forward, deflecting my enemy's attack. "If you weren't a murderous scumbag."

Palatharx growled and closed in with a rush of dexterous slashes, each one coming inches away from contact. Adrenaline roared, twisting and turning my body out of harm's way without the slightest thought.

At last, an opening in Palatharx's assault presented itself.

My eyes narrowed. *He's overextended.*

I thrust out my arm, throwing my opponent back in a surge of sky blue plasma. Palatharx toppled against the stone arena, and rose once more with sizzling flesh.

My foe leered through his wild locks. "You're strong... if only Siris had put up such a fight."

"He was a good man and an even better friend." I raised my weapon and stretched it across my arm, as my teacher once did. "Not like you'd understand."

I outstretched my ethereal wings and engaged Palatharx with a hefty two-handed slash. He matched my pace and deflected my blade with his, the clang echoing in our arena.

A violent burst of red overtook my vision, along with a vicious sting to the entire front of my body.

I clutched my freshly seared arm and panted. *Gotta give it to him, that was impressive.*

Palatharx's entire body, from the stone bottoms of his boots to the undulating strands of his hair, was alive with flitting cinder. Sinister flames twisted around his arms and legs, burning fury which immediately bent to its owner's will.

"Prepare yourself." Palatharx moved his palm along his fanged blade, and his personal inferno spread over it. "None have survived my burning wrath."

His transformation alone packed a punch. I braced myself for scorching impact. *So much power!*

I shoved my attacker back with a firm blow of the shoulder, creating an opening just wide enough for a counterattack... only it wasn't enough.

"I thought you had more in you," Palatharx scoffed then planted his feet, heaving his body weight behind the back edge of his weapon. My perception blurred as I was cast aside, and found myself snagged in a single open palm of my foe. "Take heed, this is a lesson on what true control over your power looks like."

My insides shuffled when I was skipped across the ground, each impact sending a powerful ring in my ears... each collision making everything just a bit fuzzier. By the time I'd come to a stop, I'd been laid flat on my back, absolutely paralyzed and trapped in a mental haze.

The world grew dim, and the heat gradually fizzled from my body.

"Regrettably, you've reached your undoing." Haunting steps clicked. "Now, I'll take the two shards you so graciously fetched for me... and initiate the birth of the new universe."

Palatharx lifted his fragmented crystal overhead, and a blinding white beam surged into the sky. Clouds twisted, creating a hurricane of black and red... just waiting for what came next.

With two isolated flashes, the Crystal Shards collected by Arvel and I were ripped from the Sacred Scripture, and before long the book thudded down beside me, motionless.

Come on... Each breath stung as I helplessly watched the unfolding disaster. *I need to stop this!*

"The moment is so near..." Palatharx slammed his fist into the etched surface of the battleground, forcing a pillar of light into every crevice. "Now, to deal with you."

I can still fight... I pressed everything I had against my body, but it refused to even twitch. *All I need to do is get up.*

"You see, you never did stand a chance. Your whole band of friends... Mohandar, Chad, Arvel, your Father, that dear little Kate..." Palatharx paced over and planted his boot on my chest. "They filled you with hope. They made you think you were something great, when after all, you were just another kid." He glanced off as he lifted his machete. "Perhaps I'll kill them after I'm done with you."

With lightning speed, my hand snagged the glistening edge of my executioner's weapon.

Get up.

War drums were beating in my chest. With every resounding thump, my blood grew brighter, and my grip on the sword clasped harder. The Sacred Scripture pulsed along with me, in the song of revival. My body, as if rising from the grave, slowly unfolded until I found myself standing, eye to eye with a terrified foe.

My grip tightened... and the solid blade of Palatharx's machete burst.

My chilling gaze pierced through Palatharx. "Don't threaten the people I care about... ever."

TWENTY-FIVE

"Alright guys, brace!" With Chad in one arm and Arvel in the other, I landed at the foot of the mountain. Without sparing a second, my friends wriggled free of my ironclad arms and collapsed.

Arvel stretched out on his back and sighed. "You've got the grasp of an eagle, you know?"

"Seconded." Chad shivered and brushed the frost from his exposed forearms. "Loosen up, will ya?"

I pulled my helm off and shrugged. "I could've just dropped you a few thousand feet if you want. Better safe than dead, if you ask me."

Uncomfortable silence dawned, bringing the weight of a hundred gazes on my back. With a slight turn, I beheld the petrified face of a big bearded townsman... and behind him, the entire village marketplace.

A community of mannequins watched us with their unwavering gaze.

What the... The breath fled my lungs, and the grim nature of reality set in. *You've gotta be kidding.* My face went straight into my palm.

If you fail to return the Channeling Crystal, and allow the Realms to merge... Mohandar's council bounced in the corners of my mind. *It will be a matter of hours before time itself ceases to exist.*

I took a knee with a long sigh. "We were so close."

"Easy there, lad!" A hearty chuckle came from close by. "No need to look so scared. We're shocked, that's all."

My body buckled over in response to an involuntary gag, followed by profuse wheezing.

The townsman winked. "You just jumped off of the Stairway to the Stars, the tallest mountain in Reach... and lived." An elbow dinged against my armor. "Pretty impressive, if I do say so myself."

Too close... scared the life right out of me. I gave an effigy of a smile. "Thanks. We're just passing through."

As if by cue, the entire town resumed their duties. Shoppers haggled, merchants called, and hefty men carted around wheelbarrows full of produce between the network of stalls... leaving us mere faces among the crowd.

"Let's go find something to do." Arvel tapped my back. "We don't have to leave quite yet, so let's enjoy the company of the people."

"We're on a clock, Arvel," I sighed. "I'm sorry, but I don't think we've got any time to spare."

"Come on," he put an arm on my shoulder. "Half hour, maybe an hour at the least. I don't think the Realms will explode in that amount of time, do you?"

Chad wandered off, just out of earshot.

Arvel lowered his voice, speaking with concern. "In all of our travels, I haven't seen you get rattled once." Arvel pulled off his hood. "What is it?"

I glanced up at the sky. "I'm fine."

"You're a horrible liar." Arvel's tone deepened. "Spit it out."

"Alright, alright..." I chewed on my words, "the way they were so still... had me thinking we were too late."

"I understand." Arvel crossed his arms. "But the damage gets *reversed* a little more for each one of the crystal's pieces we have. It'd be downright impossible for time to run out this early. After tonight, we'll set course for the third shard... and it'll all blow over."

I looked over at Chad and lowered my voice. "There's a slight issue with that."

For a brief second, Arvel's eyes became those of an agitated cobra.

"I know where the third shard is, and it's not even in Reach."

Arvel took a deep breath. "I need to get something before this goes any farther."

In a flash, we found ourselves in the nearest tavern, seated at a round table as Chad threw darts with a few of the commoners.

I watched as Arvel lifted an entire mug of bubbling goodness to his mouth, and downed the whole thing. Slamming it on the table, he took a moment to process what I'd given him... then spoke.

"Now... you're telling me you and another Exalted took on this guy, and not only has he made you a pair of skinned-and-ready chickens, but he's *also* gotten all three of the shards we need?" He fought off a belch, to a glorious failure. "I might as well just leave."

I laughed. "And go where?"

"I don't know, anywhere I can get a break from all these gods, and Exalted, and constant threats of everything blowing up..." He sighed. "Can we come back from this?"

"We haven't lost yet." I tapped my fingers on the table. "Sure, Drew's got a cut up arm and I'm beyond my energy reserves, but—"

"Hold on." Arvel raised his hand to the bartender. "Another, if I may." His focus returned. "Continue."

"I'll get the Shards back." I watched as the Sacred Scripture scooped up Arvel's mug. "And then we can finally put this whole ordeal behind us."

"Alright, I won't dig into it any deeper. You're wigged out enough already, talking about it's not going to make you go back any faster." Arvel winked. "But in all seriousness, kick some butt when you do."

That's what I'm talking about. I smiled. "Will do."

"Speaking of butt kicking... what are your thoughts on Chad?" Arvel watched as the bartender walked his fresh drink over. "You guys go way back, I can tell... but just by the look in your eyes, I gather he hasn't been like you for very long."

Finally.

"Dang straight." I watched Chad hurl a dart across the room, only to flat out miss and arouse the uncontrolled laughter of the entire tavern. "In all honesty, I can't quite wrap my brain around it. Chad's been my idiotic conscience since we were little, and I was the one who beat up the kids who made fun of him. When he was in his Power State... it wasn't him."

Arvel set down another sloshing mug on the table with a thud. "Kind of like he became someone else."

"Exactly." I rapped my hand against the tabletop. "And then, when I teamed up with Drew, it hit me. You remember what Chad said before he completely obliterated that golem guy?"

"Let's turn up the heat." Arvel lifted his mug, and the Sacred Scripture didn't hesitate to toast. "Like some kind of catch phrase."

I pointed to Arvel. "When Drew got ready to fight Palatharx, he said the *exact same thing.*"

Arvel twitched, and immediately engaged in a beer-induced coughing fit. He held his chest and let out a final gag. "You don't think—"

I rubbed the bristles on my chin. "He and Drew are likely body doubles, just like Siris and I. I'm pretty sure Drew took Chad over in order to fight Kharadin... I don't know what that means for Chad, but I guess we'll find out."

"Don't get ahead of yourself, friend." Arvel grinned. "Get our shards back first."

"Hey... thanks."

"No problem." Arvel adjusted his cape on his back. "Now, why don't we—"

Chad's voice tore through the commotion. "Alright everyone, this one's going right on the bull's eye!"

A vigorous eruption of orange overtook the room as a miniature missile soared across the bar.

Arvel and I locked gazes.

Chairs, tables, and the tavern wall scrambled under the force of a Chad-powered explosion.

Daylight graced the quivering image of his face, his supernatural aura slowly fizzling out. One by one, the stern expressions of the entire bar focused on the new town jester.

Chad let out a faint, unsure laugh. "At least nobody got hurt, right?"

A single brick fell onto the belly of an unfortunate man who'd been blown through the side of the tavern... and a few men got up from their benches.

Leave it to Chad...

"Wait, wait, wait!" Arvel waved his hand to the crowd. "Before you do anything..."

Everyone watched as the bowman took a gratuitously long moment to enjoy the last of his drink.

With a thump, Arvel set the empty mug down. "Alright."

We bolted out of our seats, each of us snagging one of Chad's arms along the way.

Night found us as we all laughed around the light of a bonfire, a good ten miles away from our loving friends at the foot of the mountain.

"Chad, I've never seen you so scared in my entire life." I clutched my gut, aching from over-exposure to hilarity. "We really need to get that power of yours under control."

"Can you really blame me?" Chad looked over at his new companion, the godly scripture from Grrogum, with a grimace. "I *doubt* you had much of a grip this early, either."

Memories of my training with Mohandar arose... and that infernal sphere. I looked away.

"Couple minutes of study, had it down on the first day."

Arvel perked up and put a finger in my face. "Liar, liar!"

"Shut up, Arvel!" I grunted. "Nobody asked for your opinion."

I took one last breath of pure joy, looking to the stars.

Alright... no more goofing off. No doubt I'm headed back before tomorrow morning.

My eyes narrowed.

Like Arvel said... I've got butt to kick.

TWENTY-SIX

Fragmented metal danced in the wind, the broken pieces of a former instrument of death. Each bit glistened in the presence of a freshly-kindled inferno.

The altar beneath Palatharx and I rumbled as the tension between two warriors grew stronger. One purposeful step at a time, I closed the distance between us... as burning fury grew.

Kate... Chad... Arvel... Dad... Mohandar... Everything on Earth... everything on Reach, gone. I opened my palm and welcomed the sound of raging lightning. *That's what'll happen if I lose.*

Palatharx stepped back, his hands in the air. "My blade is unbreakable... how could you—"

"If you would've talked to Siris, or even Mohandar, you'd know..." I maintained eye contact as the leather straps of my mask burned through, and the steel covering hit the stone below with a ding. "I get dangerous when I'm angry."

"I'm not scared of you, kid. It's all a façade, I'll just put you on the ground again." Palatharx heaved his weight into a right hook, only to find it trapped in my inescapable grasp.

I tightened my grip on his hand, cracking its stone shell.

"So, what're you going to do?" Palatharx looked up at the pulsing Crystal Shards. "Kill me?"

"No." My palm snagged his face, and forced a steady stream of uncontrolled voltage through his body. "What good would come from that?"

His knees buckled and cast him to the ground, covered in racing streaks of neon blue. When the attack ceased, Palatharx was a wheezing shell of his former self.

"Scripture, get the shards back." My book zipped off. "Make sure you get the third one, while you're at it."

"Mercy?" He laughed, collapsing to the stone surface below. "You do realize I'll just come back stronger, and do it all over again?"

"You won't." I knelt down and looked him in the eyes. "And if you do, I'll just put you on the ground again... however many times it takes. I didn't ask to be Exalted, but I'm not one to back out of a job."

Palatharx growled, "Spare me the virtues, we both know you're an apathetic jerk. Just because you have strength and a cause doesn't make you the *hero* they call you."

"I never said it did." I turned my back and headed off, the Sacred Scripture descending to my side. "Never said I was good, either."

"Insolent child, what are you doing?" Palatharx was now screaming beyond all sense. "Kill me!"

I didn't answer, but kept walking.

A flare of sunset orange rose behind us. "So be it."

"*Drew!*" I whipped around and threw my hands in the air. "Why?"

"If a villain this bad *asks* you to kill him..." Drew placed his boot heel on Palatharx's body, and withdrew his translucent saber from Palatharx's open back. "You do. I know it's harsh, but justice isn't warm and fuzzy."

A faint laugh came from the face-down figure of Palatharx. "See you in the new world."

A creeping fog cascaded around his body... in a few seconds, anything hinting at the Realm-wide menace was gone.

"Thanks for your help." Drew lowered his scarf and looked up at the blood-red sky. "With him gone, we can finally get the Realms fixed and get back to our lives." He clutched his bloody arm and lowered himself to the ground. "Let's just take a breather for now. We've won, after all."

The Sacred Scripture raced around me, yipping as it did so.

I sighed. "Guess you're right... all we have to do is put this thing back on its tower, and we'll be home—"

My Power State faded, giving rise to a sudden pain... like an invisible spear cut through my chest. My knees wobbled underneath me, and my breaths completely stopped.

What the... my body thumped against the ground. *Where'd I get hit from?*

"It's called *Burnout*." Drew's voice came from aside. "A technique few Exalted dare use. Burnout grants them immense pain tolerance and boosted strength, but can only be used at the end of one's Soul Energy reserves."

Would've been nice to know before I'd gone into it...

"This is why you don't use the Burnout technique unless it's your absolute last resort. In exchange for power, you cause severe damage to your body." Drew dropped to his knees, and a soft warmth spread over me. "Burnout's like an adrenaline rush for your Soul Energy. It blots out the real pain until it leaves you, then you're absolutely screwed."

Yeah, I get it... The agony ceased. *This is why Mohandar said to stay within my limits.*

"Be more careful from now on." Drew stood up, and mobility returned to my body. "If I hadn't been here to heal you, you'd have killed yourself."

"Will do." I pulled myself to my feet. "Guess I'll be seeing more of you now, huh?"

"I don't think so." Drew reached into his pocket and pulled out a box the size of his palm... an oddly familiar model. "We may be allies, but you and I are on different paths."

I picked up my mask, brushing it off as I did so. "We're both Exalted, aren't we?"

"Yeah... but I'm a little sick of it." He stroked the polished, finished wooden craft between his fingers. "You're in charge of the Channeling Crystal, but Grrogum has me out there *specifically* to fight. You gotta keep in mind that there's five more Realms... each with their own problems to solve."

He's watching over five of the Realms... and still, he came here to help take care of Palatharx?

"Anyway, there's something else I gotta do before I need to leave." He extended his hand, along with the black box. "Take this. Jen Shepard told me to pass it to you a long time ago."

"Wait, from Mom?" I accepted the gift with unintended haste. "...Thanks."

Another one? I wrapped my fingers around the lid. *What could it possibly—*

"Easy. I know you haven't seen her in... a while, but why don't you just hold on to it for a bit?" Drew snickered. "We're not gonna get many more opportunities to talk... especially since your buddy, Chad, made it into the equation."

For a brief second, we exchanged blank expressions.

I set the box down. "About that—"

"Yeah. I'm his soul bond, and I'm probably gonna give him the reins soon enough." Drew adjusted his sandy blond bangs, pausing to take a look at his blood-moistened fingers. "It's about time someone else got a turn at this job... anyway, you probably want to know how I got the box, huh?"

I took some steady breaths. "I can't say it's really bugging me."

"Truth is, some ten years ago, I apprenticed under one of the *greatest* Exalted to ever grace the Realms. Jennifer Shepard, Exalted of Cydea... she was unmatched in both power and wisdom. I won't give you the documentary version, but we travelled together between the Realms and kept them safe. Then, somewhere along the way, we went our separate ways. The last order she ever gave me was to make sure you got this package."

"Thanks, Drew." I put the box in my pocket. "I guess I'll see you around."

As I approached the Invasion Scar, the Sacred Scripture flared bright. The battleground faded, its details twisting as I walked through... before long, I was home.

***

The midday sun cast a light of tranquility upon every blade of grass as they bent to the will of the breeze... twisting along with the wildflowers, weeds and ferns of the seemingly endless meadows. Billowing clouds drifted overhead, greeting my view as I flopped onto the grass.

I can't believe Palatharx is actually gone. No more disruptions, no more obstacles. Arvel and I can fix these Realms for good, and not have to worry about them coming back together.

I took a deep breath of natural bliss.

I can't say I ever expected to make it this far... but we're so close. So close to peace.

I tracked a cloud with the face of a man as it drifted past the sun.

What am I gonna do when there's nobody left to fight?

A sudden idea popped into my head, and I whipped my phone out. With a few taps on the screen, it started ringing.

"Hey, Kate?" I smiled. "You there?"

"No, I'm not," she giggled. "Leave a message."

"I know it's been a while... sorry about that." I stroked the very top of a thistle bloom. "Things are looking like they might take a slower turn up ahead, and I was wondering..."

You're an idiot. Do you realize how close you come to getting yourself killed every day? Just let her—

"...Well?" Her voice came through muffled. "Wondering what?"

"It's been a while since I've had a chance to just relax, with all the... you know." I sat up and looked around. "I was wondering if you might want to hang out tomorrow?"

"Are you kidding me?"

I flinched. "Oh... sorry."

"No, no, not like that." A quick sigh came through. "I haven't seen you in forever! Absolutely."

I flopped back onto the ground. "Alright."

"Alright."

"Alright." I rolled my eyes at myself as I hung up. *Alright...*

I twisted in the grass, and a sturdy, block-shaped object prodded against me. *Drew's box!*

I whipped the polished wooden container out of my pocket and set it on the grass. "Here we go..." I loomed over the gift, lifting its lid. "What've we got in here, Mom?"

Under a familiar, expertly folded layer of velvety cloth, I found a small note.

Travis, my boy...

If you've gotten this one, it means Andrew's finally found you... hope you two hit it off, you've got a lot in common!

I rolled my eyes.

Don't roll your eyes, mister.

"Nice one, Mom."

Even so... let's get to the fun part. The first one I gave you was your Realm Stone... a tool to familiarize yourself with our world. This time, I've left you something much more valuable. Not even Mohandar can teach you how to use it... it's all up to you.

When you're ready, take a look... and read your final note very carefully.

I reached to the bottom of the box, and found the last piece of my own personal puzzle.

TWENTY-SEVEN

Arvel, Chad and I slowly traversed the swaying valleys of Reach... the blue sky smiled down upon us as we made the trek to return the Channeling Crystal of the Realms.

Chad lifted his arms over his head. "Home stretch."

"Finally." Arvel gave Chad a nudge. "Imagine how you'd feel if you'd been here for the whole ride."

I snickered.

Chad's eyes got big and he stuck his nose right up to mine. "What are you laughing at?"

I shook my head. "Would've taken a lot longer."

"Would not!" Chad stomped. "You saw how I—"

"Oh no, what is this weird glowy place?" I mirrored Chad's flamingo-like demeanor from the night he arrived in Reach. "This must be a government experiment."

Chad's burning Power State exploded outward. "I'm strong now, got it? You're not the only one around here who can be the hero, not anymore!"

I crossed my arms. "Think you can take me, huh?"

"I'll bet." Chad clenched his fists, burning brighter.

I responded by unleashing my inner storm. "Show me what you've got... *chicken wings.*"

"Enough." A firm grip set in on my plated shoulder. "There'll be plenty of time for you two to swing all you've got at one another once we get this crystal where it belongs."

Man's got a point... I released my Power State. *I'll beat Chad up later.*

Chad twitched his sweltering fingers. "Let me have a go at him, just a *tiny* bit."

"Not a chance." Arvel pushed the two of us apart and kept walking on. "You don't have the slightest control of your *literally* explosive personality. With an ability like yours, you'll burn up this entire valley over a whim." He outstretched his arms. "There's a lot of life here... Let's not kill things we don't need to, alright?"

"Yeah, alright." Chad's aura flickered and died. "How do I control my Super State, though?"

"First of all, it's *Power State*." I stretched my wings out. "You control it with your head, and your willpower determines potency. Mohandar's gonna give you the rundown soon enough." Something in my mind clicked. "Speaking of which, we need to get you home, and soon."

"Oh man, you're right." Chad grabbed his cheeks and squeaked. "My parents probably think I'm *dead!*"

"They haven't knocked on my door yet..." I snapped my fingers. "Oh yeah, I told Dad to tell them we've been camping."

"Wait, these books travel between the Realms, don't they?" Chad caught eye of his book, drifting along at his side. "Can I just ask it to—"

The Scripture of Grrogum spared no moment of hesitation. It encircled Chad with blinding speed, and they were gone in a blink.

Arvel and I were purely dumbfounded, staring at the empty space Chad left us.

Arvel pointed to the flattened grass. "Did he just?"

"Yeah."

"And the book?"

"Yeah."

Arvel took a brief glance at the Sacred Scripture. "I've got an idea."

The Sacred Scripture moaned quietly as it played with the meadow's puff-covered dandelions.

"I don't know..." I tapped its cover. "Hey, buddy. You think you can warp us to Daedalus Stronghold?"

My book tilted to the side and chimed.

"What do you mean you don't know?" I sighed. "Have you *never* tried it before?"

It shook its cover.

Of all its centuries of existing. I rubbed my forehead. "You want to give it a shot?"

My book yipped and zapped Arvel and I with a fizzling beam. With a pop, the valley was gone... and my insides lurched upward.

My eyes opened wide to find the same field... only from a few hundred feet straight up.

Arvel's cape fluttered around his spinning body. "What did that devil of a book do?"

Whoa, whoa, whoa! I fanned my wings out, but couldn't stabilize the descent. "Scripture, put us back on the ground!"

Pop.

Arvel and I both laid sprawled on our backs, with eyes on the sky as my jolly little book returned to study its dandelion.

I panted, and shifted my wings. "No... it can't."

Arvel snorted, and his infectious laugh spread.

***

The stars welcomed us at the end of a day filled with travel, casting their light upon our camp in a craggy mountainside. Far out in the distance, the moon peered over the horizon.

I perched on the edge of the cliff, taking in the moonlight.

It's beautiful out here. Shame we're always on the move. I squinted at a bizarre element in the cosmos. *What's that?*

A single streak of white flickered against the stars. Splintering lines expanded from it, just like a broken piece of glass... and, if I looked hard enough, the shape seemed to ripple.

"Hey, Arvel." I beat my wings and hovered beside my friend, who was sharpening the edges of his bows a few levels higher. "Take a look at this."

I pointed to the enigma, and waited as he rubbed his chin and groaned.

Man... I touched down beside Arvel and listened. *He only makes that sound when he's really thinking—*

"I don't see it."

I once again directed his attention to the tiny little crack in the night. "Right there. It looks like cracked glass, doesn't it?"

Arvel gazed out once more, and shrugged. "I don't see anything. Sorry."

Could it be like the wolf? I took off my helmet and placed it beside me. *Arvel didn't see him, but Chad did... maybe this is another Exalted only—*

"Oh, there it is!"

My face went straight into my palm.

"Yeah, that doesn't look normal." Arvel looked over to me with a serious expression. "Kind of like the sky's got a crack in it?"

"Yeah..." I chewed on the corner of my mouth. "Not like I just said it."

Arvel picked up his grinding stone and went back to work. "Let's hope it's nothing *abnormally* disruptive... but just in case, let's hustle tomorrow. We'll be at Daedalus Stronghold by the end of the day."

"Got it."

With the matter closed, I took to the skies... but I couldn't ditch a clawing feeling in my stomach.

I rolled on my back, and peered at the mystery object one last time. Immediately, the tiniest whisper creeped at the edge of my ear.

That's not human... that's a deity.

TWENTY-EIGHT

My room was silent, the entire world hushed in the presence of a scholar immersed in his studies. The chill of the breeze, the rattling of a woodpecker, not even the constant rock music playing could distract me from the task at hand.

I held my chin against my palm, each word snowballing as I read the second part of Mom's note.

Travis,

This is my last note to you. Though it pains me to say it, I've been a terrible mother. I left the life I loved for the higher calling of defending the Realms from a horrible, horrible threat. Leaving my beloved husband and you, our half-blood son, I stood up to those seeking to end life as we all knew it. The sheer truth of the matter is, people like us can either have life as a human or life as Exalted. There's no in-between. Not a day goes by where I don't wish I could come back, and make things right.

I tightened my fist, and illuminated blue blood flowed through it.

Knowing you, Travis, you'll have a hard time forgiving—

I pushed the paper aside, and it twirled to the floor. "Unbelievable."

I rose to my feet, but found myself ensnared by a single closing statement.

Travis, to put it into terms you'll understand... you're far beyond human, and beyond Exalted. You're a—

The rest had been singed off by some idiot Exalted with a short fuse.

"No..." I dropped to my knees, and scrambled to get the smoldering note. "Travis, you *idiot!*"

With what was now a cluster of cinders, I peered into the tiny wooden box. Inside was a puzzle of a gift... and I'd thrown away my only clue as to what it even was.

Swaddled in fine cloth, a spherical glass holding rays of white incandescence awaited. The lights twisted in their transparent confines.

The soft radiance reflected on the box lid, revealing writing etched into the grainy underside.

Once you open the bottle, you can't go back.

I walked off. "We'll save that for later, then."

***

Lunch rolled around, bringing Dad to a local steakhouse... where each of us dug into hearty cuts of prime rib.

Dad about choked on his drink. "How did Chad manage to turn Exalted?"

"Who knows, but he definitely saved our skins." I chuckled. "He's not as strong as I am, and can't control his powers well... but he did a good job."

"Arvel sounds pretty cool, too." Dad smiled. "Sounds like he's quite patient."

I sighed. "I wish you could see the way he and Chad bicker."

Dad's eyebrows went up.

"Chad's insufferable at times... and in contrast, Arvel's the calmest person you'll ever meet." I tapped my fingers on the table. "We were drinking in this tavern—"

Dad's expression got tense.

"*Arvel* was drinking in this tavern, and we were talking things over while Chad was playing darts. Out of the blue, Chad gets all wound up and heaves one with everything he's got... and he blew a hole right in the side of the building."

Dad felt his arm. "Takes a lot of manpower to destroy buildings with a throwing dart... you sure he's not as strong as you?"

I waved my hand to Dad. "Chad's Power State is heat based, like mine is electrically based. Combine a lot of heat with the inability to contain it, and what happens?"

"Explosions." Dad rubbed his forehead. "Not good."

I shook my head.

"So." Dad set his utensils down and leaned back. "What'd she give you?"

It took a second to catch up to Dad.

"I can't tell you for sure. I was reading the note that came with it, but then I got angry and... destroyed it."

Dad pulled the special drinks menu from its holder. "If it got you that steamed, I won't ask why. Still, describe it. Maybe I can help, for once."

I took a sip of bubbling soda. "It's this perfectly spherical bottle, like a beaker." I made a claw shape with my fingers. "About this big, and filled with light."

"Light?" Dad's eyes got big. "Oh, no... anything but that."

"The box says that once I open it, I can't go back. How can I even consider the options if I don't know what it does?" I cut into my steak.

"Listen." Dad leaned forward and looked me right in the eyes. "Do you remember how Mohandar told you that you were only *half* human?"

I nodded.

"He wasn't talking about your potential to be Exalted. Anyone can be Exalted, and Chad's living proof of it." Dad looked around the restaurant and lowered his voice. "That vial is the key to unlocking your other half. Such strength can save worlds, but it's dangerous to all of us... and even more so to yourself. I need you to promise me something, right now."

I straightened up. "What is it?"

"Promise me you won't open that bottle unless it's your absolute last resort."

"...Okay, Dad."

After we finished, we were off once more.

"Thanks for the ride." I hopped out of the truck onto unfamiliar ground. "I'll be back by six."

Dad put the truck into gear. "We live right down the road, just be back by dark."

I waved. "Yeah, of course."

Ahead was a two-floor house with a white picket fence and tannish yellow walls. A twisting sidewalk led to a teal-painted front porch, where a two-person swing rocked in the breeze. Just behind the house, twisting evergreens reached to the clouds.

Nice place. I nodded to myself. *Really nice place.*

My shoes clicked against the sidewalk as I moved around a lively flowerbed and made my way up the stairs of the porch.

Alright. I reached my hand up to knock. *It's nothing weird, so don't get weird. We're just—*

The door swung open before my knuckle could even make contact.

"Hey." Kate's emerald eyes lit up, and a smile came across her face. "...You're late."

I gave her a feigned smile. "Sorry about that... *work*, I guess you'd call it."

A moment of uncomfortable silence took over.

"Well, no use just standing here." Kate opened the door wider. "Come on in."

She bounced into her living room, where we were met by a glass coffee table and a matching sofa and loveseat both made from a lighter brown fabric. Curtains hung beside windows across the side of the room, and a potent scent of lavender expanded through the house.

Kate spun onto the far side of the couch, its soft cushions bending under her weight. "How's life?"

"Well lately, pretty heated..." I slowly took a seat at the other end of the couch. "I've had two major— "

"Nope." She clapped, loud. "Do it again."

I raised an eyebrow. "Do what?"

"You're being... awkward. Yeah, you're in my house, but *relax.*" She twirled her finger and straightened up. "Sit down again, like you normally would."

I shrugged, rose from my seat, and... did it again.

"We'll work on it." Kate slid to the center cushion of the sofa. "Anyway, continue."

I gave a nervous laugh. "I can't say all that much has happened, just the usual... fighting the bad guys, trying to keep the world from breaking." I straightened up. "Oh yeah, Chad's Exalted now."

A playful, but surprisingly firm shove came from my left. "Why wouldn't you lead with that?"

"Yeah, it's nuts. The dynamic duo's in business."

"Everyone's in the action but me." Kate sighed. "Yay."

"*You* got to plow an oar into the eye of a monster, which bought enough time for us to survive an impossible battle." I gave her a playful nudge with my elbow. "You're just as much a part of the crew as anyone... anyway, how've you been?"

"Me? I haven't done that much." She took a deep breath and leaned back. "Dad left for a job out of town yesterday, so I've been a little lonely... I've just been watching movies, and wondering what everyone else is up to."

"Movies?" I glanced around the room. "What're you into?"

"I like superhero movies." She twirled her hair and shrugged. "Sorry if that's a little strange, since you *are* one."

I shook my head with a chuckle. "Me, a superhero? Good one."

"Alright, alright..." She lifted her finger. "You wouldn't want to watch one with me, would you?"

A movie? An hour and a half of doing nothing... I nodded. "Sounds wonderful."

"Cool." She snatched up her remote to the flat-screen TV and tapped it once. "I kind of had it going when you showed up." She brushed some fuzz off the cushions of the couch. "Can you tell I cleaned up the *entire* place knowing you were coming over?"

I smiled. "Air freshener."

She propped her elbow on the back of the couch. "Yeah, I went a little overboard... you said you might be hitting a break in your hero stuff soon?"

"We've gotten all three Crystal Shards, and we're headed to put 'em back." My fingers flitted against the couch cushions.

"You won't be gone doing things all the time anymore?" Her eyes lit up. "And I won't have to worry about you—"

She covered her mouth, and her cheeks went rosy.

She worries about me? I rubbed my chin. "Yeah, at least I think. I can't say for sure, but I think Mohandar might ease up on training when there's not the pressure of large scale disaster, you know?"

She smiled, and brushed a curled strand of hair away from her eyes. "It'd be kind of nice."

"Yeah... kind of nice."

A familiar, pixelated singing crossed from behind... and the Sacred Scripture's dull blue cover poked between us.

"Oh sure." I waved my hands at my literary companion. "You're nice, too... When did you get here, anyway?"

The book gave a few sassy tones and hovered off into the halls of Kate's home.

"Hey, no messes." I pointed as it slipped out of view. "This isn't our house."

Kate raised an eyebrow. "You talk to it, now?"

I grimaced. "...Yeah."

She giggled. "You're a book whisperer."

"Hardly." I took a moment to count the list of items absolutely destroyed by the Sacred Scripture. "It's like living with a toddler. A strong and intelligent toddler."

The Sacred Scripture vocally responded from the distance.

I stayed until dark, and left Kate with a warm feeling I can't really describe. Something *missing,* something I hadn't felt since... forever. It put a spring in my step and a joy in the way I looked at things as I bounced along home, without a care in the world. Of course, that couldn't last.

In the dead of night, my teacher appeared from the air, his cloak fluttering and his staff burning from within.

"Get Chad and come to the Observatory, and quickly."

His body was silhouetted against the moon, amplifying the grave tone of his words.

"Yaris, the Lord of Domination, is alive."

TWENTY-NINE

The sun inched over the horizon, bringing light to the morning. The distant skyline became a brilliant gold, and the clouds were grayed in the presence of the burning globe behind them.

The road to Daedalus Stronghold was ahead, the final leg of our journey in Reach. Before long, we'd be ready to return the Channeling Crystal to its rightful home.

I pulled the front of my helm over my face. "You ready?"

"Last day of travel." Arvel adjusted his bows. "Let's go."

We leaned forward, ready to descend, but were stopped dead in our tracks by a fizzling sound from behind.

"Hold up, Arvel." I turned around. "What is it, Mohandar?"

My teacher rose from his knees, and his cloak caught the wind. "I was going to wait to discuss these matters with you, but time is of the essence."

Arvel angled his body to Mohandar. "And who are you?"

"I am Mohandar, Observer of the Realms and instructor of Travis." Mohandar performed a slight bow. "You need to hear this."

Arvel loosened his posture. "You have my attention."

"Matters have grown dark." Mohandar's tone lowered. "Yaris, the formerly imprisoned Lord of Domination, has been set free. With the Realms in their current condition, there's no doubt he'll make a grand entrance. In short, my friends... what little time we had has been ripped out from under us."

I rolled my tongue in my mouth. "So, what should we do?"

"Get to Daedalus Stronghold as fast as you possibly can." Mohandar clenched his fist in front of his body. "Once the Channeling Crystal is back in its place, Yaris won't be able to enter our world." Mohandar extended his staff to the clouds. "Keep an eye on this, while you're at it."

I found myself staring at the celestial anomaly from last night. It had without a doubt grown bigger... double the size.

Arvel adjusted his cape. "What is it?"

"The pathway between us and the land of the gods." Mohandar stepped out onto the edge of the mountain and gazed at it. "If it opens, Yaris' Divine Army will burst forth... Last time they walked the Realms, countless souls were lost. Do not underestimate their bloodthirst."

I bounced the thought around in my head. "So we'll fight them off."

"Easier said than done." Mohandar set his hand on my shoulder. "The Divine Army is without match, and Yaris even more so."

Arvel snickered. "This guy's done his research."

"No." Mohandar's cloak flared upward behind him. "I *lived* it. I've seen firsthand what we're up against, what kind of destruction they cause... so I urge you, with the deepest of sincerities, to make haste. In the meantime, I'll begin training Chad for battle."

"Thanks, Mohandar." I nodded. "Best of luck. You'll need it with Chad."

"Fortune is of no matter. Faith and effort make the difference." Mohandar faded back into a fine mist.

I looked over at Arvel and fanned out my wings. "Well, no use waiting."

"Truth." Arvel stretched out his arms. "Fastest way to travel, right?"

"No doubt about it." I sparked my Power State. "When the Realms are counting on you, who's got time to walk?"

Arvel plowed into me with a full-force tackle, and we dropped off the cliffside. With the plummet to boost us, we forged on.

***

Towering walls of polished white stone gleamed in the setting sun. Numerous buildings jutted up from within, but one in particular stood out... the rising spire of Daedalus Tower. A hollow pocket in its head framed the sun eye of twilight, like a lighthouse watching our approach.

"Hey, bud." Arvel wheezed in my grasp. "Can you put me down? I gotta—"

I brought us to a swift halt and set him on the flat grassland below.

"Arvel, if you needed to be on the ground, why didn't you say—" I turned away. "Whoa."

Arvel dropped to his knees and gagged a few times... then fired away.

I cringed at the sound. "Man, that's really coming out."

"Little bit for the plants, eh?" Arvel wiped his mouth and stood up.

The Sacred Scripture threw a fit of obscure, high-pitched cries, and twisted its cover in protest.

"Yeah," I chuckled. "Just take a breather, alright? I'm sure we have time."

The ground beneath us writhed in a fit of rage. Trees toppled, soil cracked and split, and... Arvel heaved once more.

This is starting to feel like London...

Eventually, the commotion died down and I turned my focus to the sky.

The gateway to doom swelled, now large enough to devour clouds that strayed too close.

Arvel slugged me on the shoulder. "You were saying?"

I extended my hand. "Just aim off to the side, try not to stain my wings."

With a forceful boom, we ascended.

Arvel pointed up ahead. "You see that?"

My eyes went numb from a brutal flash, ears screeching as a blitzkrieg of air swatted us down. After being dragged by the gale forces, I lifted my head and shook myself back to life.

A billow of crimson smoke rose above the distant city.

We can't catch a break, can we?

THIRTY

The Observatory was quiet as Mohandar conducted one of his legendary sermons. Chad and I found ourselves inside a massive pyramid-shaped room with a perfectly square floor of midnight tiles.

Our teacher levitated with arms out to his sides. "So... in Palatharx's efforts, he unleashed the Mad Deity Yaris to lay waste to the Realms. You two are valuable assets to make sure that doesn't happen. To conclude... we need to get to work, and fast." Mohandar folded his arms. "Young Chad, are you alright?"

My friend stood petrified, skin paler than snow and legs quivering. "You want us to do *what?*" His voice echoed off the walls from sheer volume. "Please, tell me I didn't hear you right!"

"In the event Travis runs out of time, I need you to be prepared." Mohandar descended with grace. "Not only will you stand against the Divine Army of Yaris, you'll need to be prepared to face the Lord of Domination himself."

"Look at us!" Chad wiggled my arm. "Do you *really* think Travis and I are going to have a shred of a chance against such terrible odds? He's just one guy, and I... while I hate to admit it, have *zero* control over my Power State."

"You doubt my abilities." Mohandar's cloak began to flutter. "In a few days' time, I'll have you disciplined enough to give Travis a run for his money." Mohandar stretched. "Now then... let's begin." He rose into the air with grace, landing between Chad and me. "Travis, most of this will be review. I hope that's alright."

I smirked. "Gotta keep the foundations strong, right?"

Mohandar's really calm... Even under the circumstances, he's playing it off like we've got it covered. Even I know we're in serious trouble here. Reach is starting to show signs of collapsing... earthquakes, explosions, not to mention the gigantic portal in the—

Before long, Mohandar had us side by side and training away.

Mohandar held his fist to his chest. "To activate your Power State by will, you must search deep within and find the connection between yourself and your book."

I watched as Chad squinted and strained to reach his inner being... to no avail.

"Travis."

I straightened up. "Yes, sir."

Chad snorted. "Since when do you call *anyone* sir?"

"Since I figured out Mohandar can put just about anyone on their back with one finger." I tensed my muscles. "What is it, Mohandar?"

"Please demonstrate your transition to Power State. Perhaps a visual example will provide some aid."

"Sure thing." I puffed my chest out, and a flow of electricity followed. "Better?"

A blistering heat expanded by my side, marking Chad's ascension. "Now, that's more like it! What's next?"

"Sparring... but first, I'll introduce Chad to the elementary principles of control." Mohandar approached and squeezed Chad's skinny arm. "...So it's not a simple boxing match."

"Did you hear that?" Chad's head snapped toward me. "We're gonna fight."

"You better believe it." I nodded. *And I'll show you what I'm made of.*

"Pay attention, Chad." Mohandar held out his palm, and a brilliant flow of violet energy twisted from it. "Can you grab hold of your Power State, like so?"

I remember this torture.

Chad mirrored Mohandar in posture and aura. "Sure."

"Good." Mohandar lowered his view and studied Chad's glow. "Next, using only the imagery in your mind, forge a sphere out of your Power State."

Here we go... I snickered. *Let the pain begin.*

Chad's palm flashed, and produced a wispy globe of luminous heat... and it was one-hundred percent perfect. "Like this?"

"What is that?" The veins of my neck popped out, and I grabbed Chad by the shoulders. "That took me *days* to get!"

Bang!

Chad's rupturing focus sent me flying.

"Now, now, everyone learns at a different pace," Mohandar laughed. "The more intelligent one is, the easier it is to—" Mohandar caught himself. "I shouldn't put it that way. The more imaginative and calculating one is, the easier it is to bend their energy."

Chad lost control of his laughter. "Did you hear that? You're an idiot!"

"Alright, buddy..." I pulled myself to my feet and cracked my knuckles. "Get ready."

Chad's eyes got big, and he squeaked. "We're fighting already?"

"Perfect." Mohandar took a single, floating bound, and retreated to the corner of the room. "Go until someone's Power State fails."

"Awesome." I allowed my electric fury to surge through my body. "Ready, Chad?"

"Um..." Chad's voice trembled. "No."

"Too bad."

I plowed into Chad with a high-powered tackle, knocking him backward and off his feet.

He recovered, bouncing from the ground as he did so. "Playing rough, huh?"

"This is a fight, Chad." I tightened my fist, and sparks danced on my knuckles. "Rough is the only way to play."

He smiled, the air around him sizzling. "Bring it."

We both pushed to the middle of the battleground, and engaged. Heat sweltered, bodies flew, tiles shattered, and the Observatory shook as raging lightning clashed against burning embers.

By the end, both of us were collapsed on our backs, absolutely spent. The entire floor was singed from a blend of unbearable heat and crackling thunder, and the tiles were broken beyond recognition.

"Travis, I gotta give you credit..." Chad panted between his words. "You're way stronger than I could've thought. You didn't even use your sword, either."

I scoffed. "This isn't Reach."

"I'm talking about your Power State sword..." Chad shifted a hand to the top of his belly. "The one you make from your energy."

"Oh." I stretched. *He's got more in him than I thought, but we're in totally different leagues. I didn't even get to use half of my real strength.* I smiled to myself. *Can't wait to see what he'll do after he's learned a bit.*

"Well done." Mohandar's body flopped in between us, creating a stoner's triangle in the process. "We're done for today. Rest, and come back tomorrow. The harder you work yourselves, the more you can handle."

I checked the time. *Looks like I need to go... I can't be late again.*

*****

The midday sun warmed the edges of my skin as I stood at the bottom of a long, easy hill leading to the twisting trunk of a Japanese maple. Songbirds flittered on thin branches, crooning in a never-ending game of cat and mouse.

Kate shifted her weight onto one leg and studied the hill. "What's so special about this place?"

"I'll tell you when we're at the top."

"Interesting..." Kate followed with a bouncing step. "When you said you wanted to show me something cool, I was thinking a drawing or an ability, something like—"

Her eyes got big when they met the endless view at the hill's crest. Her hand cradled over her lips, and liquid diamonds eased their way down her cheeks.

What do I do? I set my hand on her shoulder. "You okay?"

"Yeah..." She made her way to the maple and took a seat at its base. "Just give me a minute."

She breathed slow, and gave a hesitant laugh. "Sorry... I had no idea this was even here."

"I get it." I leaned back against the grainy bark of the tree. "To tell you the truth, I didn't know about this place either until my dad brought me here. Apparently it's an important place in my family."

She turned with a pure, sincere smile embellished by the sunlight. "Do tell."

She looks great today. More than usual, anyway. I should tell her that. Nah, don't be weird... I should probably answer her.

"This is where my mom and dad met." I knocked on the support behind us. "Dad was just sitting here reading, and she just showed up."

Kate raised her eyebrows. "You never really talk about your mom... if it's alright to ask, what was she like?"

I brushed the grass off my jeans. "She was beautiful, patient, more loving than anyone on the entire planet. Hair the color of ivory, and skin smoother than silk. At least, that's how I remember her."

Should I tell her?

"Just recently, I found out Mom wasn't quite what she seemed." I sighed. "Turns out she was Exalted, just like me. A note from her, as well as a guy I met, said she never died in the hospital. Instead, she left." I shrugged. "Off to fight the bad guys somewhere. Nobody knows if she'd dead... alive... if she's even okay."

"Jeez, that's rough." Kate's eyes went down to the grass. "I know how loss feels, but not knowing is a totally different ball game... sorry."

"It's fine." I smiled. "Sharing takes a bit of the edge off."

She propped her elbow on a branch of the tree. "You hardly ever talk to anybody about the important stuff... just bounce it around in that head of yours."

"You're not wrong." I sighed. "With Dad, we kind of just know what's up."

"I know how you feel." She reached up and plucked a leaf off the tree, rubbing it between her fingers. "You're the only person I really tell anything to. Something about you, from the moment you beat up those two slime balls at school... just feels right."

Oh, no.

"Kate..." I gently set my hand on her shoulder and put a little space between us. "I appreciate how much trust you have in me, but I'm really not that great of a guy. Chad and I have known each other all of our lives, and he'll tell you straight up I'm a jack— "

"Hush." She put her finger over my lips. "Would you stop trying to be all humble and heroic for a second and let a girl talk?"

I shied away. "Go ahead."

"You're a good man, Travis." She curled her fingers around my wrist and lowered it off of her shoulder. "Tough when you need to be... maybe a little rough on the edges, but you're good. My dad leaves on week-long work trips every month. I haven't worried even half as much for him as I do when you disappear to go fight." She looked me straight in the eyes with pure sincerity. "Not knowing if I'll see you again hurts me, and you can tell me all the bad things you believe about yourself. It won't change a thing."

What am I supposed to do with all of this? You can't, Travis! At any moment, an angry god and his army could descend upon these worlds, and you'll be one of the few who fight against him. The odds don't look good.

"Kate..." I sighed. "As much as I want to, I can't ever promise to be here forever. A massive, fate-decisive problem is coming in hot. If time runs out... my life is a trivial cost to pay if it means the world stays safe."

"I know, Travis." Her hand shifted, and the soft touch of her fingers slid between mine. "All the more reason to savor this moment... right now."

My heart melted inside, and every part of me went fuzzy. *Anything could happen tomorrow. All we have is today. Just... let go.*

Kate's long, full eyelashes batted once as her eyes went closed. Ever so slowly, she drew closer...

her hand squeezed mine, and my last bit of reason fluttered to the wind.

I gingerly brushed her hair away from her eyes, stroking the edge of her cheek. A smile curled at the edges of her lips... and I leaned in.

A sudden, profound rush of steaming air blew into us.

"Man, this book can really get places." Chad's voice shattered the moment like a hammer on glass. "Hey Travis, you want to—"

Kate's cheeks flushed pink. She smiled as her eyebrows lifted, with a hint of disappointment. Her hand peeled out of mine, saying nothing.

...Talk about bad timing.

Thirty-One

he path to Daedalus Stronghold burst apart with a bellowing cry. Earth split, trees toppled, and the sky grew dark red as Arvel and I soared through the chaos.

"That explosion came from inside the city." Arvel held tight as I made a swooping turn. "Can't be good."

Reality struck me like a brick. *We're out of time.*

I pushed harder, each flap of my wings accelerating us toward Daedalus Stronghold. "Hold on. This won't be a smooth ride."

A fresh fissure roared open beneath us, spewing hot lava from the depths.

I flipped to the side, and arced us away from a fiery demise. "If I'd known we were cutting it so close, I'd have suggested splitting up."

"No way I'd let you face the end of the world alone," Arvel laughed. "Don't flatter yourself."

The Sacred Scripture fueled my Power State, and we blasted even faster.

I twisted, turned, and corkscrewed through a labyrinth of flame, my lungs biting more and more with every beat.

Come on, Travis... Sweat beaded on my forehead. *Push harder!*

Arvel banged on my helm. "Look out!"

A bursting flash marked the entrance of an unavoidable obstacle... a skyscraper had toppled into Reach. I curled my wings around Arvel and prepared for the infernal blitz to come.

I winced at the army of tiny blades created by a shattered window. *Not bad, I can take—*

A supporting layer of pure concrete laid into us... followed by an audible crack.

I bit my lip, but howled inside. *Not good.*

I'd loosened up at the worst time... just long enough to earn another brutal snap. The glass jingled upon our exit, spilling Arvel and I out onto the breaking ground.

"Travis!" Arvel pushed his hood off and ran over, his cloak in tatters. "Are you alright?"

I pushed myself off the ground. "My wings are shot, but we need to keep going." My crimson-stained appendages flopped on my back, lifeless. In spite of the pure agony, I pressed on.

Arvel followed, right on my heels. "Only half a mile left... we can make it!"

In the near distance, Daedalus Stronghold awaited our arrival.

"Don't let your mind trick you." Arvel pulled ahead. "If you stop to catch your breath—"

The singed grass below burst open, flinging Arvel and I straight toward a pit of liquid incineration.

My eyes scanned for a solution. *Physics!*

My Power State burned within...

"Arvel!" I snagged his hand. "Get ready!"

I thrust my open palm downward and fired off a powerful burst of plasma. Arvel and I immediately became a pair of living mortar shells, arcing over the cataclysm... and the city walls. We crashed into what remained of a garden, and the rumbling disaster hushed.

I groaned and raised my arms. "We made it."

"You're out of juice..." Arvel lifted me to my feet. "No time to rest, we have to keep going."

The streets were full of scrambling citizens and ironclad guards making a futile attempt to maintain order.

A long, wide set of ivory stairs led to an equally polished tower surging up to the clouds. At last, the vigilant and stately form of Daedalus Tower was *here*... majestic even amidst the calamity.

"At last." Arvel took to the steps. "If it were under better circumstances, I'd celebrate."

I ground my teeth under the biting pain in my wings. "When we get close enough, the Sacred Scripture will—"

Broken ivory soared when firm impact set in ahead.

"A human archer and an Exalted with broken wings... not to mention an exhausted Power State." A low, comfortable laugh followed. "How nice."

The fog cleared, revealing a specter of a man with a gigantic fanged machete. He stood, slowly, and smiled.

"You must be Palatharx." Arvel twirled his bows off his back and drew. "You're the last thing we need right now."

I readied my sword, isolated from the help of my Power State. *We don't have time for this!*

"Hello, Travis." A machete, fanged and the size of a man, gleamed in the dusk. "Did you miss me?"

I dropped into fighting stance. "Last time I checked, you were lying face down in no man's land."

"No." Palatharx flipped his twisting hair. "Another miscalculation... when you've got a purpose as *grand* as mine, there's no time to die."

"Doesn't matter." Arvel readied his bows. "We're here to stop you."

Palatharx gripped his weapon with both hands and rushed forward. "Go ahead and try!"

THIRTY-TWO

My senses sharpened, pulling me out of the chaos. *Another jump, huh? Heck of a time... just when Arvel and I got where we needed to be.*

I leaned on the kitchen table, fingers fidgeting after giving Dad the rundown of the situation. All was quiet in the house as he took a long drink.

Dad set his beer aside and sighed, rubbing his hands. "We're out of time."

"Out of time and out of options." I looked over at the Sacred Scripture. "I'm headed for the battlefield today."

"To take on Yaris and his Divine Army." Dad leaned back in his seat. "Don't know if I should be proud or horrified." He ground his teeth. "When the Realms do collide, how much time will we have?" A light bulb went on in his head. "What'll happen to you when both of your bodies are in the same world?"

"Beats me." I ran my hand along the tabletop. "I'll ask Mohandar when we meet up. Speaking of which... he's agreed to give you refuge in the Observatory, but he'll still be on the front lines with Chad and I."

"Boy, you listen to me." Dad stood and put his finger in my face. "If any son of mine is going straight to war for the entirety of the world, he's *going* to take his father with him. If you get yourself killed out there and I could've done something—"

I have to be careful about how I word this... I rose from my chair and opened the refrigerator. *Think before you open your mouth.*

"Dad." I pulled a pitcher of water out and poured myself a drink. "You've been my mentor and guardian for years. With all due respect, if you step foot in the crossfire of a thousand individuals as strong as I am, if not *stronger,* you won't last a minute." I looked at him over my shoulder. "The guys I've fought had the power to level cities. The way Mohandar talks about this divine army... they've got what it takes to make a clean sweep of the entire world."

"You remind me of your mother." He leaned back in his chair and sighed. "Make sure you're prepared before you go. Take your mask, a sweatshirt, and—"

"I'll be alright, Dad." I wrapped my arms around him. "No matter what it takes, we'll win this."

"Okay, okay." He stood and squeezed me between two dense forearms. "Get out there and show 'em what you're made of."

Before that could take place, though... I had one last knot to tie up.

My steps led me to the front porch of a banana-yellow home, where I stared at a neatly folded envelope in my hand.

Should I go in and talk to her? I scratched the bottom of my chin. *No, I wrote her a letter for a reason. If I try to say anything, it won't come out right. Just like she said, I've only got the day in front of me. If there's no tomorrow... this is what I need to do.*

I slowly opened the screen, and eased the smooth paper of the envelope under the door.

A quick, unannounced creak stopped me dead in my tracks... and I found myself face to face with reality.

"Travis." Kate's eyebrows went up and she took a peek at my hand. "What're you doing here?" She stepped outside, and closed the door behind her.

I offered her the letter, and my heart grew heavy. *Every word's true.*

She accepted my offering with caution. "...It's time, then."

I wrapped my arms around her and held her for a long moment of stillness. Gradually, she returned the embrace... and let all else fade.

"Please, read it." I took one last breath of her intoxicating aroma and let go. "I really mean it."

She nodded, quivering just a little.

"Bye, Kate."

"Bye..."

I took my leave and headed for the sky... my emotions refusing to stay behind.

Kate,

I'm sorry. I wish I could've told you about this sooner... but things have taken a turn. What was once a mere worry has become reality. Yaris, an evil god set to destroy the Realms, has been freed. It's up to me and a few friends to keep him from destroying everything... the grass, the sky, the trees, the people around us... we all have something we hold truly special.

For me, it's all of these things.

And you.

If there's such a thing as love, however stupid I may be, I'd boldly say I've felt it with you. Not a doubt in my mind. What happened on the hill (or I should say, "almost" happened) yesterday, was... unforgettable. It pains me to leave like this, not knowing if I'll ever come back, but I can't really say I have a choice. Either I go fight, or we lose everything. Seems like there's a pattern in the Exalted business, huh?

Anyway, what I'm trying to say is... I don't know what's going to happen. If I fail to return, know you've given me a piece of myself. Something I'd have never found if we hadn't crossed paths. I'm going to give it my all out there, for the sake of everything and everyone.

Don't worry about what could happen, Kate. Somehow, whatever the cost, we'll win this. Like you said, we've got no day but today... my today will be spent securing your tomorrow.

Yours Truly, Travis

(Fair warning: Mohandar's going to pick you and your dad up in about ten minutes. You'll be safe in the Observatory.)

***

I spotted my destination, and descended to the edge of a vast overlook... where Mohandar first gave me the chance to be Exalted. After glancing about the area, I took a seat underneath the land's wooded guardian.

I'm the first one. I delved into the pockets of my jeans. *Time to take care of this, then.*

Mom's empty gift boxes gleamed in the falling sun as I studied them for the last time. With a little help from my Power State, I dug a nook underneath the roots of the Japanese maple and placed both of them, along with the entire collection of notes, under the care of the hill's sentinel.

"If anyone's fit to watch over these, it's you." I cradled the shining glass globe in my palm. "You've seen the whole story unfold, after all."

Mom's final gift—the contained light—bent and twisted in its prison.

What could possibly be in this thing that's so dangerous?

"Greetings, Exalted One." A phantasmal wind blew across my body. "You're early, as usual... ready to save the world?"

I tucked the bottle away in my pocket. "Ready as I can be."

Mohandar tightened his grip on his staff. "It will be an honor to fight alongside you."

I looked past him. "Where's Chad?"

Mohandar looked out onto the horizon. "Late."

"Figures..." I chuckled. "You keep training him, you'll learn real quick."

A car door thumped behind us. "Don't worry, guys. The savior of the Realms has arrived!"

"Travis." Mohandar pointed his staff out to the reddening skyline. "Out there."

A tiny streak, formed in the emptiness of the air... cracking away reality like glass. In seconds, it stretched from one side of the valley to the other, and unleashed a haunting moan.

I straightened my posture. "Yaris?"

Mohandar nodded. "...And friends."

The crack swelled, opening our world and unveiling a legion of silhouettes. If I hadn't known they were the enemy, their glory would've had me awestruck. Instead, lurid tension built. The sky became blinding white as the barriers between Realms shattered, smashing Earth and Reach into one... Clouds dissipated as the gateway to our foes rumbled wide, and a gale force blasted into us.

I braced under the coming storm. *That's how you make an entrance.*

The atmospheric assault settled, revealing the nature of the battlefield... Towering trees from Reach loomed in the once clear valleys, and the sky took on the deep crimson of calamity. Daedalus Stronghold was at the heart of it all, smoldering and beckoning rescue. The gates of war opened wide, and a focused ray of radiance dropped into the city.

An all commanding voice rumbled, forcing the world into submission.

"Mortals... you and your beloved Realms have met their end."

Mohandar, Chad and I stood shoulder to shoulder, staring death in the face.

So, this is what we're up against... should be one heck of a fight.

Chad and I readied our Power States, and Mohandar grasped his staff.

"How long do we have, Mohandar?"

"Not long. Get the Channeling Crystal in place, and it won't matter." Mohandar leapt off the cliffside. "Onward!"

"You heard the man." I pulled my steel mask over my face and unveiled my radiant wings. "Showtime."

THIRTY-THREE

Mohandar, Chad and I soared into the fray... hundreds of blurs plummeted from the gateway above, each one arriving with force. Our world was under siege, and the three of us were all that stood between mankind and a burning end.

Wait a minute. I passed my hand over my pocket, where my Realm Stone seared away. *Shouldn't I have switched to Siris' body?*

"You won't be able to switch." Mohandar read my mind. "Your active body needs to be petrified before you can. Seeing as Reach and Earth are one... that's not going to happen." He decelerated and flew beside us. "I have a plan."

"For once, *somebody* does." Chad shifted in my grasp. "Let's hear it."

"We'll stick together and avoid being overrun. Landing at the city gates, we'll fight straight to the tower. If we were to go airborne, we'd attract the attention of the entire battalion." Mohandar pointed up ahead. "Once we're through, Chad... you'll stay with me and keep the pressure off of Travis." Mohandar looked over to me. "We're counting on *you* to plant the Channeling Crystal."

"Slight problem." I tightened my focus on the city ahead, now covered in dancing embers. "Palatharx is back... Arvel and I were about to fight him—"

"I'm well aware, Travis." Mohandar's staff pulsed its lavender glow. "Just leave him to me."

Chad wiggled. "Who's *pal of farts?*"

Mohandar plummeted downward. "Dive, now!"

I descended to the scorched earth, and released Chad.

The massive iron doors of Daedalus Stronghold laid blown-out, each half curled on itself and resting against the earth... a pair of fallen giants. Cinders danced around them, giving a grim light to our company.

Twelve beings donned in elegant, swirling armor straightened and broadened their posture. Each stood at seven feet tall, and brandished fine spear-like weapons with blades on each end. Their faces were entirely concealed by headpieces, funneling into crests arching over their backs.

"Exalted." One twirled his weapon and assumed a fighting stance, mirrored by the others. "At the ready, brethren!"

"I give you..." Mohandar stomped, and a gust of wind erupted from him. "The Divine Army."

Chad and I each took a side of Mohandar, our Power States blazing.

"This is your only chance, mortals." More dropped from the sky like rain. "Submit now, and your deaths will be swift."

"So arrogant..." Mohandar tightened his fist, smoldering with unbridled power. "You forget who I am."

In a blink, Mohandar *became* the wind. I watched in amazement as he single-handedly tore apart the ranks guarding the gate. Like bowling pins, each and every one was catapulted backwards, slamming into the walls of Daedalus Stronghold.

"Well, then." The great Observer appeared, and forged on. "Let's go."

"Right—" Chad started into full sprint to keep up. "Yes, sir!"

I laughed and followed. "You get it now, don't you?"

"Yep." Chad nodded, puffing along the way. "I'd hate to get on his bad side."

"If we don't pull our weight, we will." I unleashed my wings and soared ahead. "Let's get in there and show 'em he's not the only one to worry about."

"This is the easy part." Mohandar's cape fluttered. "Travis, we'll need your strength for what's to come." He shifted and fired a swift energy blast to the side. "The true fight starts now."

The buildings parted and revealed a wall of shields. Behind the phalanx, Daedalus Tower released a steady beam of turquoise energy directly into the portal.

A leading officer of the Divine Army broke from the ranks. "Insolent one, surrender now! Leave the body and—"

"Over my rotting corpse!"

Arvel.

My ally, wrapped in a bloodied and tattered gray cloak, loomed over the limp body of a winged knight. His posture and fierce tenacity embodied the silver eagle on his neck. He remained perched, glaring at the ring of halberd-wielding beings surrounding him.

"This is my friend." He loaded an arrow into each one of his bows, one by one. "Unless you all start shooting confetti out of your butts, I'm not gonna budge."

"So be it."

Before my mind could even comprehend the situation, my body threw itself into harm's way. I snagged the handle of a descending halberd and pulled. The weapon's wielder toppled off his feet, and couldn't resist as I dragged him into his companions. In seconds, they were scattered and motionless.

I lifted my mask. "Hey, Arvel."

"What the... it's you!" Arvel trapped me in his arms. "You're uglier than usual."

"Why do you think I wear this?" I chuckled and once again veiled my face. "Hope you haven't had too much trouble while I was gone."

"Wasn't so bad." Arvel smirked. "Palatharx nearly had me done for, but he pulled out once these shiny lunatics showed up. Believe me, they're a lot tougher than they look."

"Palatharx could be anywhere, then." Mohandar looked out to the growing ranks of Yaris' army. "Probably waiting for you to return the Channeling Crystal, Travis."

I clenched my fists. "I don't care."

"Close in, brothers." The Divine Army advanced. "They've sealed their fates."

Chad opened his palms, each one popping out a blazing sphere. "I'll blow a hole in their ranks."

We waited as he focused, the globes in his hands growing brighter and more intense. Sweat beaded on his forehead, his breathing grew heavy... and the air began to swelter.

Any time now...

"Firing!" Chad extended his arms and brought his wrists together.

Each sphere dissolved, becoming two twisting lines of tangerine heat. They corkscrewed and bent, surging the center of the marching battalion.

Arvel scratched his head. "Was that supposed to—"

He smiled. "Patience."

Under a sudden burst of flame, a virtual supernova the size of a house blasted forth. Just like Chad said, a clean hole in the formation waited to be exploited.

Nice one, Chad.

"Don't just stand there!" Chad gave me a shove. "Go!"

I spread my wings and blasted toward the tower, met by a few airborne soldiers.

One met a clean slash across the torso. Another, an energy blast to the face. Then... a familiar face.

"When will you learn to *expect* me?"

I twisted my body and knocked Palatharx away with a heavy strike of the heel. "Not this time, pal. I'm on a clock."

I closed in on the peak of the tower with Palatharx, a flaming red missile, hot on my tail.

A stone-dressed fist clocked into my jaw, and my ears rang. Without a moment's rest, two more solid blows sent me spinning backwards.

"Nice try." My hand shot forward and snagged his continued assault. "But you made a mistake."

A flurry of sun-colored darts tore my pursuer from the sky... buying just enough time.

Thanks, Chad.

I pointed to the empty space in the tower, void of its missing heart. "Scripture, place the Channeling Crystal!"

My book opened, glowing brighter than the sun... all else faded as its divinity spread, blotting out the world with its pure glory. In the obscurity, three individual surges arose... each marking the emergence of a Crystal Shard. They swirled around one another, drawing closer until a ring like a massive bell tower sounded far and wide.

United once more, the heart of Reach bolted back into place at the head of Daedalus Tower... inciting a powerful moan from the structure itself.

A spire of pale flame erupted from Daedalus Tower and poured into the gateway to Yaris' world.

In a whirling tempest of shouts, cries, and fizzling light, the portal caved... dragging what remained of the Divine Army back where they had come from.

Chaos subdued. The tower's beam hushed and flowers began to bloom between burned grass and bodies of soldiers, both human and godly.

Palatharx floated to my side, looking up at the pure blue sky. "You've won, haven't you?"

Kate, Dad, everybody... you're safe now.

I glided back and leaned on the ivory surface of the tower. "Give it a week, something else will be trying to destroy the world by then. You're not gonna be a total jerk and break the Crystal, are you?"

Palatharx looked out into the distance. "Waste of energy."

Huh. Looks like I finally wore him out.

"...Especially when you're already dead."

In seconds, the Realm Stone in my pocket went from calm and cold to scorching.

The details of the world blurred... elements of Earth and Reach separating back into their rightful places.

An unseen force ensnared and petrified me.

"Yes, you've separated Earth and Reach for good." Palatharx laughed. "Your friends may be safe for now, but you're not going anywhere... We have somebody to visit."

The gateway in the sky burst open once more, and my body rocketed upward.

Not good, not good, not good!

Before I could begin to comprehend the matter, the portal closed... sealing me off from any help or escape.

I was in the throne room of a deity.

THIRTY-FOUR

I found myself flat on my stomach against cold, glossy metal. "Oh, Yaris?" Footsteps patted beside my head. "I've fulfilled your request. Now, may we have a little talk?"

A deep, rasping voice rumbled in response.

"Speak, mortal."

I planted my fist against the floor and lifted my body up. *Why am I on the ground?*

Ahead was a platform as long and wide as a football field, with Palatharx marking its farthermost end. A waving trail of royal purple velvet worked its way all the way down the silver length, guided by pillars of ivory. At the other end was a pair of arching staircases made from floating slabs. Like magnets, the disconnected pathways bent out and around one another, creating a bridge to the center.

A gigantic throne the size of a two-story house rested underneath a dome-shaped construct, shedding the light of the cosmos on its keeper. Tapping his titanic, translucent fingers on the platinum arms of his resting place was the face of intimidation himself.

Yaris.

His metal headdress curved over the absence of his face, like an iron hood. Massive chrome plates layered around his body, hiding most of the deity's near-transparent flesh. His anatomy, however, seemed largely human... aside from the fact that his left arm melded into a world-splitting scythe at the end, leaving only his right hand as a sign of humanity. In a way, he reminded me of Mohandar... a massive, terrifying Mohandar.

"Great One," Palatharx said, extending his leg and bowing with grace. "I know you seek to wipe these Realms clean to form a new and glorious order. I wish to assist you in realizing your goal."

"Oh, do you?" Yaris sat up in his throne, sending tremors through the entire platform. "Tell me, what do *you* get out of obliterating life as you know it?"

Yeah, Palatharx. I stumbled to my feet. *What's in it for you?*

"We've been over this already, my lord." Palatharx extended his blade to Yaris. "We share a common dream, to forge a world where evil, and all suffering, no longer exist."

Yaris hesitated, but began to bellow, clutching his gut with his only hand. Before long, the deity was in hysterics.

Palatharx's eyes narrowed. "That wasn't a joke."

"That's why it's so *hilarious!*" Yaris pointed down to Palatharx from afar. "You actually believe I would let someone rule *beside* me... you'd even go so far as to think you're worthy of the position."

Palatharx bit his lip as Yaris silently brought his giant palm in front of his face.

"You really think I've forgotten?" He turned his gaze. "You think I *forgot* when you and your allies threw me into the abyss, to suffer in agony for twelve ages? Think again!"

What?

The universe trembled as Yaris twisted and thrust his hand forward, unleashing a spear of judgment upon Palatharx. It bored straight through, leaving a sizzling hole where his chest once was.

"Should've..." Palatharx's body tipped... and fell. "...Never left."

I knelt down beside Palatharx, only to find the heat fading from an empty vessel. "What do you mean?"

"Exalted. First generation." Yaris set his arm on his throne. "They obliterated my Divine Army and sealed me away to be forgotten. They were always a little prone to chasing lofty dreams."

Palatharx, a first generation Exalted... I brushed Palatharx's eyes closed. *Who'd have thought?*

"Now, to the important matters." Yaris cleared his absence of a throat. "You."

I glared at him from the corner of my eye. "What do you want?"

Dense, clanging metal surfaced as Yaris' entire army gripped their weapons from four levitating platforms around us.

"Careful." Yaris extended his arms. "You don't want to disrespect a god, do you? I have quite the temper... and if you can't see, I'm perfectly content."

I'm not buying that sham.

"Whatever." I cracked my knuckles. "What do you want, *sir?*"

Yaris chuckled. "No, no, this is about what *you* want."

"Me?" I broadened my chest. "What do you care about what I want?"

"You wish to see the best for everyone you love and *beyond*." Yaris ran his fingers along his scythe-arm. "You act in their best interest, not your own. For such a man, I have an offer."

Stay sharp, Travis.

"Unlike Palatharx, who was driven to meet his own dreams, so far as to betray his former allies, you have a certain fidelity, allegiance to life itself." Yaris relaxed, leaning back. "I've been watching you from my prison, and I believe you're exactly the type to serve as my council and successor... to bring light to these Realms and free every living thing from the chaos of their very nature."

I scoffed. "By killing everyone where they stand?"

"Don't resist an offer of mercy." Yaris' posture tensed. "If you attempt to stand in my way, you'll end up like that maggot beside you. Deities can only be slain by other deities, so don't even—"

"Shut up."

"What?" Yaris' hand began to quiver. "Are you saying—"

"I said shut your egotistic mouth. I couldn't care less about what you think I am, or how invincible you tell yourself you are." I clenched my fists and readied my Power State. "You're threatening the lives of people who can't do a thing to protect themselves, people who didn't do anything to deserve death. I'm gonna give it to you straight."

"Royal Guard." Yaris snapped his fingers. "Take care of—"

My fuse blew. "My name is Travis Shepard, and I'm giving *you* one chance for mercy. No way I'm letting you past me, to wreak havoc for your cold heart's content. To answer your offer, no. I think you're full of crap, and you need to be taught a lesson in the meaning of life!"

"How disappointing." He tapped his scythe against the throne, and it tolled like a bell. "Meet your death."

Four tremor-emitting booms arose just ahead, and I found myself facing Yaris' Royal Guard. These titans were composed entirely of gold, and bore dense, large-backed bodies which hunched as they went up. Each had four thick arms with three-fingered hands and stout legs.

Three of them backed away to reveal an individual with a body marked in white oil, resting a greataxe on one hulking shoulder. It shuffled forward with heavy steps and loomed over me, engaging a warrior's stare-off.

"Think one of you will do the trick?" I cracked my knuckles. "We'll see."

A vile hiss came from my foe, and the axe came down. With a quick flash of reflex, I managed to duck between its legs.

Time to assess... I cocked my arm back. *That armor's definitely too thick to use your sword. Try a blunt attack to one of the joints.*

The metallic ankle of my enemy slid into view, and I lashed out. This triggered a groan and a violent counterattack from the giant, catapulting me airborne.

Good hit. I manifested my wings and squared off. *Gotta keep distance... otherwise I might get cut in half.*

The construct's thick back split open, unleashing a barrage of bladed missiles in my direction.

I did a barrel roll and evaded the incoming swarm. *Okay, so it has good range, too... what can I do?*

The crisp gleam coursed over the fine metal of my opponent's body.

That's right! They're all made of gold... a spectacular conductor.

I clenched my fist, grabbed hold of my inner tempest... and dove as the embodiment of the storm.

In a mess of flying sparks and dancing metal, I plowed *through* the enemy. Its lifeless body toppled to the side, coursing with bolts of electricity.

The others readied their weapons and rushed forward, unaware of the strength of a lone Exalted.

I smiled and grabbed the titanic handle of my fallen enemy's axe, planted my feet and heaved the weapon... sending it clean into the closest one.

Adrenaline flowed, pumping into every one of my muscles. With a furious shout, I raced ahead, leaving the last of my attackers to wither in the residual fury of my strengthening power.

"Yaris!" I sprang into the air and cocked my fist back. "Stand up and fight!"

The silver deity rose from his seat... and exhaled.

My momentum reversed and landed me grounded once again, a mere fly under the swatter. *That force came from his breath?*

"As you wish, Exalted One." He marched down from his throne with steps of dominance, loosening his weapon arm. "Know that in all my existence, I've never seen my Royal Guard defeated... let alone so *easily*." He pushed out his chest, and ghostly steam wisped from every crevice in his armor. "Quite frankly, it *angers* me."

"Good." I nodded to the Scripture and intensified my Power State. "Maybe it'll teach you not to underestimate your opponents."

Yaris growled and leaned into a swipe of his scythe, splitting the air as I evaded fast enough to only get a few of my hairs trimmed. More strikes followed, each one accelerating as the assault continued. At the slightest opening, I zipped behind him and readied every ounce of my energy.

Opening in the armor... My eyes scanned every inch of his broad shoulder. *There!*

My arm extended forward, driving the weaponized manifestation of my soul between the edges of two interlocking plates. Upon entry, a massive explosion of sky-blue fury set off, and threw me away from the flinching deity.

Got him! I unleashed everything I had... blasts, slashes, bare-knuckle blows, every bit of fight I had went straight into the recovering Yaris. *Is this it?*

"How... how are you so powerful?" Yaris dropped to a knee, and let out a long, shaky breath. "No mortal can damage me, especially not Exalted."

"Effort." I flipped over Yaris and landed in front of his empty face. "If you don't try, you don't get anywhere."

"Legend has it that a hero was destined to be my killer. Half man, half god." His shoulders drooped. "It appears that the hero is..."

I readied my blade.

He chuckled. "...*Not you.*"

Palatharx's voice pierced the stillness.

"Travis, look out!"

The force of a tsunami struck me from behind, casting me through the empty pieces of Yaris' armor and tumbling across the platform.

Standing before me was the glowing, star-forged manifestation of the giant. In shape, he appeared the same... only every part of him was spiraled together from pure light. Where he once had silver plating, he now wore the fibers of the sun, extending into a vast number of tendrils spreading out from his shoulders.

"Did you not know that I have an incarnate and *disincarnate* form?" Yaris laughed. "All bodies are weak, especially in comparison to the full might of a deity... you asked for my full power, and now you'll get it. Behold!"

I pulled myself to my feet and dodged another swipe of his scythe, but fell prey to the merciless explosion of fiery wrath which followed. Adrift in the air, I couldn't evade a precise column of plasma burning from Yaris' face.

A crisp ding slowed the whole experience down.

As I whirled back toward the stairs, bits of steel spiraled away... my peripheral vision returned, and the soft hugging on the back of my head released.

Kate's mask had been shattered to pieces.

My singed back struck the floor. My shirt had been burned clean off, leaving only exposed skin and, thankfully, my pants. I went to reach into my pocket, but for some reason... couldn't. With a quick turn, I saw why.

My arm!

Hanging only by a few threads of skin, it thumped against the left side of my torso... lifeless.

"Aw..." Yaris stretched his arm. "Did I rip off the little bitty boy's arm? So *fragile.*"

Down to the wire. With wounds like this, it won't be long until I bleed out... Exalted or not.

I flicked my wrist to summon my ethereal sword, and with one stinging swipe, it was done.

Gone. I bit my lip as a thump teased my ears. "Scripture, can you slow the bleeding?"

My book shook its cover and whined.

"Don't worry, buddy." I smiled and blocked out the pain. "We've still got one trick up our sleeves."

I'm at the limits of what I can do, and there's no way I can use Burnout... there's only one option left. My hand dove into my pocket and my fingers wrapped around a firm glass orb... and raised it in the cradle of my palm. *Sorry, Dad.*

I tightened my grip, and shattered the vial.

THIRTY-FIVE

The breath left my lungs and the world faded... I was alone, petrified in endless darkness.

A voice filled my head. *"Travis... you just took the last step to becoming who you are. As you're listening, you'll notice your body is going to start hurting... bad."*

I buckled over, punched in the gut by an invisible force.

"This pain, coursing through you, is the gift you just accepted. The glass orb contained something known as the Light of the Living. Right now, it's intertwining with your soul, establishing itself as the supreme nature of your being."

My eyes began to water, and my legs trembled beneath me. Unseen fiends were clawing at every inch of my flesh, tearing deeper into my conscience as the seconds went on.

"The Light of the Living is the purest light, only used to birth gods. Any mortal who absorbs it will meet a swift end at its hand."

Mom gave me death... as a gift? I fought to breathe, unable to move in the stillness.

"Relax. If you were going to die, you would've already. Just endure a little longer, and you'll see just how hollow you were before."

My heart shed its electric blue aura, taking up the pale white of the stars. With every pulse, it grew... until my entire body showcased its relentless glow.

"Now, Travis... rise, and show Yaris what it means to be a hero."

Control returned to my body... and the radiance faded. I was left wheezing in the presence of my executioner.

"Your Power State is gone." Yaris stomped toward me. "You've lost."

"What it means to be a hero."

Death descended, and my eyes grew wide as the tip of Yaris' scythe fell mere inches away from my face.

Something in the back of my head clicked, like the trigger of a gun.

The Light of the Living surged from within, a raging tornado tearing its way to the heavens. Stars ducked out of the way, and Yaris was thrown off balance against a virtual tempest.

And his name was Travis Shepard.

My war cry shook the universe... stars burst in the distance, comets raged, and the whole platform rumbled... until it gave way to a soft white glow. My entire body radiated with the essence of dawn, and my eyes filled with radiance as I stared down Yaris.

The divine might in my hands made the Power State seem like a childish toy... completely inferior. My arm was gone, but all doubt and all fear had been extinguished. The air of victory shrouded my piercing gaze.

"Yaris." My voice echoed, as if thousands were speaking at once. "That legendary demigod you're so afraid of... it's me."

He squared off his posture, but his knees gave him away.

I opened my palm and began to shape a weapon from my essence... a gigantic curved greatsword as long as my body. By human limits, the blade would be impossible to wield even with two hands... yet I hoisted it to my shoulder with a single arm.

I extended the blade toward him. "It's time for both of us to face fate."

I sailed into battle. Turning my weight in midair, my sword crushed through Yaris' shoulder armor. He roared and responded with a counter of his scythe, parried expertly... *impossibly,* by my greatsword. His guard opened up long enough for me to land a vertical strike to his calf, bringing him to his knees.

Too heavy. I opened my palm and allowed my weapon to fizzle away. *Let's try something else.*

My legs ached when my entire body was pushed down, assaulted by the stream of flame pouring from Yaris' open face.

"Powerful..." He leaned down closer. "But still, not enough."

To think this same attack completely obliterated me a few seconds ago... Ever so slowly, I stood up straight and squinted into the infernal assault. *I can see what Dad was saying. This strength...*

I pulled my fist back and loosed a punch toward Yaris. The wind itself rushed into action, forcing the flames back on their wielder.

It'd be absolutely horrifying in the wrong hands.

I leapt up and gave Yaris a hard clock to the face, knocking him to the side.

"Impressive." Yaris straightened up and backed off. "It seems you've managed to take on the false guise of a god... a *Pseudo-Deity*."

I closed in with a slow, but purposeful walk. "Point being?"

"You contend with me, now." Yaris plowed his fist into the platform, barely missing. "However, you still deal minimal damage."

The silver beneath us split into thousands of fragments as Yaris withdrew his fist. One by one, his broken pieces recovered, until he'd returned to perfect condition.

He heals? I readied my arm with a growl. *Guess I'll just have to push harder!*

I sailed through the next attack and plowed into him with an armada of blows, breaking through every defense he could've thrown at me. By the time I needed breath, all that remained was a twisted, broken representation of what used to be.

I wiped the blood from my mouth. "Try recovering from that."

"Gladly." The broken body snapped and twisted until Yaris once again rose from ruins. "Even with this level of strength, you cannot—" He paused, looking past me. "How are you still alive?"

"You know, Travis... I like your tenacity." A scarlet glow arose from behind. "It reminds me of something I lost a long time ago."

I ducked away from Yaris just in time to evade a sinister ray of desolation... a combined assault of red and black energy, boring its way straight into Yaris' chest. Through it all, I saw Palatharx burst from Yaris' back, leaving his machete embedded in the stricken deity.

"The heart..." Absolutely siphoned, Palatharx collapsed. "Source of his healing."

"He's wrong." Yaris retreated and placed his scythe over his open chest. "One loses sense with a hole in their body, I'm sure he's—"

Thank you, Palatharx.

"My first time fighting was an invasion... a purely evil being by the name of Ulanog. A lot like you, actually... the whole world domination thing." I focused my mind. "Thing I learned is, when you put pure, *righteous* energy in the heart of something dark and twisted like him, they can't handle it."

"Too late." Yaris pulled his guard away, revealing a near-closed wound. "The hole's been—"

"Let's see what happens to you."

I opened my palm, and an army of lightning bolts overthrew the mad deity with their fury. Taking hold of Yaris' twisted heart, they spread and brought him to his knees... the weight of justice upon him.

Yaris attempted to speak, but all that came out was a garbled croak.

He buckled over.... and the universe lit up white.

I sheltered my eyes. *Wow, it worked.*

Silence filled the ruined throne room... pillars were toppled and crumbled, banners ripped, and the shattered pieces of the platform danced through space. A graveyard of armor marked the ruins of the Divine Army, forgotten along with the ashes of their lord.

A sense of peace set in on my heart. "We actually did it."

I hopped between the broken pieces of the platform and knelt down beside Palatharx, who began to radiate a dull crimson glow. Slowly, his bloody wound closed, and he took deep breaths.

"Look, Shepard..." He sighed. "I've come to a realization."

I raised an eyebrow.

"I may have helped you in the end, but it doesn't outweigh the amount of evil I've done." He lowered his gaze. "Kill me. It's what I deserve."

Drew's words echoed in my ears. *If a villain this bad asks you to kill them, you do it.*

I took a moment to think... then raised my fist, surging with power.

"Good choice."

I brought it down, giving him a nice and playful smack. "Get up."

Palatharx raised his head, absolutely dumbfounded.

"Yeah, I'd say you deserve to be shut down, too..." I extended my hand and lifted him. "But if we always got what we deserved, we wouldn't be quite the same people, would we?"

He nodded, and paced off toward Yaris' remains.

"Hey." I collected what remained of my shirt. "If you ever want to join the good guys, I'm sure they'd have you back."

"You really are stupid." Palatharx gave a hint of a laugh. "No."

It took me a few seconds to catch up. "Then why'd you help me?"

"Like I said." He kept on. "You reminded me of something I lost a long time ago."

"What?"

"Passion." He stopped. "In the old days, when we took on the lunatic Yaris for the first time, I was just like you. Odds didn't matter, as long as there was hope... then I lost someone very close. I set out on my quest for the new world. Somewhere along the line, I lost myself."

Weird. I gritted my teeth. *Where's all this coming from?*

"Originally, I wanted to take Yaris' power for myself. If a mortal somehow dethrones a god, they get their power." He lifted his machete and brushed it off. "All I have to do is take a seat on his throne."

There it is. I shrugged. "Without your tip, I'd have never won. Go ahead, take your prize."

"Nah." He smirked. "I don't really want it anymore. Some people just aren't fit to be gods."

With that said, he planted his feet and heaved his blade, the very thing that claimed the life of Siris, into space.

"That blade worked for evil... I think it's time to let the old Palatharx die, and begin a new chapter." He came back to me with a single bound. "Thank you, Travis Shepard."

"Alright, enough with the charade." I watched as he walked right past me. "Stop trying to be all sentimental, we both know the egotistic jerk you really are."

"Shut up." As he walked away, his body became transparent. "Tell Mohandar not to come looking for me... See you around, kid."

Just like that, Palatharx was gone. The Sacred Scripture and I stood in the middle of an empty throne room... *somewhere.*

I looked around, then at the book. "How the heck do we get out of here?"

It danced through the open air, singing suggestions.

"No way." I shook my head. "Do you remember what happened last time? You dropped Arvel and I into the middle of the sky!"

My book moaned and got closer.

"I guess you're right... it is our only option." I rolled the idea around. "Scripture, if you really think you can do it—"

I landed hard on my back, against the chilled surface of... more metal.

"I swear, if we're in the same freaking place—" I froze.

Chad, Arvel, Dad and Kate all stared my way with gigantic eyes. Behind them were the wide-stretching windows of the Observatory, dead silent in the richest moment of awkwardness in my entire life.

I lifted my hand. "Hey—"

In a chorus of shouts, they all jumped on me and cut off my already restricted breathing capability.

In just a few seconds, it all stopped, as Dad easily passed his hand over my left shoulder.

He took a long, deep breath. "Your arm."

"It's fine, Dad." I gently grabbed his wrist and lowered it away. "We won... with a little help from an unlikely ally."

His posture relaxed, and he had a seat in front of me. "At least you're alive."

I looked around the room. "Where's Mohandar?"

"Looking for you." Arvel patted my back. "He's worried sick."

A puff of fog arose in the distant corner of the room.

"Grave news, friends..." Mohandar emerged from the mist with his head low. "While the Realms have been parted, and Yaris vanquished, it appears Travis gave his life doing so."

"Travis?" I scratched my chin. "Don't worry about him, he's a total jerk."

"By the gods and all that exists, he *lives!*" A blur of violet pounded me into the ground. "How did you get back?"

"The Sacred Scripture managed to blip us here." I pushed him back. "Can I get up?"

Mohandar pulled me to my feet and backed away. "My apologies, Exalted One, I was just so worried. Is there anything I can do for you?"

"A shirt would be greatly appreciated." I slapped the side of my burned, exposed chest... and blushed a little when I made eye contact with Kate. "I'm only nudist when I'm home alone."

Dad fake coughed. "Wonderful image."

Chad pulled off his sweatshirt and handed it to me.

"Thanks."

I lifted it up, and accepted the *true* greatest challenge of my Exalted career... putting on a long-sleeved shirt with one arm.

Silky hands lent a bit of help in my struggle.

When I popped out of the shirt's neck, I froze at the sight of two deep green jewels for eyes.

"Hey." Kate smiled and coaxed her hand behind my head. "You made it back."

My heart grew fuzzy, and my knees weak. "Kate—"

My senses dulled and my balance went backward... taking Kate down with me.

Immediate commotion roused between Chad, Arvel, and Kate, but two voices cut through the banter.

Dad gave a long sigh. "Anything we can do about his arm?"

"Don't worry, Wade." Mohandar's footsteps clicked as he paced off. "I've got just the thing."

EPILOGUE

The porch swing creaked as it swayed back and forth. All was peaceful... the breeze coaxed the world around, tickling the trees and the endless fields. The scent of wildflowers in bloom permeated the air, blending with the wafting pine needles as I relaxed without a thing on my mind. Just the gentle swaying of the swing, and the soft touch of my love, whose arms curled around mine.

Kate rested against my shoulder. "Getting used to it yet?"

I shifted, and brought my new, completely mechanical left arm forward. The prosthetic moved with otherworldly grace between a network of metal rods. It shared the very same characteristics as Mohandar's staff, forged from midnight gray metal, and emitting the soft radiance of my resting indigo soul.

"Actually, it's not bad. Turns out, Mohandar's a real craftsman. He built this thing from scratch." I rotated my hand and gave her a light touch to the nose. "Accurate enough to make small, soft moves just like that."

Kate smiled and sat up. "Can I feel it?"

"Here." I turned, and extended my synthetic palm.

She flipped her hair, and gingerly grazed her fingers along the edges... as if for research. After a long inspection, she presented her own hand, and I gently slid my fingers in between hers.

"A little cold." She released a brief sigh before taking my other hand. "I like this one better."

"Really?" I spun my mechanical wrist all the way around in its joint. "This one makes me like a *cyborg*."

"Believe me." She playfully rolled her eyes. "I know."

I leaned back on the swing and rocked us back and forth. "Still... an arm's an arm."

"Yeah, but how are you going to keep it hidden for school?" She cozied back up and stroked my hair. "People aren't exactly going to react too well when they see you roll in with a *very* high-tech prosthetic."

"I'll cover it up." I watched as a butterfly flittered its way past us. "You know, being Exalted... maybe I'll just not go to school. It's not like I'll find a better career."

"Yeah, right!" Dad's voice rumbled from inside. "Hero or not, my boy's gonna get an education."

"Well..." I shrugged. "I've still got a month or two to figure it all out."

"Um, Travis?" She giggled. "School starts *next week*."

"No, no, no... I met Mohandar in June, fought in London in July, fought Yaris two weeks ago..." I froze up. "What's today?"

"Today, young sir," she said, giving me a soft poke on the shoulder, "is the thirteenth day of August."

"...Well, that's not good." I looked over to Kate. "I'll have to work on my tolerance levels, that's for sure. If I punch any of those idiots in school now... they'll die."

"All the more reason to keep training."

Mohandar's cloak flowed down over the rail of the deck as he perched, watching the two of us.

"I see you've learned to use your arm." He stepped down. "Good."

I nodded. "Thanks, Mohandar... I really appreciate it."

"Seeing as you're in prime condition again, are you ready to *get back out there?*" He clutched his staff, and the upper portion began its majestic whirl. "The Realms never sleep, especially not for you."

"You heard the man." I gave Kate's hand a soft squeeze. "I have to go."

She shrugged. "I'm not stopping you."

"Bye." I glanced at Mohandar before giving her a quick smooch on the cheek.

"Get back here, mister." Just as I turned to leave, she snagged me by my sleeve and pulled me back. "You can do better than that."

She pulled me close, and our lips touched for a wonderful few seconds.

Mohandar stepped off the porch and cleared his throat. "Whenever you're ready, Travis."

"Better." Kate gently eased back. "Don't do anything *abnormally* stupid out there."

I bounced down the stairs, then followed Mohandar through the atmosphere and into the far reaches of the Realms.

"So, Mohandar." I soared up alongside my master. "Where are we headed?"

"Don't know." Mohandar looked off into the far beyond. "Wherever there's trouble."

A smile crossed my face.

Let's go.

ABOUT THE AUTHOR

Teague Rudacille is a young author fresh out of high school, enthralled by the drama and action of heroic tales. When he's not polishing his swordsmanship or spending time with the family, he's looking for ways to spin captivating stories with powerful emotion.

Connect:
trudacilleauthor@gmail.com

 trudacilleauthor

 @trudacilleauthor